Bloody Iced Bullet

By Andrew McGregor

Bloodied Wehrmacht Series

Book 1

Prologue

November 1942 on the banks of the River Volga. The German Army advance into the Caucasus Mountains in search of the Russian oilfields has halted for the winter as the bitter fighting in Stalingrad takes centre stage.

The German Air Force, the Luftwaffe, has virtually driven the Red Air Force from the skies.

The Germans, confident in taking the city that holds Stalin's name, strip their flanks of troops to bolster their forces fighting inside the city...for just one last push to decide the battle and the outcome of the war.

To the south of Stalingrad, on a thinly held front line stretching hundreds of miles, small groups of German troops are dispersed across positions held by their allies of the Fourth Romanian Army. In the north, it is a similar story, the Romanian Third Army bolstered by resting German troops.

As winter approaches and temperatures drop, the soldiers bed down in their positions, consoled by the thought that they will not have to fight through another Russian winter in the bitter sub-zero temperatures. Temperatures that the Russian Army is more than accustomed to.

Press releases advise the front line troops of the impending collapse of the Russian Army and state. The drive to the banks of the Volga had produced few prisoners and seen most Red Army units retreat before the mighty and victorious German Sixth Army...that Germany would finally win this war against Mother Russia within days or a couple of weeks at most. Hitler had even proclaimed it in radio broadcasts.

Common belief was the Russians were making one 'last stand' in the city that held Stalin's name...that the Russian Army was finished, the bitter war in the east was nearly over...that this was the end of communism.

The front was relatively quiet. Soldiers sat in their warm bunkers writing home to family and sweethearts, their conversations and thoughts of the coming Christmas and the dawn of a new world.

A new world where the German Reich stretches from the English Channel coast to the Ural Mountains deep in Russia and beyond.

The men on the front line believed that they would soon be going home......

Introduction

It was snowing heavily, the large flakes falling all around the dugout, slowly collecting and blanketing the wooden and earth structure cut into the side of the small hill, the numerous boxes and equipment that lay around the entrance slowly becoming covered by the falling snow. He sighed heavily, his exhaled breath spiralling and rising in the cold surrounding air, creating a cloud and adding further condensation to his lips, this instantly freezing. The inhale of oxygen always slightly uncomfortable as the freezing air entered his lungs before warming to his body temperature.

The scarf covering his mouth was becoming frozen again from the condensation of exhaled breath as he exerted himself, the battle between his body warming the material from the inside and the external temperature continuing relentlessly. The cold bit at his exposed flesh, his nose and eyes painful in the piercing frost. He had to blink more often to ensure the moisture in his eyes did not freeze and the condensation that froze to his eyelashes had to be regularly broken off by brushing his gloved hand across them to prevent restriction to his vision.

He stamped his feet, the freshly fallen snow crunching beneath his boots. The severe cold was infiltrating the two layers of socks and straw he had pushed into the boots, nipping cruelly at his feet and toes...this was going to be a cold night, even colder than last night he mused. At least the cloud cover would prevent the heaviest of frosts which was the bitterest night to endure, almost too much for human flesh to stand. His second guard duty would be the hardest if the cloud cleared, the temperatures dropping mercilessly in a clear sky.

He looked east, seeing only 5 or 6 metres to his front, the snow now falling so thickly it seemed to form an impenetrable curtain around him, a suffocating blanket of cold that must be resisted for survival. He considered to himself, deep inside, 'if they attacked now, they would not even find us, let alone us see them coming.' Yet it was very quiet, he knew there was a sentry to his left and to his right, but how far now? They were maybe thirty metres apart before it started snowing, but now he would struggle to find them. He realised he should not move too far or he would become disorientated, losing the dugout's entrance...that it would probably mean death if he wandered anywhere other than his bunker. Being lost in the fields around this position would eventually lead to death from exposure, his body temperature dropping slowly over time, his blood beginning to slow in his veins. The panic that would overcome him would simply hasten his end, reducing his temperature more rapidly and causing further confusion and disorientation.

Grinning ironically underneath the scarf wrapped round his mouth, he cleared his negative mood, determining a different line of thought. Who would ever have thought of this situation? The actions that had led to this place? He watched as the warmer air he exhaled swirled with the snowflakes as they fell, disrupting their descent. The air and flakes playfully embracing each other as the temperature of the air dropped and in less than a metre away the stillness and calm returned, the severe temperature seeming to slow and dissipate any signs of life.

He turned to his left, 'north' he prompted himself. Stamping his feet again, blowing onto his hands, although this made little difference, his hands remained cold and numb in their gloves. He knew he should make only two or three steps and perhaps be able to see the light near the bunker, the small fire he had prepared earlier with the other sentry. He looked down as if to trace his footsteps back to the warmth, sensing a stab of uncertainty, the realisation the fallen snow had now covered them.

He gingerly stepped forward in the shroud of snow, one cautious and frightened step...two steps, three steps...he hesitated, staring into the swirling white maelstrom...he could not see a flickering light. He strained his ears to listen, the crumpling of snow under his feet having been the only sound. A jab of fear swept through him, dancing across his spine...the thought, 'was he going the wrong way?' He could not call out, he dare not call out...perhaps another step? The fear of disorientation rising, he gingerly stepped forward slowly, aware he could be moving further from safety...squinting, he could still see nothing, no light of any kind, the concern becoming more intense. His eyes narrowed, he slowly turned though 360 degrees, adopting his father's teachings, to turn his feet to 90 degrees each time to ensure he did not lose direction.

The shroud of snow continued, the heavy flakes falling to earth, obscuring his view and limiting visibility to now less than two metres. Stood there motionless in the snow, he felt utter loneliness...complete isolation. Strangely he had known this feeling for some time now, but recently it had subsided...this was a harsh reminder. There were many times in the last year he had thought of this loneliness, struggled with faith and loyalty, but always concluded that fate had chosen this path and that it would be difficult, if not impossible to change what had happened, to alter what he was now. After all, it was in a way achieving what his parents and neighbours had always talked about with their subdued whispers and mutterings. He had confused and conflicting feelings...both of guilt and loyalty...

He stiffened, had he heard something? He realised he had become distracted and had lost his fear, his thoughts focussing him. He heard a muffled voice in front of him, and stepped forward cautiously, taking the rifle slowly and quietly from his shoulder, lifting it to his waist in anticipation of challenging. Then a shadow in the blizzard, slightly visible through the thick falling flakes, he stepped forward half a step in curiosity. The shadow moved slightly towards him, his excitement rising as he recognised the outline, his muscles relaxing as he heard again a whispered 'Wo bist du?'

'Heir', he hissed back, lowering his rifle. The slim outline grew bigger and a pair of welcoming dark brown eyes and narrow smiling young face emerged through the darkness. The soldier eyed him up and down, the smile widening to a grin, his fears subsiding further inside him. This was the man he knew as Udet, a young soldier of perhaps 22 years with a positive outlook and friendly demeanour, always ready with a comment or quip at the retorts from the others. The man was saying something he did not understand and nodding, beckoning him forward. As the two men became alongside each other, the young man slapped his back comfortingly. He relaxed further, shrugging off the thoughts that had distracted and concerned him. The other soldier was a similar height and dressed as him with a scarf over his nose and mouth, the steel helmet covering his short brown hair frosted. The soldier placed a gloved hand on his shoulder in order to guide him, whispering into his ear, 'Kommen sie mit'. He smelt hot food in the man's breath and after a couple of steps could see the light from the dugout nearby. His feeling of loneliness melted away and a warmer feeling of camaraderie overcame him. Stepping nearer to the light, the soldier guided him with a reassuring hand.

The man reached forward and grasped the several sheets of tent cloth that had been strung up as a makeshift door to the dugout and pulled them back slightly, pushing him through the opening, patting him on the back as he did so. The soldier then turned round into the cold, acknowledging with a sigh his turn on duty had come, 'Scheisse! Das is Kalt.' The thick fall of snowflakes swirled around him as the tent material fell back into place.

He exhaled, feeling the warmth of the dugout hit the exposed features of his face like a wave, the skin tingling as it regained warmth, re-energising with life. The smell of a fire and some food reaching his nostrils, this aroma tinged with the smell of unwashed bodies.

The dugout had been made with winter in mind, with the wall placed directly in front of the door, from which you went either right or left into the one main room. Both options had a further tent flap to negotiate, thus providing some additional shelter from the all-enveloping, advancing cold.

He hesitated, slowly dusting the snow from his overcoat and reaching purposefully for his helmet, removing it quickly so as not to lose the straw he had packed into it for further warmth. Turning right, he stepped forward towards the tent flap. Noticing the scrawled message scratched into the wood to his left, he touched it briefly, then reached out and grasped the tent material. Drawing it back slowly, he leant to his right to slip through the opening into the room, the action to minimise heat loss. He brushed against the scrawled message and stepped into the room, pulling his scarf down from over his mouth.

The message was a stark reminder of the fall of a comrade, the author having scratched it with his bayonet into the thick bark before leaving the safety of the dugout to take food to a forward foxhole. All soldiers leaving the dugout would now touch it 'for luck', sometimes pausing to reflect. Its author, a kind, engaging teenager with blonde hair and blue eyes, always ready to share a joke, always smiling...had died after a shot to the head by a Russian sniper.

It read boldly, 'Wilkommen zu Stalingrad. Ein Kristall Fortress Platz an der Volga.'

Outside it continued to snow heavily.

Chapter One: Camaraderie

The dugout was a rough square with a compact stove at the back exuding warmth. Its chimney was very small to reduce the advance of the cold, thus leaking some smoke into the room. This created a thin layer of smoke which hung and twisted slowly near the low beamed ceiling. Three candles placed around the sides added further light to the stove, their glows dancing and flickering across the wooden logged walls of the dugout, casting fleeting shadows from distortions and cracks in the bark.

Three soldiers sat or lay around the space, collected between the candles, almost filling the room completely. All still wore their greatcoats, but had removed their helmets, this closeness creating further warmth. The group looked up as he entered, acknowledging his presence with a nod or fleeting smile. Their rifles, including a medium machine gun, were stacked in a small side hollow, with a tarpaulin sheet laid beneath the weapons to avoid dirt.

To the far right, a soldier beckoned him forward, 'Come sit with me, my friend.' The officer smiled welcomingly, 'We are in for a cold night I think.' He swung back to the radio in the corner, turning the volume down. The radio set was placed on a makeshift table created from two ration boxes, the officer sitting on another.

He nodded, smiling slightly as he stepped forward...the man was his closest comrade of this group having spent many an hour talking with him, becoming a close friend over the last nine months. Responding to the welcome, he proceeded towards the corner, carefully stepping over outstretched legs and lowering his head to reach the back of the room. Arriving beside the officer, he crouched down next to him, slowly easing his legs onto the floor, using his arms against the wall of the dugout to lower his body. This man had once saved his life and he owed him his loyalty, he felt comfortable giving this commitment.

The officer continued with the radio, jotting down some notes onto his small notepad next to the machine and lowering the earphones. Reaching out with his right hand, he picked up an opened ration tin next to the radio, and scraped some food from the interior of the tin with a knife. He turned to face him smiling, depositing the morsels into his mouth as he did so, the candle light flickering across his angled features.

This man had piercing blue eyes and was clean shaven, a very particular habit he commenced every morning upon rising. He had high cheek bones and dark blond hair and he estimated his age at around 25, a little younger than himself. The man usually wore his helmet at all times, but this evening had discarded it to the left of the radio, his hair unkempt and matted after a day pressed down under the combat helmet.

The officer smiled as he swallowed his food and indicated for the man to lean forward, a glint in his eye, 'There is heavy fighting in the north today…good that we are south of that mess.' He was speaking in a low voice to seemingly not disturb the others, 'It seems the Russian bear still has some teeth yet, eh, 'Hase'?' He winked, the nickname 'Hase' one of the officer's invention and it had been explained it meant 'bunny'…a term of endearment.

He smiled at the officer's behaviour, one of a school ground gossip, the delight he exuded in telling him information that was not normally extended to someone like him or of his rank was quite engaging. It was apparent this officer liked him and they had spent considerable time travelling with each other.

He cleared his throat, whispering in response, 'Is the fighting heading this way?'

The officer's eyes narrowed, his mood darkening, 'I don't think so…but we had better be ready and awake in case there is movement here. It will be very cold later as the skies clear.' He shifted on the supply box, 'Will you take the 0500 watch? I need someone out there who's alert.' The officer then began collecting some more morsels from the bottom of the mess tin, scraping with his knife, glancing back at him for a response.

He nodded, replying instinctively, 'Yes, I will be ready for 0500 until first light.' The dreaded thought of the bitter cold entering his mind again.

'Good…very good. Thank you Hase, that has put my mind at rest. Keep a fire lit for some warmth if you like and I will see you are relieved as early as possible. Now I believe we will have visitors shortly with some food and drink. Stay next to me, so we can chat…' The officer grinned, '…and can both try and understand Tatu together. Apparently he has had a delivery today and wants to come over and *surprise us!*' He laughed, emphasising the expected arrival.

He recalled Tatu was the name of the Romanian Army quartermaster. A solid, fatherly figure with disordered grey hair and moustache…a very popular man with this and the adjacent unit and quite a character he mused. Tatu's endearing ability to generate some of the tastiest recipes from seemingly limited or non-existent rations was a form of amusement to the soldiers and a talent that was cherished by both units.

The stillness and subdued mood of the bunker was suddenly broken as they were startled by a cheer of announcement from the entrance. The tent cover was thrown back, and the six feet tall, stout figure of the Romanian quartermaster stood in the doorway, his face flushed red with alcohol mixed with the short walk in the freezing temperatures. The man wore a large army overcoat and was carrying a bottle in either hand. 'Mein Kameraden!' He exclaimed, grinning, 'A feast to share! Come…make room for your friends and allies.' He stumbled forward into the room, another stout Romanian soldier entering behind him carrying a box, the aroma of freshly cooked food now beginning to circulate around the room.

The soldiers in the dugout started to shuffle to the side, sitting up from their half lying positions to create room for the new arrivals, smiles of anticipation beginning to form on their faces.

Tatu stepped purposefully further into the small room, avoiding outstretched legs and handing a bottle to one of the resting soldiers eagerly awaiting the sustenance and warm offerings. He then lowered himself by leaning on this young man's shoulder with his free hand until he was squatted on the floor, his legs crossed.

'Come Petru,' he indicated by a jerk of his head to the other Romanian soldier, 'Place my feast on the ground here.' He indicated to the small space created by the soldiers in front of him. The other Romanian carefully leant across him, placing the box on the ground, a shy smile flicking across his face, his eyes darting to the officer opposite before retreating a step.

'Meinen Dammen und Herren!' Tatu announced, indicating to the topless ammunition box with both hands, 'Here is the food from your Romanian allies.' He grinned widely, removing his cap to show his unkempt grey hair, dusting the top of his head as to clear imaginary snow from it. Then he drew his hand down across his moustache as if settling it and reached behind him, producing a knife from a scabbard on his belt. He turned, grinning to the officer, 'We have Ciorba (Meatball soup), Sarmale (Stuffed Cabbage Rolls), Mititei (grilled ground meat) and to wash it down with, Secarica (caraway flavoured vodka) and a rare treat, a bottle of Hornica (plum brandy).'

A cheer spread across the bunker as the realisation of a party became instantly apparent, Tatu beginning to prise the metal lids from the full containers of food allowing a nourishing steam and aroma to fill the bunker. He glanced to his countryman, 'Here Petru...join us, you helped carry it all.' With this, Petru smiled warmly and shuffled forward on his knees to be near his friend, in his hand a spoon. 'You can also take the blame if they don't like the food!' Tatu delivered the punchline as his friend leant forward to help, causing him to hesitate and look up disapprovingly. The room exploded with laughter, with Petru grinning as he appreciated the joke was to break the ice and introduce him. Tatu continued, 'We have been friends for years have we not Petru?' He looked at his friend with obvious fondness in his eyes, slapping him on the shoulder, 'We used to make furniture together in Bucharest, joined up together and here we are...far from home, entertaining the troops...eh, my friend?' Petru nodded, a cautious embarrassed smile slipping across his face. Tatu continued, 'He doesn't say much...but when he does, it is usually important. Mind you...I believe he does not get much time to talk when I am here!' Tatu smiled, glancing around the grinning group, 'Now let's eat and drink together as friends!'

The expectant grinning soldiers began to rummage and locate their spoons from their pockets and packs in the expectation of the feast on offer.

Tatu passed a bottle of the Secarica to the officer, 'Here my friend, lets drink to both our units' success!' He retrieved another bottle from the inside of his jacket and removed the cork with his teeth, spitting it onto the floor of the dugout, 'Petru and I are now both your humble friends, Herr Leutnant.'

The officer grinned, indicating to both with the extended bottle, 'Thank you Tatu…and welcome Petru.' He swigged deeply, passing the bottle to Hase and indicating he should drink too. Nodding, he stated with a wink, 'This will help you sleep before your early start.'

Tatu looked across, 'Ah, young Hase, you must drink too…we are all friends here.' Pointing the head of his bottle at him, the stout quartermaster was beaming with a smile from to ear to ear, 'I told Petru I would introduce him to you all so let us have some introductions so we can all be friends…eh, Hausser?' He turned back to the officer again. 'We met your unit's baby, Udet, outside, Herr Leutnant. He seems to not like the cold of the steppe, maybe more suited to a fireside chat, eh?'

Hausser smiled, 'He is a good soldier…if young and cheeky. We should look after him Tatu, he will maybe look after us when we are older, even if we have to teach him some manners.' The smile broke into a grin, 'As for the others, they are Gunther, Raynor and Meino.' He indicated to the men individually with an outstretched hand, the soldiers returning a nod to Tatu and Petru as all were now chewing vigorously on the food that had been provided. Meino raised his bottle in salute and swigged from it, a cheeky smile spreading across his unshaven face.

The gathering continued, with Tatu holding an audience as he described the actions and the persuading he had completed to gain the rations they had received tonight from the nearby supply depot at Novosad and elsewhere. The Leutnant agreed that it was difficult to obtain some supplies but that they should be all happy to be fed such good food this far from home. This prompted the subject to move onto loved ones and those that were left at home, with the men passing crumpled photos around and recounting happy times with their families and sweethearts.

Petru had become visibly emotional as he had recounted his family in Bucharest. Tatu had placed a comforting hand on his friend's shoulder as Petru explained his family of three children and spoke warmly of how he had met his wife. One of his three children was 'of sickness', he disclosed, so they would spend extra time and care with him. Tatu explained that they would regularly meet at Petru's house for a meal and drinks and that the generous hospitality that Petru and his wife displayed should prompt them to open an Inn. Tatu had winked as he reminded Petru that at all times only his wife should complete the cooking in this inn and this re-established the high spirits within the group as Petru frowned in jest, embraced by grins from around the room.

Wary that he would have to rise early for guard duty, Hase had shuffled to the corner of the room and found a spot that would enable him to half lie on the straw that cushioned the bunker floor, reducing the cold from the earth below. With his feet near the stove, a full stomach of hot food and a warm friendly atmosphere he began to be overcome with drowsiness. He listened to the men talking, with the candles flickering across their faces. The camaraderie creating further warmth in the isolated dugout.

He sleepily watched as the men chatted, occasionally swigging from their communal bottles and telling stories of their previous exploits, their voices becoming strangely distant. Sleep was approaching as he wrapped himself snugly into his greatcoat. Curled up near the stove, he was now quite warm, yawning occasionally his eyes becoming heavy...the voices even more distant until he heard them no more. Submitting to his exhaustion, he closed his eyes for the last time that day.

Chapter Two: The Darkest Hour

'Hase!' He could hear his name being whispered firmly in the distance. 'Hase!' Then a firm prod to his shoulder, jerking him from his deep slumber and towards reality. His eyelids flickered, then opened.

He sat up quickly, Meino's face close to his. 'It's your time my friend,' Meino whispered. He shook his head, to fight off the groggy sickness and rubbed his eyes wearily. Next to him, Udet stirred in his sleep, having lay down beside him to gain warmth.

Slowly he looked round the dugout, now darker apart from one flickering candle and the glow emanating from the stove.

Meino flicked his chin with the top two fingers of his right hand, 'Time to get up sleepy.' He grinned, 'Use my scarf as well as yours out there as it is very cold.' Meino picked up his helmet from the ground and started pushing a handful of straw into it with his fist, 'Here, this may help.' He handed him the metal helmet and extended his hand, offering to pull Hase up.

Hase grasped Meino's arm at the elbow, the strength lifting him up to a crouched position, allowing him to refrain from wakening the others. Udet shifted in his sleep next to him, his young almost childlike face just visible under his greatcoat collar. As he stepped over the young soldier, Meino slowly and purposefully changed places with him, the vacated spot the only available space on the bunker floor with everyone sleeping.

Meino winked, whispering, 'The Romanians are to your right and left if you need company and their patrol should be back soon. So stay alert.' He raised his finger to his lips, grinning, 'Now get out of here...can't you see I am trying to sleep.' Meino's eyes then narrowed in concern, 'Remember...fall asleep out there and it will be the last thing you do. So take care my friend...keep moving.'

Hase carefully picked his way across the dugout avoiding the sleeping men, grasped his rifle from near the door where he had left it the previous night and walked sideways through the first tarpaulin flap. Stopping just inside the second set of material, he could feel the creeping cold touch his face and spread across his features, the frost seeming to reach out to him. Hesitating further, he purposefully and slowly wrapped the scarves across his mouth, doubling them up when he could and using Meino's across his forehead. This would make his eyes the only part of his face that would be exposed to the elements. Placing his helmet purposefully onto his head, he pulled it down onto the scarf, pushing any stray straw up under the rim. Drawing breath, he pulled the flap back and stepped out of the dugout into the snow and freezing air. Feeling the ice crack under his initial footstep, the crunch of tightly packed snow the only sound with each step as he walked out into the darkness.

The engulfing air was bitterly cold with the frost seeming to nip at his flesh under his greatcoat and uniform. It had now stopped snowing and the sky was clear with the stars shining brightly. He paused for a moment to look at the splendour of the late night sky, his condensed breath freezing on the scarf as soon as he exhaled. This air was considerably colder than the previous night, and stung at his eyes as the moisture began to freeze. This increased his blinking to combat the slightly misted vision, his breathing becoming short and rasped as the air was restricted through the freezing scarf.

He decided to keep moving to attempt to ward of the creeping cold, slowly and purposefully trudging through the snow to the edge of the emplacement the bunker was situated in. Facing slightly to the south east he peered cautiously out through a gap in the top of the earthworks. They had dug this position some 4-6 weeks ago, creating a high earth wall for cover and to restrict any enemy snipers view. Over time and with heavy snowfall, the wall had now become a slope on the other side, the addition of barbed wire placed to delay or perturb attackers.

Hase knew that facing him was a field which stretched off into the distance and declined away from their position at approximately 500 metres. The decline led into a gully with a wide stream and a small copse of trees to the right on the edge of the depression. Beyond the gully were some further fields and beyond that more open land that led to the banks of the Volga, or so the Leutnant had told him, as yet they had not advanced that far. To the north and slightly to the east lay the banks of Lake Sarpa, and some distance to the south, another large expanse of water, Lake Tsatsa. The soldiers regularly joked with irony that their close proximity to the water at this time of year chilled the air and increased the likelihood of thick freezing fog drifting across from the lakes. This had caused the nicknaming of these positions, 'the blinding defence' by the neighbouring units.

The flatness of the land offered little protection from a biting cold wind, but he was encouraged that this was not the case this early morning. The air was freezing but still, a welcome rest from wind-chill. A low deep white mist seemed to hang in the air for some distance away across the fields, but this could not be determined due to the darkness. He considered this mist would disperse in the morning sun, but would offer reduced visibility until then.

Hase squinted to stare into the distance, trying to see further...but realised there was little point. He had always been taught to spot a particular landmark in mist or darkness, then he could judge if conditions were becoming better or worse as time passed. He determined to do this once the edge had come off the darkness and remembered a grouping of bushes to his left that he had utilised before for this purpose, making a mental note to look for them in a short time.

He turned to the left...north, and slowly trudged through the deep snow towards the neighbouring Romanian unit, glancing to his right over the emplacement wall every few steps. Cautiously, he peered into the gloom, being mindful to keep moving and keep the glances brief and sporadic to avoid predictability, a precaution against someone looking in towards their position down a rifle sight.

The snow crunched beneath his boots and he began to feel the temperature in his feet reduce, the cold nipping at his toes first, Hase having to half crouch in places to ensure he did not expose his head above the snow covered earthworks. He entered a trench, and after some twenty metres, reached the end of the section his unit was responsible for, peering out towards the Romanian position some fifteen metres further to his north. Seeing a briefly raised hand in greeting from the edge of the Romanian trench, he returned the greeting and turned to retrace his steps and repeat the exercise to the south.

Hase considered he could start a fire for some warmth, but discounted the temptation, reminding himself that a fire in darkness provides excellent silhouettes for snipers. Even in this reduced visibility and with obstacles protecting him, the fire and any comfort he could gain from it would have to wait until it was lighter.

Reaching a slight bend in the trench, he peered out to the east once more, becoming aware he could now just make out the outline of the bushes he had considered a good marking point, these were now directly to his front. It was slightly lighter than earlier, but the mist was reducing visibility considerably as it hung in the air, hugging the landscape, distorting images on the steppe. He surmised it was unlikely he would see the copse of trees at this early hour or even in these conditions...so the bushes would be his marker on his return to this spot.

He turned back south and continued trudging through the earthworks and on into the southern trench, reaching the edge of the defensive position after a short time. Receiving the same brief wave from the Romanian position to the south, this time a machine gun emplacement, he returned the gesture, turned and began the trudge back north again. The frost was now attempting to seep through his clothing, his feet having become numb in the intense cold. He hesitated briefly to try and see the copse of trees to his east, but this landmark was still shrouded in mist and darkness and beyond his sight. He considered it may be another hour before he could see the trees in any detail.

Hase returned to the earthworks and paused to stamp his feet, blowing into his gloves, the escaping warmer condensed breath rising slowly into the early morning sky. He was tempted to re-enter the bunker for a snatch of warmth to reduce the chill he was now feeling, but realised the temptation to stay in the comfort of the dugout room would be probably too much to resist. He discounted this, estimating that it would be only a matter of time before he could light a fire now as the dawn was approaching…he just had to be patient…this was his duty.

He continued into the northern trench, the snow crumpling below his feet to keep him company. Only now he had his own foot prints from before to guide his footing, so this reduced the effort considerably. His mind wandered in the early morning cold, first considering that he would gather some of the stored firewood on his return to the emplacement to prepare for an early morning fire, his focus returning to his basic need for warmth. This thought led him to recall the collections of firewood he had completed for his father and family in his childhood, the fond memories of the family around an evening fire discussing the day. His father puffing on his pipe in the corner of the room as they chatted about the dinner they had just consumed, his mother's considerable efforts in their small kitchen and what they intended to do the following day. He smiled, realising he had a warmth towards people that smoked pipes due to his childhood experiences, relating this to his father's kindness and efforts to educate and protect him from harm through advice.

Hase reached the slight bend in the trench and paused to look out over the snow towards the bushes, lowering the rifle from his shoulder and leaning it against the trench wall, making a mental note to keep the muzzle clear from the snow. The bushes were now a little more distinct in the early morning light. Although it was still dark, the edge had come off the darkness and he was able to see right up to the frozen foliage, no longer just seeing an outline, but more clearly. Beyond this the mist hung heavily in the air, restricting further vision.

He blew on his gloves again and stamped his feet, the cold seeming to creep through his greatcoat and uniform in waves, trying to find the thinnest spot or gap. It nipped at his toes through his boots, straw and the two pairs of socks and froze the condensed breath in his scarf, making his breathing more laboured with the slight rasp as the warm breath fought against the frozen cloth.

Hase smiled to himself as he remembered coming in from the cold as a boy, his mother would always make sure a roaring fire was awaiting him and his father's return home to warmth when the weather was bitter outside. They would sit talking like excited children about the day, eagerly awaiting the food his mother was preparing, the mouth-watering aromas escaping from the small kitchen simply adding to their excitement.

A chill suddenly went down his spine…but this was not the cold. He squinted out across the snow, leaning forward as he did so, straining to peer further into the gloom. Concentrating his gaze to the right of the bushes where he had glimpsed what he thought was movement, realising immediately he had forgotten to collect any flares as he left the dugout. The use of a flare was the way of warning the neighbouring units to a potential threat to the line and he had left them in the emplacement, his weariness undermining his thinking. Momentarily he was entranced by his mistake, cursing himself for a serious error if indeed there was a threat out there, hidden in the snow.

Continuing to stare at the bushes, Hase began mentally scolding himself for his stupidity and potentially letting his comrades down. He squinted into the gloom further, becoming aware it now seemed to be colder than before, aware that this was now his senses sharpening to the potential danger. He consoled himself with the idea if there was nothing there he could retrace his steps and pick up a flare at the dugout as he passed.

Then a jerk of nervous energy, his suspicion confirmed as he glimpsed the bushes move slightly. He reached down slowly for his rifle, considering fleetingly that a small animal could be responsible for the movement and then discounting this. His mouth became dry in his realisation this was probably a Russian engineer, checking the ground for mines or traps...as yet unaware that he had been seen as the darkness receded.

Now he could just glimpse the top of the Russian soldier's helmet, confirming his fears. The man obviously thought he was still enveloped by the mist and could not be observed. He was slowly sweeping snow to the side, feeling for any mines that may have been concealed...his role in a Russian penal or punishment battalion confirmed due to a previous mistake. The only salvation to survive the posting and be deployed back to an ordinary unit, thus making him a desperate and dangerous adversary.

In the trench, Hase slowly and carefully raised his rifle, aware that any sound would alert any other hidden enemies. He was wary that this man would not pose a difficult shot at this distance, that the shot would alert nearby units to the potential danger if there were more Russian soldiers approaching. He slowly leant his head into the rifle to look down the sight...his mouth was dry and he could almost hear his heart beating...it seemed so strong and loud, pounding in his chest with the nervousness and adrenalin.

The Russian helmet had moved slightly towards the bushes as the man struggled to clear the area surrounding him. The Russian was older than others, in his early forties, and slower due to an old injury he had sustained in his right leg, but this was of no interest to the commissars. He was now working hard, wary the light of day was approaching and that he was running late in his duties, that most of his countrymen were further forward than his position. This had made him careless in his urgency to catch up and avoid any further penalty or discipline.

Looking down the rifle sights, Hase could clearly see the Russian helmet was shaking as the man worked feverishly to clear the frozen snow. He began to deliberately breathe deeply to compose himself and moved his finger slowly to the trigger, preparing to take the shot.

As his gloved finger touched the trigger, a muffled shout from the left distracted him. He glanced towards where the northern Romanian position would be to hear a short crack as the flare was launched into the air. Hase looked back down the sight to take the shot but the helmet was gone, the Russian now lying flat on his back in the snow having reacted to the shout.

Both men looked up, watching as the flare began to fall from high in the sky, its glow pulsing in the darkness, mesmerising in its sinister beauty. The light seeming to drift and curl in the cold air before being enveloped into the mist, shadows flickering within the shroud as the light died.

The nervous Romanian sentry was taking no chances at what he believed he had glimpsed and pulled the bolt on the machine gun he was manning, the loud crack echoing across the German trench in the still early morning. Hase glanced back down the rifle sight to see if he had a shot, but it was now too late.

He jumped as tracer bullets flew across the snow to his left and disappeared into the night, the rattling of the firing sweeping across the positions. The Romanian soldier hesitated briefly, shouted for assistance and then reapplied pressure to the trigger. His fear intoxicating as the lone sentries were in a vulnerable position if an attack was to be launched from this close to their positions.

Discounting the shot, Hase moved his head upright, glancing right as he heard the machine gun to the south begin to fire in unison with its counterpart, the Romanian soldiers taking no chances and firing wildly into the misty darkness.

The Russian penal battalion was now caught in the open field, closer to the German position than their own with approaching light. They had no option but to await discovery or attack before more German and Romanian soldiers were alerted and manned their positions. Instinctively, together, they rose up from the snow in unison with a shout of 'Hurrah', their officer cocking his pistol as he struggled from the snow, readying himself for any signs of retreat or cowardice.

Hase tensed and moved his head to squint down the sights of his rifle towards the bushes again, attempting to gain a further sight of the helmet. His eyes widened in shock as the Russians rose up in front of his position, making him jump. The soldiers were only some 20 metres away, with most wearing white camouflage uniforms. Biting his lip beneath his scarf, he realised now he had spotted one of the most distant and had simply presumed he was the nearest. He gasped in surprise when he realised how close the Russians had got to their position, shocking him into inaction for a second.

A Russian soldier directly in front of him, some 15 metres away, saw the German helmet and raised his rifle…this reality and danger shook him from his inaction, he spun his rifle to the right and the weapon jolted into his shoulder as he pulled the trigger, the Russian dropping his rifle and falling backwards into the snow, the bullet hitting him mid chest and shattering his ribcage.

Shaking, he fumbled with the bolt of the rifle in his thick gloves, finally grasping it tightly and pulling it back. Raising the weapon, he fired again, hitting another Russian that was waving a pistol directly to his front. The bullet hitting the man in the arm, spinning the soldier around and knocking him backwards into the deep snow with the ferocity of the impact.

Hase became aware that the Russians were struggling in the deep frosted snow, having to make high steps to progress through it, the iced surface resistant to their movement. They were advancing slowly and clumsily towards his position, but they now knew where he was and targeted his position. He ducked instinctively as bullets flew in his direction, splattering on the side of the trench and throwing snow and dirt over his back.

He turned and ran desperately at a crouch from the position, back towards the dugout…to defend it and get his comrades out to safety. A grenade exploded behind him and he briefly glanced over his shoulder, realising that the explosion had occurred where he had been standing. He swallowed hard, understanding that he must have stepped over the grenade or it landed just after he turned to run. The thought propelling him forward, bullets splattering around him on the tops and sides of the trench.

The Russian infantry were struggling where they faced the Romanian machine guns, but had managed to get behind the arc of the guns in front of the German position and were now reaching the barbed wire below the front of the emplacement and trenches.

Hase ran half crouched, half stumbling along the short trench and into the emplacement as a grenade exploded just behind the emplacement wall to his right. He lunged towards the doorway of the dugout, tripping and falling forwards as Hausser stepped through the tarpaulin curtain. The young commander's MP40 (Maschinenpistole 40) submachine gun was rising as he fired a burst over Hase's head, towards the wall of the emplacement, toppling two Russian soldiers into the wire.

Udet and Meino emerged from the dugout behind him with a rifle and MP40 respectively. Udet instinctively stooped and grabbed Hase's arm, pulling him to his feet, 'Kommen sie, Hase,' Udet exclaimed, his voice shaking.

As he scrambled upwards from the ground, their eyes met and he stared briefly into Udet's face. He saw the concern for him…but also fear, the link was broken by Hausser's shouting. 'Get the machine gun up…drive them back!' The officer turned to them abruptly, barking his orders, 'You two! Get anyone who gets through!' The commander fired another burst of his MP40 felling two more Russians emerging from the southern trench.

Hase looked round as Meino fired his MP40 over to the right, the target unseen to him as he rose from the ground. Grabbing the bolt of his rifle, he reloaded and raised it to fire as the Russians began to come up over the side of the emplacement. Pulling the trigger, a Russian fell backwards off the emplacement wall, the bullet hitting him in the throat. Behind them Gunther and Raynor burst through the tarpaulin with the unit's large machine gun, an MG34.

'Get that up on the wall you two!' Hausser shouted frantically, turning to Raynor, 'Udet…go with Meino and clear the right trench! Hase with me, we will go left!' He fired again at the Russians struggling in the wire and felled three more. 'Move quickly before they use grenades! We are too close together! This is it, men!'

Hase glimpsed Meino grab Udet's shoulder as they approached the right trench, the Austrian firing into it, hitting an approaching Russian in the stomach as the youngster followed. Udet advanced to Meino's side, half crouched, his rifle raised nervously. Hase turned and cautiously approached the left trench, seeing it was empty up to the bend. Grasping his rifle more tightly as he advanced cautiously, the fear and nausea rising through his stomach.

At his side, Hausser rose briefly and fired over the emplacement wall, hitting two Russians in the wire, forcing the others to drop back down the slope. Hase glanced back, seeing Gunther pull the empty ammunition box from the sandbagged wall that was used to cover the firing position, Raynor lifting the MG34 into the gap, in the same instance pulling the trigger, the flashing muzzle sending tracers into the advancing Russians. Gunther dropped to his knees and began vigorously opening an ammunition box with his bayonet.

Hausser slapped his shoulder, refocussing him forward, 'Come Hase, let's go hunting, I feel these Russians were not ready to attack else we would be gone now. Cover my back as I clear them out of our position.' The commander advanced half-crouched into the trench with his submachine gun pointing menacingly at waist height.

They neared the bend in the trench, the rattle of machine guns from the north and south a comforting sound, providing extra courage. Hausser peered around the corner and then stole a glance above the top of the damaged trench. Crouching down again, he turned to him, his face close, 'They seem to be heading back now Hase, I think...have a look if you like.'

Hase quickly popped his head up over the trench wall, seeing several Russian soldiers wading away through the snow as quickly as they could away from their positions...now some 30 metres away. Darkened figures were beginning to disappear into the thick mist as it swirled around them, seeming to pull them forward into the shroud. He noticed visibility was better now with the dawn now nearly upon them, he was now able to see the bushes and trees faintly to the south through the haze.

The older Russian, having crawled to hide amongst the bushes, observed the young helmeted soldier glance out over the trench. He recognised that this was the young man who had injured the commissar as he urged the penal battalion on. He smiled to himself...a good soldier perhaps, his aim inaccurate with the stress of battle. It had left the job of finishing the hated commissar off to himself in the confusion. He looked over to the dead Russian official some 4 feet away. He had dragged him there, with the commissar thinking he was to be saved, placing both his legs over the commissar's arms to reduce any struggle. Looking into the hated man's face, he had slowly inserted his bayonet into the man's neck just in front of his spine, watching the terror in the man's eyes as he purposefully hesitated, then tearing the blade forward. This inflicted the death he had planned for the miserable bully all along, one he had learnt in the gangs of Kiev as a younger man during the revolution, the German's shot had simply created the opportunity. He smiled and stroked his greying beard, now stained with streaks of blood. This weak, cowardly man could bully him no more and hide behind a uniform using the excuse of the Party's will or orders. He had inflicted a well-deserved end to him, his life forfeit for his crimes.

Shrugging, he turned cautiously in the snow and crawled back slowly towards the Russian line, wiping the commissar's blood off as he went. This day was to be a very long one and many more would die, no one would notice this wretch once the number of corpses had risen.

Chapter Three: The Descent

Hase looked round, the area in front of their position now quiet, the machine guns to either side silent. Both he and Hausser were still at the bend in the trench north of their emplacement, every so often hearing a wounded man moan from the field to the east as he lay dying in the snow. These desperate pleas for help seemed to tear at his soul in his willingness to provide comfort and mercy, but it was too dangerous to go out and try to help in this light, the Russians would also have snipers posted. He considered that the action had taken perhaps all of 10 minutes, but it had seemed longer…much longer.

Hausser inserted a new magazine into his MP40 and turned to him, 'Well young Hase, we drove them off…but I don't think their hearts were really in it.' The young officer turned and grinned at him, tapping his friends helmet, 'Let's go and check on our neighbours shall we?'

With this, Hausser glanced around the bend in the trench warily and shouted across to the Romanian position, advising them a friend was coming from the south. The reply was welcoming as per the units' prior arrangements for the day, Hausser immediately bolting half-crouched out of the trench towards the safety of the Romanian line. Once there the officer turned and indicated for Hase to follow.

He held his breath as he prepared to run across the gap, wary that Hausser's actions may have alerted a Russian sniper in the snow of his forthcoming appearance. He drew a deep breath and lunged forward, half crouched, holding his rifle in his right hand, his other hand on his helmet. Gasping as he reached the Romanian trench, sliding against the eastern wall, he was greeted by a young Romanian soldier grinning at him. The man crouched next to Hausser and was possibly in his early twenties, winking mischievously at Hase's fear.

The officer turned to face him, a warm smile forming on his lips upon observing the relief on the man's face, 'I will go and speak to the commander here. See if you can find Tatu and if the old fool is still alive with his friend. Maybe he will have a late breakfast ready?' Hausser turned and darted off along the trench, leaving him alone with the Romanian soldier.

'Tatu, da!' The grinning Romanian soldier exclaimed, giving directions with an outstretched right arm and hand and gesturing for him to follow the trench and fork off to the left. Hase nodded and proceeded along the trench, wary that the Romanians had placed seemingly sporadic log sided fire points in the right side of their defences which differed from his own group's smaller emplacements.

He followed the young soldier's directions and these proved accurate. The left fork in the trench twisted back and forth for about twenty metres and then descended a gradual slope, finally opening up into a large emplacement, set before a small wood on the western edge, the trees heavily laden with snow. The Romanians had obviously considered their quartermaster valuable and in need of a regular supply of wood to keep them nourished with warmly cooked food.

On his journey, he passed soldiers coming from the quartermaster's kitchen a couple of times. Both were laden with mess tins full of steaming stew, indicating the cooking had not stopped in the face of an enemy attack. In the narrow trench, the obstacle of another soldier had only been overcome by both parties passing each other whilst moving sideways, the Romanian soldiers grinning at his obvious discomfort. The close proximity to food making him now aware how hungry he had become after the stress of the attack.

The quartermaster's emplacement had a dugout in its northern wall and a large roaring fire in its centre. Hase stopped by the fire to seek warmth and felt the heat emanating from the flames across his face, the steam beginning to rise from the scarf across his mouth as the frost melted further. His outstretched hands also began to emanate steam from the frost on the gloves, his feet beginning to tingle as warmer blood returned to them, the flames spitting as moisture fell into the heat.

'Ah, young Hase!' The exclamation was clearly Tatu's voice and he spun round, startled. The stout quartermaster stood at the entrance to the dugout with his hands on his hips, legs apart, beaming at his new guest, 'Not perturbed by our Russian friends trying to come for breakfast then?' Tatu let out a short laugh, 'I have some food for you if you are hungry...'

Hase nodded, smiling, realising his hunger further now that the cold was subsiding. He grinned at Tatu's joviality, the robust Romanian a pleasing sight seemingly wrapped head to foot in some sort of elaborate fur jacket, with thick felt boots. The older Romanian seemed to glide across the snow as he moved to stoke the fire, indicating behind, 'We store rations and supplies in the bunker and in other areas of the trench system...it avoids a direct hit from artillery...'

Tatu's suddenly froze, and turned to look directly at him, his eyes a piercing stare, the Romanian's face immediately becoming very serious, his eyes narrowing and a frown appearing on his lips. He raised his hand as if to silence the young soldier, the Romanian quartermaster seemed to be sensing the air as if breathing it in. There was a number of distant thuds and Tatu broke his stare, glancing towards the dugout entrance. Realising the door to the dugout was now beyond reach, the Romanian looked back at him, his features stern, 'I think our Russian friends are perhaps unamused.' Tatu exclaimed, 'Get down!'

The whoosh of shells filled the air, both men dropping to the ground, thrusting their faces into the snow. The crump of shells around the emplacement threw snow and earth over them as they lay face down with their hands over their heads. The trees cracked as a shell landed in the small copse sending branches and snow flying into the emplacement, scattering sparks from the fire onto the two prone figures.

Hase could hear the explosions all around their positions and some screams from the forward defences. The noise was deafening as the whooshing and crumps of the explosions in snow merged to form a seeming wall of noise washing over them like a wave.

Then as soon as it had started...the wall of noise stopped. Both men lay there in anticipation, slowly and cautiously raising their snow covered heads to look at each other. Tatu seemed to be sniffing the air, the smell of the scorched explosions filled their nostrils, almost overpowering their senses...but the Romanian was straining to use a different sense.

Petru poked his head out of the dugout curiously, 'Have they finished?' He stammered, clearly shaken by the ordeal, forcing a smile as he glimpsed Hase.

'Shush' Tatu scolded his friend, turning his head in disdain to look at the dugout entrance.

The silence was almost complete when a crack from the wood on the fire broke the three men's concentration, making them physically jerk in surprise. Then the sounds of a slight squealing noise, distant yet distinct.

Tatu's eyes widened in horror, his voice broken, 'Russkie Tanks!' Both men scrambled to their feet, looking at each other in confusion. Tatu was the first to react, turning to address his countryman, 'Get the guns and the brandy, Petru, we are going to show these Russian pigs how Romanians fight!'

Petru nodded grimly and disappeared back into the dugout as they heard the machine guns begin to fire again some fifty metres away to the east. Petru reappeared from the darkened emplacement and tossed a submachine gun to Tatu's outstretched hand, lifting the strap of a bag over his shoulder and grinning at the younger soldier, winking.

Tatu checked the chamber of his weapon, a PPSH41 Russian submachine gun, and turned to face the entrance to the trench, indicating for them to follow him. As they approached the opening, the Romanian quartermaster almost collided with Hausser running towards them down the narrow passageway, his submachine gun in his right hand, Tatu grabbing the officer's tunic to prevent him from falling backwards as he slipped.

'Ivan is bringing up tanks.' Hausser exclaimed, breathless, 'This is a major attack it seems, there were no reports of them massing forces in this area.' He gasped, 'Tatu, how many anti-tank weapons have your men got?'

'Not many my friend and those that we have are old. Let's see if we can get close enough to give them a taste of Romanian brandy.' Tatu replied sternly, 'We will come to your emplacement to help…Let's go!'

'OK, this way,' Hausser exclaimed. 'The trenches are under direct fire.' The officer indicated for the men to turn away from the trench and make their way round to the position from the west. Jumping out of the quartermaster's emplacement, they slipped down a slope to the south west of the position and ran half crouched along a small depression behind the line, coming out just behind the German dugout. They ran into the back of the emplacement, jumping over discarded boxes, ducking their shoulders upon hearing a shell whistle overhead and land behind them with a loud crump as it exploded in the snow behind.

Raynor turned his head to see them arrive, his eyes wide with fear, his mouth wording, 'Panzer Alarm' before turning back to fire the machine gun, his shoulder shaking as the weapon fired through the emplacement wall. Gunther had stacked the spare ammunition cases opened and around his friend and was himself laying a bundle of grenades out between him and Raynor in anticipation of a Russian approach.

Hausser ran to him, grabbed his shoulder and shouted 'Udet?' Gunther pointed down the right hand trench and picked up his rifle, leant against the wall of the emplacement.

Hausser now turned to him, grabbing his arms, 'Hase, you and the others cover the left trench, I am going to radio command for support.' The young officer pushed him away towards the trench and ran to the dugout entrance, disappearing inside.

Watching Hausser disappear into the dugout, Hase turned and ran half crouched into the trench, ducking instinctively at an explosion just outside the emplacement to the right, throwing earth and snow down onto them.

Glancing back, Tatu and Petru were behind him, solemn expressions of determination on their faces, a glint of fear in Petru's eyes...a cold stare in Tatu's.

Hase reached the bend in the trench and stole a glance over the wall. The scene in front of him was mesmerising...the mist still hung low, but was now further back...the machine guns of both sides of his position firing into the swirling gloom, the visibility low. The mist would swirl as the Russian soldiers exited its embrace to be then targeted by the machine guns as they moved into their arc of 45-90 degrees to their front. He watched as five Russians were cut down as they advanced from the misty fog in front of the MG34's position.

Tatu grabbed his shoulder and pulled him below the wall of the trench as bullets spattered across the ground in front of their position. The Romanian was shouting in his ear, 'Focus, young Hase or today will be your last! Keep your head down, fire a shot then move position!'

Petru had pushed past them and was now nearing the end of the trench, indicating a greeting of support to the young Romanian soldier opposite, receiving a forced terrified smile in return.

Another shell landed just short of the trench, sending scattered frozen earth and snow on top of them, all instinctively ducking further below the walls of the walkway as they heard the whoosh of another shell heading in towards their position.

Tatu shouted to his friend as the earth from the explosion fell onto them, 'Get the brandy ready Petru...we will not have time later.'

Petru nodded, delving into the bag he was carrying and producing two bottles. Both had rags hanging from their corks and he placed them carefully onto the ground. Dropping two submachine gun magazines for Tatu's weapon next to them, then checking the breach of his own rifle.

Tatu stole a quick glance over the trench wall and swore loudly, 'The tanks are getting near.'

Hase raised his head above the wall briefly, seeing a flash in the mist, a dark outline behind, the mist swirling downwards and sucked under the hull of the sloped hulled tank as it emerged from the shroud. Flashes started from the metal monster's forward machine guns directly at the German emplacement, the ducked Russian infantry emerging from the mist behind their tank, using it for cover.

His eyes widened in fear as he saw two other tanks emerge from the white gloom, their machine guns firing, infantry sheltering behind them. Ducking back down, he clenched his hands round his Kar 98 rifle. Stammering, he turned to Tatu, 'How will we stop the tanks?'

Tatu and his eyes met and he gained the understanding that the situation was very serious. Tatu slowly placed his hand on the young soldier's shoulder, 'Go and help your countrymen young Hase, Petru and I will hold this place.' The Romanian then grasped the hesitant young man's greatcoat lapels with both hands, moving his face close to his, 'Now GO!'

Tatu pulled him past his left shoulder and pushed him down the trench, Hase stumbling forward with the momentum, scrambling back towards the emplacement, almost on his hands and knees. He heard the shells whine overhead and crumple behind the dugout. The machine gun was firing continuously and he heard several clanks as the Romanians tried to engage the tanks with their aging anti-tank weapons, the projectiles from their weapons bouncing off the thick forward steel armour plate. The noises began to swirl around him as he focussed on the dugout's entrance, earth splattering around him as the shells burst behind and around the emplacement. He forced himself forward towards his goal and safety, half scrambling across the snow and covered boxes and equipment.

He threw himself through the dugouts tarpaulin, landing on the floor of the room half inside the tent flap. Glancing up, he saw Hausser shouting into the microphone, a radio earphone pressed to his ear, 'I repeat...Tank attack...enemy attacking in force...we need support!'

The radio crackled back, dispersed with the loud shell explosions and machine gun fire outside, dust and loosened earth falling from the dugout's roof.

'Scheisse!' Hausser shouted in frustration, dropping the radio equipment. He turned, staring incredulously at him, 'They say hold the line...that there is no support available. The enemy is attacking along a wider front, support deployed south of here. Enemy breaking through.' Hausser's eyes were widened in exasperation, his mind confused in its efforts to grasp a possible successful solution.

Hausser shook his head, mentally summarising the situation. The young officer stepped back and without warning raised his MP40 and fired a burst into the radio, shattering it. 'Destroy equipment!' The officer hesitated, turning to face him, then grabbed a sack next to his makeshift desk, tossing it to him, 'Hase, take the grenades and give to the men out there...they will need them.' Hausser took two steps towards him, indicating over Hase's shoulder, 'Come on, let's go!'

Both men pushed out through the tarpaulin, the noises of war reaching fever pitch. The clunking of the old anti-tank weapons against the Russian tanks as they moved slowly up was nerve wracking, the explosions behind the position to engage possible reinforcements made the men instinctively duck as the shattered earth and snow fell onto and around them. The machine gun was still firing, with Gunther preparing a new barrel for the weapon.

Hausser realised the danger that changing the barrel would bring...without the gun firing they could be overwhelmed by Russian infantry. The officer ran forward, shouting at Gunther, 'How long?'

Raynor frantically shouted back, 'This barrel is nearly done...its overheated too much, Herr Leutnant!' His eyed were wide with fear, the sweat pouring down his face, 'I don't think we can change it fast enough...the Russkies are behind their tanks, but will be all over us before we get it firing again.'

Hase ran forward, half crouched, throwing himself against the emplacement wall and pushing himself against it with his left shoulder. Glancing briefly over the wall and down the decline, he realised in horror there were now six tanks in the field before them. Two had lost tracks and were stationary as a result of the anti-tank fire, but had turned their attention on the culprits and were firing at the Romanian positions in an attempt to silence the gunners. The other four tanks were slowly moving towards their positions, their tracks spinning in the deep snow, attempting to gain grip and traction.

He pushed himself up with his left hand and ran into the right hand trench, towards Udet and Meino. They acknowledged him with cautious nods as he reached them, the men both crouched in the trench. Udet's face was contorted with fear, Meino's hand on his shoulder for brief comfort.

Hase dropped a number of grenades on the ground before them and looked up, seeing both realised the danger of the situation from the strain in their eyes.

His mouth was dry, licking his lips, he turned to proceed back to the emplacement. The machine gun jammed suddenly, stopping him in his tracks…the barrel finally giving up, the jam occurring due to the its warping. Both Raynor and Gunther struggled frantically with the weapon, pulling it from its firing position and fighting with the barrel, their hands scorching from the hot metal. He realised they had left it too late…the bullet jammed in the barrel now far more serious.

He stole a glance over the trench wall, seeing that the Russian soldiers had now realised the machine gun had stopped firing, cautiously moving out from the back of their prospective tanks. The machine gun was still firing to the south, Hase watching the Russian tank turrets slowly turn towards it, determining to concentrate their fire.

The air filled with shouts of 'Hurrah' as the Russian infantry seemed to collectively realise the machine gun would not fire. They broke from the cover of their tanks and swarmed forward towards the machine gun position. As he watched, the nearest Russian T34's barrel flashed as it fired at the Romanian machine gun, two more flashes from other tanks quickly followed. Instinctively glancing round as if following the shell, the explosion ripped the roof off the Romanian gun emplacement, killing the crew instantly and destroying the machine...the firing on their right flank fell silent.

More 'Hurrah's' echoed as the Russian infantry rose from the snow in front of the destroyed Romanian gun, and began advancing towards the Romanian riflemen that had been protecting the now silent machine gun. The riflemen began frantically trying to pick off the mass of advancing infantry, attempting to make every bullet count.

Hase looked back to see the two German infantry still struggling with the machine gun, hearing the whine and rasp of one of the tank's engines as it began to ascend the other side of the slope of the emplacement. He shouted a warning at the two soldiers, and could hear Udet shouting behind him, but the noise of battle and the tanks' engines drowned them both out. Raynor turned slightly and made eye contact with him, looking up from the weapon briefly, desperation on his face. Then he disappeared as the wall of the emplacement collapsed backwards under the weight of the tank, burying the machine gunners. The T34 tank's tracks spun in the air as it fell forward onto the collapsed wall and the buried soldiers, crushing them instantly. Udet grabbed Hase's shoulder, the scream of frustration from the young soldier behind him in reaction to what they had just seen, their eyes transfixed on the scene.

Meino was shouting frantically at them, spurring him from his fixated stare on the gruesome scene. Realising what Meino's intention was as his mind cleared, he spun round and pushed Udet back to distract him, focussing the young soldier and breaking his stare. Frantically, they both grasped at the metal objects from the snow at their feet, furiously unscrewing the stick grenade bases. The grenades primed, they lobbed them over the walls of the trench, hearing the resulting crumpled explosions breaking the attack as Russian infantry were thrown back down the slopes.

Hase looked to his right, Meino firing his MP40 furiously over the trench wall, shouting desperately for them to move, the flashes from his submachine gun surreally lighting up the experienced soldier's face. This demonic sight spurred him into action, feeling the adrenalin surge through him. Turning, he grabbed the shoulder straps of Udet's overcoat and pulled the younger soldier towards him, back towards the emplacement and the only way out.

The two soldiers took three steps in approach to the clearing and stopped in the trench, their hopes shattered. The Russian tank had advanced across the emplacement and was grinding its tracks into the dugout. Behind it, Russian infantry began to surge over and through the broken emplacement walls, their rifles with bayonets fixed, the 'Hurrahs' ringing in their ears. Udet grasped his shoulder in fear, both men realising their escape route was about to be cut. In response, he raised his rifle in exasperation, wary this weapon was no longer enough to defend them against such odds.

The world seemed to slow, as both men hesitated, tightly grasping their weapons, their stomachs churning in desperation. For a second hopelessness overwhelmed them, the situation seeming unsurmountable as the Russians surged into the emplacement. Then time moved forward dramatically, the Russians being met with an explosion of bullets from Tatu's and Hausser's submachine guns as they exited the trench opposite. Firing as they came, the advancing brown uniformed Russians twisting, shuddering and fell all around, screams filling the air as the muzzles flashed opposite.

Petru ran out behind them half crouched and across to the left seemingly with a flame in his hand. With one jump he landed on the back of the tank as it crushed the dugout beneath its tracks, the front of the tank crashing downwards into the room they occupied the night before. Its engine growled, the tracks skidding on the screeching broken wood as the driver revved the motor in an attempt to climb the back wall of the dugout. Under the immense weight, the wood shattered and cracked, splinters flying from the grinding tracks, plumes of exhaust billowing as the engines roared.

Petru scrambled onto the turret and grasped the hatch, wrenching it open and throwing the flaming bottle inside. He jerked his body back as the flames rushed skywards through the opening, the bottle smashing and the brandy ignited inside the tank, creating an inferno. Petru leapt off to the right side of the tank, rolling as he hit the ground, the momentum of the tank pushing him forward. Then the tank jolted, its engine stalling, the muffled crews distorted screams echoing from within the metal cabin. A burning crewman attempted to climb through the flames, his head rising through the turret as he scrambled desperately to escape the inferno below.

Tatu jumped onto the back of the tank, his immense jacket billowing behind him with the forward motion. He knocked the crewman back into the tank with the butt of his submachine gun, flipped the gun in his hands and fired a burst into the open hatch, the inside of smouldering the tank falling silent. Jumping from the tank, he joined Petru, turning to call the others forward towards them, beckoning with his free hand.

Hausser responded, firing his submachine gun through the gap in the emplacement wall, shouting and indicating desperately for the men to follow Tatu and Petru over the destroyed dugout. In response, both surged forward, with Hase half pulling Udet as he attempted to gain his footing in the snow. Both young men half scrambled across the smashed emplacement, Meino passing the hole in the embankment behind them, the experienced soldier tossed his last remaining grenade through the gap. The soldiers ran half crouched towards their Romanian comrades, Hausser covering the gap in the wall with his submachine gun. Once the men had passed, the officer quickly turned and followed them, shaking his head in frustration. The whining of approaching tank tracks down the slope to the east and distant shooting with muffled gunfire to the south and north the only sounds now. The battle was lost.

Once the men had safely left the destroyed emplacement, they swiftly retraced their steps into and along the depression following Tatu and Petru. Wary of distant Russian voices now either side of the slight ravine, they held their weapons at the ready, moving as silently as possible. Their progress was cautious but swift, taking care not to make too much noise in their haste, with no talking. Upon nearing the Romanian quartermaster's emplacement, Tatu led the party sharply left through a thicket and into the small wood that had bordered his emplacement. Cautiously they all disappeared into the snow laden trees and bushes.

In the centre of the small copse of trees they came upon a small narrow ditch that had been cleared. The young Romanian soldier Hase had seen in the trench greeted them with a strained smile, a look of near panic and bewilderment on his face. His relief at not being left alone evident, but the severe stress of what had just happened clear from the strained expression on his face and the white knuckles tightly grasping his rifle. Tatu, it seemed, had briefed the teenager on where to come and what to collect on the way.

Hausser indicated for them all to get into the trench and they all proceeded to drop into the narrow man-made defence, the sounds of sporadic distant shots in their ears coming from the Romanian positions. All were exhausted from their ordeal and stood half crouched in the trench gasping for air until they recovered their composure, the whine of distant tank tracks now evident to the north and south.

The rations in the mess tins the young Romanian soldier had stored in the trench earlier were readily received and welcomed, the men not having eaten yet that day. These were opened and the soldiers slowly munching on the food, a cold Romanian stew, as they began to realise the situation they were in and what they had overcome.

The officer crouched and then sat on the edge of the trench, removing his helmet and holding it in his hand, visibly tired and seeming to be lost deep in thought for a moment as the men chewed.

Hausser then began to talk slowly in a low voice. He explained that this trench was the best place to hide whilst the Russian front line passed them by, that the enemy were hopefully moving too fast to check on small obstacles like this wood. He quickly advised the demoralised men that he would go and keep an eye on the Russians and that they should wait here in the trench. The officer then stated he would make a decision on what to do when he returned. They were instructed to eat and remain as quiet as possible in the trench, but to be highly alert at all times, in case of discovery or curious Russian Infantry.

The young officer instructed Meino and Udet to assume sentry duty on opposite edges of the small wood, stating that they should inform the others of anyone approaching the trees immediately. But that everyone should avoid contact with the enemy at all costs, that this would clearly mean the end of them all as they were too few in number to defend themselves for long. The six men nodded in grim agreement, accepting the hopelessness of the situation.

Meino and Udet then checked their weapons and left cautiously to assume their positions, with Hausser advising he would move between the two as support and to gain information on the overall situation the group faced. The expressions of grim concern, the stress of their situation and danger they faced etched on their faces.

The remaining four soldiers sat in the trench and slowly ate in solemn silence, the stresses of their situation playing heavily on their minds, all lost in their individual thoughts. The food was semi congealed, and the air quality in the wood poor, the temperature in the enclosed atmosphere of the thicket low. They were all were aware that lighting a fire would immediately alert the Russians to their situation. To the north and south they could hear the distant noises of an army advancing, the squealing of tank tracks and revving of engines as the vehicles struggled in the deep snow. Occasionally they would hear the distant murmur of voices, or a distant shout causing them to tense and reach for their weapons.

Hausser disappeared for some time and returned once everyone had completed their improvised meal. He ushered them closer, assuming a seated position on the edge of the ditch. Aware he was to brief them on the situation, all four men leant forward intently as he began to speak in a whisper, 'I have been to the outskirts of the wood. This is an excellent hiding place and we must thank our host, Tatu, to who we owe our survival. It does not look as though the Russians have considered looking in here.'

Tatu nodded appreciatively, seeming to be slightly embarrassed. Petru placed a friendly hand on his shoulder.

Hausser continued, his tone a low whisper and solemn, 'The Russians have broken our lines and are advancing westwards seemingly at speed. They have tanks and infantry carriers and their front line is now probably quite some distance to our west. There is fighting to the north and more distantly, to the south it seems, but at present we are in the middle of the Russian advance, or perhaps slightly to the north of the centre. At the moment the Russians are advancing on both sides of this wood, and with a little luck they will not find us here. My view is to move north at dusk or after nightfall...eventually we will re-join an allied unit.'

Hausser paused to let the information sink in, then drew a deep breath and continued, 'This is a major offensive by the Russians I think, so it may take some time to stabilise the front and for our armies to destroy this incursion.' A brief smile crossing his face as he glanced at Tatu, 'The Romanian 20th Infantry division should be to our north and they are a good unit, they should hold for us and others to join them I think. That is my decision gentleman and I think the best one.'

The men nodded silently, all lost in solemn thought, the loss of their comrades a heavy burden. Their eyes were wide with the shock of what had happened and their faces grim with the realisation of the position they faced.

Petru broke the silence, the others turning to hear his low whispered words, 'Many of our men died and will die today...too many, I think that is enough. I think we must get warm clothing and more food and go north, this mess will take some time to recover. We need to sleep now, and move tonight...I think it is best too. This position on Sarpa Lakes has gone.' His voice was shaky, but his expression focussed and determined, his eyes a fixed stare as if looking at something in the distance, looking back towards his homeland, 'Yes...we sleep now, we must...we will be cold for a long time now I think.'

Chapter Four: Isolation

Hase knelt motionless in the bushes, having crept slowly and meticulously to this spot avoiding creating any sound, his breath heavy as he felt the chill in the air across the bridge of his nose. It was late afternoon and he had just awoken after a drifting fitful sleep, his mind still groggy from the last snatched few minutes of final deep slumber in the ditch. The light was receding slowly across the open and clear sky, and he could begin to feel the temperature dropping further as he looked out over the field to the north. This was the route they would follow shortly…leaving the safety and secluded gloom of the thick bushes and trees to head north into the open countryside. The snow crumpled softly beneath his foot as he shifted his weight, aware that his decision on the safety of the land in front of him would determine the group's initial movement.

The field in front of him lay empty, the silence inviting. The tracks of many vehicles had disrupted and churned up the deep snow, leaving many ruts and grooves in what had been an almost perfect scene in peacetime.

He began to consider this day's events. In the distance to his right lay the Romanian positions, overrun and destroyed. There were probably many dead there, perhaps people he could have known in a different time. He felt some allegiance with them, understanding how it must have felt to face tanks without effective weapons. He remembered the feeling of frustration and helplessness, the escalating desperation as the tanks approached, seeming impervious to their defensive fire. The descent into an emotional state of utter futility, wary at all times that any attempt to turn and run would result in instant death without cover as you were crushed or the tanks' machine guns cut you down.

Hase swallowed hard, clearing his head, forcing his concentration to move from his thoughts. Hesitating, he became aware of a distant sound…straining to hear, his eyes moving to the horizon, then upwards…a plane was approaching, flying relatively low it seemed. He watched as the fighter seemed to hang in the air as it flew directly towards his position. He stiffened, considering if the pilot knew he was there? Then dismissed this, the plane was too high and far away...the flight path a coincidence, the pilot looking below, surveying the ground beneath him. The plane seemed to crawl across the sky, but this was simply the illusion of it flying directly towards him. Hase smiled beneath the scarf wrapped tightly across his mouth at his initial thoughts of being discovered...he was hiding from any potential enemy infantry patrols and he had briefly considered a plane above him could see him in bushes? How little faith he had in his concealment, his jaw hardening as he realised this response was an indication of how afraid he now was of discovery.

The drones of the plane's engines were becoming clearly audible across the frozen expanse and he watched as the pilot slowly banked to the right, turning the aircraft east and probably now beginning to cross over above Lake Sarpa. Hase glimpsed the distant yellow tips on the wings of the aircraft and could just briefly make out black crosses in the fading light before the German plane levelled out and began to climb away to the east.

He swallowed again to clear his throat, this time to attempt to disperse the desperate sickly feeling rising from his stomach. The plane indicated to him how far safety was from him now, untouchable, out of reach and out with his control...they were now truly alone.

The plane had been sent out for reconnaissance, to discover the distance of the enemy breakthrough. It had taken virtually all day for the situation to now become clear, for the true extent of the potential danger the army on the Volga now faced. With the chaos that had ensued after the initial assault and a heavy ground fog and cloud cover, it was late afternoon before a fighter had been sent south to finally determine the situation and to confirm the broken radio reports. The pilot had flown across the lakes and reached the fighting to the south...then circling back, checking for surviving or trapped units. He had reported back and been instructed to check again, resulting in this, his final circle in fading light with low fuel. He radioed back his findings to the airfield in Stalingrad, the report being conveyed to the command centre and then back to Berlin via enigma machine.

'Report from Pitomnik airfield 20th November 1942 (Evening): Reconnaissance sweep, southern sector, Stalingrad front completed. Enemy breakthrough in the Sarpa Lakes area in force. No surviving defensive units seen in sector. Fighting to north and south of breakthrough ongoing. Enemy units advancing to the west. Fading light prevents further flight.'

Hausser had instructed Hase to position himself here, to monitor the route they would take to the north whilst the rest of the men prepared themselves. He had been concealed in the bushes for nearly an hour and had nothing to report, considering the Russians were probably now using the roads, the nearest to the south of them. But he had not seen any patrols…were they not patrolling the area, searching for and picking off any survivors?

The temperature was now becoming extreme as the darkness approached, the extent of his vision across the snow to his north diminishing in the fading light. He looked up, observing the sheer beauty of the clear night sky and the sharply lit stars emerging, the darkness slowly descending and providing startling clarity to the many sparkling lights across the heavens. His breath condensed and shallow now as the temperature began to bite at his chest as he inhaled, he began to experience the frost closing in around his limbs and nip at his fingers and toes, the night sky both beautiful but deadly in the extreme cold. But tonight there was no reassurance of a forthcoming warm meal or fire as a conclusion to sentry duty…the stove and sheltering dugout were gone…now a distant memory.

He thought back to that afternoon, trying to distract himself from the mood that was descending upon him…but these thoughts too were bleak. He had slept briefly in the trench after their improvised meal, the adrenalin still flowing through him with the fear of being discovered preventing any revitalising rest. His fitful sleep had been disturbed by Tatu and Petru returning from a scavenging visit to the quartermaster's dugout. They had completed this excursion to retrieve further clothing and some more food for their night walk. It had been a bleak choice, a dangerous retrieval of supplies and clothing or potential death from exposure on the Russian steppe at night. Both men spoke Russian, so had considered their chances high if challenged due to their unconventional dress, possession and personal familiarity with Russian weapons. Hausser had reluctantly agreed to them going.

Petru had been clearly emotionally disturbed by the experience and sat alone in silence at the end of the trench after returning. Tatu explained that the emplacement was virtually untouched, as the Russians had been spurred on in their advance, with little time to explore.

They had discovered a severely wounded Romanian soldier in the dugout. Having crawled there in desperation to escape the advancing Russians, there was a blood trail across the snow in the emplacement and the young man was close to death when they found him. The young soldier was only 21 years old, but had sustained a severe stomach and leg wound and was slowly bleeding to death, knowing that there were no medics and no help available, he was fully aware the end was near.

Tatu explained in a solemn and determined manner how they had given the wounded man some brandy to try and dull the pain he was suffering. That he had accepted this willingly, knowing it would help him on his way, but that the young soldier had struggled to swallow the strong liquid, spluttering and coughing up blood from his wounds.

The wounded soldier explained painfully that the Russians had captured some injured Romanians, but that their commissar had then intervened, preventing any mercy. He had ordered the wounded be stripped of their uniforms and left in the snow to freeze. The Russian political officer then set fire to their uniforms as they watched...condemning them to their fate in the bitter cold.

The soldier had continued choking back tears, stating he had 'played dead' and with the blood he had lost from his wounds, the Russians had presumed his actions to be reality. Once the Russians had moved quickly away in their advance, spurred on by their commissar, he had crawled to the only spot he knew may be safe, the quartermaster's dugout. He considered he may find clothing here to take back for the wounded, but he was too weak and exhausted upon his arrival from blood loss to return to them.

Tatu explained that Petru had crept back to the front position with some clothing to see if he could help, but that he had been too late. The injured soldiers had sustained further injuries from another Russian unit that had followed the advance. Petru placed his head in his hands at this point, a moan of frustration escaping from his lips as he began to sob uncontrollably.

Tatu lowered his voice, whispering that the wounded men had been butchered. Determining it probably had been a Russian penal battalion that had been let loose on the helpless soldiers, spurred on by a commissar's hatred. Some men had been tortured and others simply bayoneted and left to bleed to death. That when Petru had arrived he had had to scare off some wolves, feasting on the recently deceased with their blood still warm. There was evidence that a couple had initially tried to resist the ravenous animals, but had been overcome quickly, the victims simply being too weak to fight them off. When Petru had arrived, all the men were dead...there were no survivors.

He continued, advising that the young Romanian soldier had died in his arms, choking on the blood that had filled his lungs and throat. He had held him for some time until Petru returned, then the two men collected some food and clothing and returned to the wood. Tatu leant forward to finish, stating solemnly that the hardest act had been to leave the young man in the dugout, but this would look to any prying Russians that there were no survivors.

Tatu then observed his audience closely, seeing that Udet, Meino and Hase were aghast at what had been explained. Looking directly into Udet's and then Hase's eyes he had spoken almost reflectively, seeming distant, 'I will remember that soldier and that I left him alone for the rest of my life. But you too must remember him...for this shows what the enemy will do to you if you surrender. You are young, and may hesitate…the Russian will not…always remember that.' He spoke slowly to ensure he was understood. 'This fighting is different now…vicious and without mercy. This young man was Nicu's best friend, so I will tell him. That is best.' With this, he rose abruptly and turned, creeping into the undergrowth towards the young Romanian. The youthful soldier posted to the edge of the wood to observe, the message a heavy burden to carry.

As Tatu had departed, Hase had turned to look at Udet, his eyes moist. Udet was staring fixated into the trench, a desperate look of defeat in his eyes. Meino's eyes were determined, his experience overcoming any outward emotion, but Hase saw the sadness deep within him.

It was Petru who had finally broken the grim silence. The Romanian spoke as he stared into the distance, only turning to look directly at the younger soldiers as he finished, his eyes seeming to stare deeply into them. 'We will move soon. Hase…go to the north side of the wood. Go and check the land we will cross; it will soon get dark…we will come then. We have a long walk ahead of us tonight and it will be cold, very cold.' With this, the Romanian had tossed him a felt balaclava and socks they had brought from the dugout, 'Wear these, you will need them.'

Hase turned sharply, startled by a rustle of the bushes behind him. Hausser was approaching him cautiously, half crouched through the undergrowth, the officer's submachine gun in his left hand, a pack in the other. The officer outstretched his right hand and indicated for him to take the pack, Hase realising the others were behind the young commander, all weighted down with packs presumably filled with food and extra ammunition. All nodded to him as they caught up with Hausser, slowly spreading into a semi-circle around him.

Hausser shifted uncomfortably, turning to be able to address him and the others, speaking in a whisper, 'Remember what I told you…spread out. We need to look like a Russian patrol to anyone that sees us.' The men nodded grimly, all wearing the felt balaclavas and scarves across their faces, a shield from the intense cold...their helmets now glistening with the frost that was forming across the metal.

Hausser turned to him, 'So, young Hase...what is out there?' The officer's breath was condensed in the extreme cold and he was now aware the temperature was considerably lower than it had been earlier.

'There has been no movement, sir.' He replied, wary of all eyes upon him, 'There seem to be no patrols...are the Russians sticking to the roads?'

Hausser's eyes narrowed, 'Either that or they think we are all gone from here and are in dugouts and the villages.' His eyes slowly surveying the group one by one.

Hase's eyes slowly followed Hausser's around the small group and it was then he realised the soldier called Nicu was next to Tatu, the young Romanian's eyes staring at the ground expressionless, the shock of the cold and the loss of his friend evident in his strained eyes. The others, Udet, Meino, Tatu and Petru all returned the eye contact, a look of camaraderie in their eyes, Tatu winking cheekily to instil comfort in the young soldier.

Hausser's inspection completed, he stiffened, 'Let's go.' Turning, and rising from his crouched position, the young commander stepped from the cover of the bushes and into the field, the crunch of the snow announcing his departure.

Slowly the others followed one by one, spreading out to about 5 metres apart to advance across the field. The seven men stepped cautiously across and between the frozen ruts in the snow which impeded their progress, the grooves formed from tank and half tracked vehicles running right to left indicating the enemies' earlier route of advance. The soldiers held their weapons at a 45-degree angle across their bodies as they advanced, prepared to react to any possible threat.

The iced snow cracked with each soldier's step, the intense cold having crystallised every part of the landscape, the moonlight causing the surface of the snow to sparkle as the dim rays reacted to the frosted snow. They made slow progress, having to raise their boots when they sank through the ice that had formed on top of the snow...scanning to the limits of their visibility in the gloom, straining their eyes and ears for any sign of hostile life.

The night sky was vicious, yet intensely beautiful in the extreme temperature, the stars seeming brighter and sharper than on any other time the men had looked at the heavens. It was minus fourteen degrees Celsius...the temperature was still dropping.

Chapter Five: Song of the Volga Boatmen

The fisherman's lodge had sat on the western shores of Lake Sarpa for nearly forty years. Provided by the state, it was mostly frequented by burlaks (barge haulers from the Volga) and was used as a rest point and an area for these men and their families to relax at. The fishing in the lake was good with many fresh water varieties for the parties of workers to feast from. Regular large gatherings occurred there in peacetime, especially during the warm summer days and the many visitors had added to the small grouping of buildings over the years.

The collection of buildings comprised of a main hall and gathering point fixed to the boathouse, a small smoking shed, tool/storage shed for netting and garage for the communist party automobiles when dignitaries visited. The buildings were surrounded by the earth walls of a depression or ravine…the only entry or exit, a small track to the north. A short wooden pier stretched out into the lake, used to tether the one or two man rowing boats from the boathouse when several families gathered to celebrate the warmer months. In the summer evenings, the children would play on the lake's edge with the observing adults sitting and drinking on the pier. The older relatives would usually remain in the main hall and cheerfully watch their offspring and families through the glass doors facing the lake. The families would sleep in the main hall or in one of the several tents stored in the outbuildings.

The buildings had fallen into some disrepair since the outset of war over a year previously and the visitor numbers had decreased dramatically since the summer. Rumours of the advance of the German armies towards the area in the summer of 1942 had become more and more widespread, demoralising the regular visitors and preventing any mood for a large gathering or party. Collective fear had quickly eliminated the energy for the journey from the city and motivation for a recreational retreat.

In the late autumn of the year the Romanian 20th Infantry Division had set up a forward command post at the small collection of buildings, hastily departing earlier the previous morning upon realising the extensive attack that was about to fall upon them from the east. With the lake surface frozen heavily in the extreme temperature, Russian infantry had approached silently on skis across the ice. The Russians had opened fire sporadically at the rapidly departing command vehicles, forcing them to abandon a considerable quantity of supplies in their desperation to escape being overrun and ultimately destroyed. Several Romanians had been wounded or killed in the skirmish and they lay around the buildings. The wounded had been left in the snow to die from exposure, the cold overcoming most of them during the morning and early afternoon.

The new occupants were a small patrol from a Russian penal battalion on their mission to sweep the area for survivors and deserters. After suffering some quite extreme casualties in the initial assault, the unit had been broken up and scattered across the area to prevent the escape of surviving enemy units to the city that lay to the north. The brutal and vicious tactics of such a unit were ideal for chasing down and murdering disorientated small groups of soldiers that were desperately attempting to escape. No prisoners were expected and therefore none were taken...no questions were asked...the disillusioned and bitter men assigned to the unit eager to extract revenge for their circumstances on an enemy that was finally weakened. Two surviving wounded Romanians, weakened by the extreme temperatures had experienced their brutality first hand, both being kicked to death as they attempted to crawl away. The assailants laughing as the victims' bones cracked, maliciously taunting the men as they begged for mercy, their lives extinguished as sport.

The fifteen men now sat or lay around the meeting hall, warming themselves on the open roaring fire that they had built. They had used their daily portion of Vodka earlier that evening, but had then found six bottles of Romanian brandy amongst the hastily discarded supply crates lying outside the buildings. These boxes had been placed to the left of the fire and their contents were now being passed around the men as they lazed next to the fire, the strong fiery liquid being slowly consumed as they boasted of their kills and brutality for the day. The fire was utilised to warm the food thoroughly, on the end of bayonets or by placing the tins in the fire for the meals to warm through. As the evening progressed, the men had eaten their fill and had now adopted a more liquid diet. Slowly each man began becoming more absorbed in the high spirits of the group, the common bond of bitterness and hatred focussed into the emotional release of slaughtering their enemy.

Only one sentry stood at a window, facing south, but the alcohol slowly began to overcome the men's caution, complacency and a group feeling of power from the elaborate stories beginning to distract them. The sentry spent more and more time turned to face the group as the stories became more exaggerated, the laughter and bravado becoming more extreme.

The stories of killing powerful enemies in exaggerated numbers was infectious and the need to 'outdo' the last storyteller too enticing. In reality their victims had been the wounded or men weakened by the cold, perhaps a day hiding in low temperatures with limited winter clothing. Most offered little or no resistance, several had begged for help. The men boasted overpowering groups two or three times their actual size, changing weak and wounded men into fully fit well armed enemies in their elaborate stories.

They hardly noticed the soldier that slowly moved to the edge of the gathering, a quiet man who did not quite fit into the group. The man had listened intently to others' stories and realised he had no story to match or share, his first confirmed kill that day being his hated commissar, butchered in no man's land...something he realised he could not discuss.

Alone, he had continued during that morning, butchering and torturing any wounded he had found, their cries for mercy going unnoticed in his need for satisfaction. His thrill of perpetuating and prolonging their agony and terror...he gained power from their fear, eventually ending their lives when he got bored of their whining and crying. His chosen weapon of torture was his sheath knife...to him, a glorious weapon of pleasure and ultimate destruction, the long blade usually drenched in blood when he had completed his gruesome and grisly task.

Around midday he had narrowly escaped being caught with his last victim, a Russian captain approaching him only a short distance from the body. He had seen the suspicion in the man's eyes, the extensive blood on his clothing a clear indication something was not right. He had thought quickly and overturned the suspicions of the captain describing how he had attempted to save a mortally wounded comrade, but had ultimately failed. The captain had ordered him to come to the fisherman's lodge…to await the returning patrols.

He had hastily departed upon receipt of the order completing the five mile distance to the lonely buildings in three hours. Shortly after his departure the captain had found his last victim, the shock of the discovery and consideration of what had occurred making the officer physically retch. The victim had had some of his organs removed, and by the look on the poor soldiers face, this torture had been accomplished whist he was still alive.

The soldier in his forties slipped silently from the meeting hall, quietly closing the glass door that faced the pier behind him, the cold air hitting his face and freezing the condensation in his beard as he turned from the building. The piercing cold a reminder of the harshness of existence on the Russian Steppe in winter, the clear sharp skies reducing the temperature to almost unbearable levels. The stars sparkled brightly above him, the freezing air intensifying the sight. The frost clinging and embracing the wooden pier, the solidified water grasping the pier supports in almost a crushing embrace.

Only one of the half-drunk soldiers observed him leave, the departure of the older soldier pleasing him. This soldier found the older man's presence unnerving…even creepy…the way the older man stared at the soldiers as if examining them physically. With the door closing, he shrugged and swigged from his bottle, the thought that the strange older man may freeze to death a fleeting thought that made him smile briefly before refocussing his blurred gaze on the fire.

There was a freezing breeze sweeping in from the lake as the man shuffled through the snow, his walk restricted due to his right leg injury. He skirted the main hall and struggled slowly in the deep snow towards his goal, the smoking house. Reaching the tightly closed door, he unhooked the two catches above and below the door handle and pulled the tight door outwards. The steam poured from the opening as he slipped inside, the frost in the hut now melted. The heat engulfed him as he ducked his head to enter the small hut, closing the door behind him. He had earlier set a strong fire in the stove in the small room, warming the small cabin. The outbuilding had been insulated to smoke fish in the colder months, and he had chosen it for this reason, realising the structure would also provide some sound proofing.

He turned slowly, the lantern he had attached to the ceiling swaying slightly as he had nudged it on entering, the light cascading across the small room. He reached up and steadied the light before removing his heavy overcoat, dropping this cumbersome hindrance, grasping the handle of his sheath knife at his waist as if to mentally check it was still there.

The moan from the other side of the room sounded alarmed, the shuffling and scraping of hobnailed boots on the wooden floor of the smoke house scratching the rough floorboards as the other man in the smoking house attempted to move away from the bearded man at the doorway. The actions were futile, the young soldier bound and gagged tightly to the rough wooden fish racks at the end of the room. The young soldier had struggled behind the end of the rack with his head against the wall of the hut, his body wedged between the rack and the wall. His brain was filled with panic…he did not know how he had got to this place, or where he was. He remembered riding his motorbike towards the command post to deliver his message, the message in his despatch case. He remembered finding the bodies in the snow outside…he remembered entering the main hall cautiously, his pistol drawn. Then he remembered nothing, falling perhaps…then nothing. His mind was darting from thought to thought. His head hurt on the left side, excruciating pain and he realised there was congealed blood on the side of his face…but how had he got here, what was this building?

The bearded Russian shuffled across the floor, his right leg tired from the day's efforts. He moved slowly and deliberately, knowing the other man was helpless to protect himself now. Knowing he was watching him...the fear rising within the man was delightful, he could almost sense it. He could almost feel the man's breathing becoming sharper, more frequent as his fear became more intense.

The Russian smiled fleetingly, the young German despatch rider had no idea what horrors were about to occur in this small shed. He had no idea what was about to happen to him...the sensual pleasure the Russian would draw from the squirming he could inflict on this human over time. He would push the young blonde German beyond his wildest nightmares of pain.

The Russian's tongue slipped across his lips as he considered slowly removing parts of the young soldier's body as his victim writhed in pain. The portions of skin he would slowly carve from his legs and torso as he progressed up and down the young man's body. Slowly the young man would succumb to his inevitable fate, realising the struggle was futile, his resistance becoming simple whimpering. Eventually he would beg to die, but this was one of the Russian's most cherished parts of this exercise as he could then begin the final parts of his fantasy. Slowly inserting his sheath knife into the most private of areas and openings in the young victim's body, allowing the release of more and more blood and approaching the climax of his adventure, during which his victim would succumb to death. Once this was accomplished he would slowly and carefully remove the victim's organs, embracing their remaining warmth. This was to be his special pleasure, not only a German soldier, but a young one. Up until now his victims had all been the allies of the tethered soldier, 'the stupid and filthy Romanians' he mused to himself.

The German was now struggling with the ropes around his wrists, seeming to sense the fate that was about to befall him, his panic beginning to become apparent. His moaning becoming frantic, the scarf across his mouth so tight he was unable to form words. His natural sense of survival was screaming in his head...to escape, to run from here, to preserve his life. He was eighteen...he had seen into this Russian's eyes in the dim light of the shed...he had also observed the arousal and awakening of a madman. He knew he had to get away from this man, but the ropes were tied too tight, his struggling useless, his assailant well versed in such restraint. His legs were tied, but apart and to the rack and a hook on the wall. This intensified his struggling, understanding that something was extremely wrong for him to be in this position. His head was clear now, the dull pain from the injury throbbing but his eyes wide with fear, his throat and mouth dry.

The Russian was now facing the young German, stood less than a metre from him, watching him as he struggled. A smile formed on the Russian's face...he knew his captive could not escape, the bonds that held him expertly applied. He had learnt this in the backstreets of Kiev, where no one noticed the occasional missing youth, the investigations by the Russian police always inept and incompetent. When war had broken out he had joined up and the army had posted him here, to be stationed on the Volga. Now no one would stop him, no one would find out his actions in this carnage. He smiled further, this war was gratifying, providing ample weak victims for his pleasures. The madness began materialising in his eyes in the form of a hard stare at his victim...his lips were moist, the lust rising within him.

The Russian slowly drew the sheath knife from its leather scabbard on his belt with his right hand. His smile broadened as he observed the German's eyes widen further, his struggling ceasing momentarily as his victim realised that this was a horror beyond the comprehension of his young years. The struggling then began again, with more panic and vigour as the Russian knelt down to begin his ritual, his left hand grasping the German soldier's left thigh tightly near his crotch. The Russian leant forward beginning to apply the full force of his weight through his arm down onto the German's leg, the whimpering and moaning becoming intense as the young soldier tensed his body, trying desperately to move against this further restriction...but it was no use. Slowly the Russian inserted the knife into the fabric of the German uniform at an angle just under the knee. The tip of the sharp blade easily cutting through the uniform at the seam and touching the young man's leg. The Russian smiled further as the sound of the tearing fabric pleased him, the moaning of his victim increasing as the cold blade touched his flesh.

The German squirmed, sheer terror now overcoming him...but the ropes were too tight and confining. He could only tense his muscles, attempting to pull his thigh towards him as the blade slipped slowly up the outside of his inner thigh. The tip of the large steel blade drawing blood as it progressed up his leg to his crotch.

The despatch rider closed his eyes, tears flowing down his cheeks, his chest clenched tightly with a feeling of sickness, he sobbed in desperation. He began to blank out the horror of the reality, feeling helpless to the actions of his captor. He could see his mother smiling, her outstretched arms as he returned home from his initial training, the last days before being posted to Russia. This was to be his big adventure, he could almost feel her embrace and warmth, her safety.

He felt the stale sharp breaths of the Russian on his face, the fetid smell of his uniform and body odour and the sound of the tearing fabric. He felt the blade nick his skin near his right calf, the stinging of scratches that now ran down both his legs.

The Russian was breathing heavily, his excitement rising in anticipation of his game and what was to come. He glanced at the young German's face, almost childlike he mused, his victim's eyes screwed tightly closed and tears flowing freely down his cheeks. The Russian almost felt pity, but the blood lust was more intense, overcoming any other feelings he had for his victim. His lips wet with anticipation, he slowly ran the blade edge down the young man's leg drawing blood.

The German felt the knife touch his skin again, this time the pressure was slightly stronger and he whimpered loudly, knowing the man was deliberately cutting him. A feeling of helplessness overcoming him, the nausea rising from his stomach. He felt the cold air sweep over his body, nipping at his now exposed flesh, his mind flickering in confusion.

The young German despatch rider heard the gasp of breath to his right, an exasperated hiss, 'Was ist...'. Then heard a frantic scrapping, a crack and then a crash. Shadows flickered before his tightly closed eyes and the knife was swiftly withdrawn. Cautiously, but still intensely frightened, he opened his eyes slightly, the light, tears and panic the cause of his vision to be blurred initially.

His mind struggled to recognise the face before him. He saw the scarf wrapped across the man's mouth and nose, the iced frost across his eyebrows, helmet and uniform. He felt the cold emanating from the man as he looked into his eyes and saw compassion and fear…fear for him. Steam was beginning to rise from the man's uniform, he was looking into the brown eyes of Udet.

Udet crouched in front of him, briefly checking his wounds before producing his bayonet from underneath his overcoat to cut his bonds. As the terrified captive's hands dropped when freed, his vision became clouded again, then as darkness overcame him as he passed out.

Chapter Six: Kristallnacht

They had been trudging through the iced landscape for some time now. The methodical and deliberate steps initially breaking the frozen surface of the snow when they had commenced their journey…but in the preceding hour they had been able to make better progress. Their weight was now held by the iced surface as the temperature had dropped further, solidifying the snow beneath the surface.

Hausser had led the men diagonally across to the north east. His aim to reach the banks of Lake Sarpa, considering that this would perhaps limit their exposure to an enemy that would be unlikely to be near the ice at night and only inland. There would also be perhaps the added bonus of lake mist to assist them in the earlier hours of the morning. The initial trek to the lake should have taken about an hour, but in reality the task took 3 hours. Caution was high and the thoughts of the grim reality they now faced etched deeply on their minds promoted frequent stops to check the way ahead. Slowly over this time, the caution and trepidation had transformed into a grim determination to continue against the odds as the temperature dropped further. The men had begun to realise the lack of Russian presence in open country and that the intense cold was assisting their cause. The temperature had dropped further to a bitter level upon approach to the frozen water's edge, but all were aware that nature's cold embrace would deter any enemy from the area. With this providing further assurance, they were now progressing slowly northwards along the western banks of the lake.

Wary that the landscape, cold and monotony of the men's progress would dull senses and limit alertness, Hausser insisted the soldiers answer individual questions regarding their service and surroundings. He had explained his reasoning to the men as they left the cover of the copse of trees, that this was a tactic adopted during the previous winter when they observed slow reactions from patrols and sentries.

Hase had watched Hausser explain this slowly as they had started their walk through the snow, methodically stating the reasoning and ensuring each soldier understood the importance of alertness. That individually they should resist the temptation to become mentally numbed to the cold, surroundings and repetitive walk. That succumbing to these feelings would reduce their effectiveness and reaction time, and that this would spread through the group making them vulnerable to any events that may occur.

As he observed, Hausser explain this to the men he realised the care the officer had for them, for their individual survival. The emphasis the young commander had placed on each soldier understanding what was needed of them individually, requiring them to acknowledge they wanted to survive. That this commitment was essential to demonstrated his determination for them to progress through this danger, to a perceived safety beyond. The commander had held his gloved hand on several of their shoulders as he explained and Udet had received a knock on his helmet in an attempt at humour when he had been slow to respond.

The fear in Udet had been evident in his eyes and Hausser had explained to the young soldier that this was simply a fear of the unknown, that reassurance would come once they had progressed further. Udet had nodded solemnly and the others had listened intently, the breathing of the group seeming to be hushed as Hausser had spoken, as if each man understood the meaning applied to him also.

These actions seemed to slowly transform the low spirits of the group as they progressed, the responses becoming more projected, less withdrawn as they moved. Hase admired this attention to detail in his commander and the resulting effect. This endeared him to the man further and he began to realise that a new loyalty and feeling of belonging was beginning to emerge from his doubt and uncertainty. He realised he was seen as part of the team, a member of the unit, something he had not considered before...a feeling that comforted him, deep in his chest.

The snow sparkled in the moonlight and from the bright stars as they had advanced through the cold, the crackling of ice and crunching of compacting snow beneath their boots as their individual weight was applied. Occasionally a man would slip or stumble as the iced surface of the snow gave way, or they overcame a rut in the earth beneath the enveloped landscape. As time passed this happened less and less frequently as the snow froze through...the temperature was dropping further.

Each man's overcoat slowly began to gain a thin layer of frozen condensation covering it as the temperature fell, the darkened fabric gradually turning a peppered white. Their bodies became unable to sustain warmth to more than the first layer of clothing, the felt clothing provided by the Romanian quartermaster providing a welcome insulator. The frost extended to their metal helmets, as the last remaining moisture crystallising in the air.

The frost also restricted breathing, freezing the moisture in the scarves across each man's mouth, turning each exhale into a rasp as the warmth battled against the external temperatures. Each inhale of breath was wheezed as the men's bodies struggled against the cold temperatures. Their condensed exhaled breath now hung in the air as they progressed, the cold now seeming to still all life and existence.

The night sky was breath-taking in this temperature, the stars seeming to be sharper and brighter than at any time the men had witnessed before. The air was so still and crisp in the low temperature that vision was completely unimpeded, the darkness seeming overwhelming were it not for the sharpness and focus of the lights that pierced through the oblivion of space.

Each soldier now had a felt balaclava which insulated his face, covering their nose and mouth, with the scarf added for extra protection against the elements. This welcome Romanian addition covered their neck and tucked into their uniform, adding to the straw packed into their helmets to retain warmth.

But the cold swept into their eyes, turning them bloodshot as their bodies resisted the fierce temperature, each individual forced to blink more frequently to prevent the moisture in their eyes solidifying. Occasionally, they would each have to brush the frozen condensation from their eyebrows and scarf to assist vision and breathing further.

Hase had listened to the men talk and answer Hausser's questions as they walked. The soldiers had spoken individually of their personal situations, their words forcibly pushed through the half frozen scarf and felt masking their mouths and noses. The strain of talking whilst walking in these temperatures was initially hard and misunderstood, but then slowly collective realisation became apparent as the numbing and piercing cold dulled their minds when they did not converse. Hausser would break the conversations and predictability by demanding the men look at particular objects, then jump from the expected recipient of a question to an individual that had not spoken for a while.

Hausser had initially targeted Tatu, knowing this would guide the group's train of thought and exploit their fondness for him. Tatu had obliged, understanding this reasoning and knowing the objective, then quickly asked Hausser a question in return to establish a routine in the men's minds.

Hase had listened as Hausser and Tatu had exchanged information, then watched and listened to the other four men talk.

Tatu had informed the men that he had signed up for the army with Petru as an adventure, that the Russians had threatened Romania and taken her beloved territory as a 'bully' next door would do. That this was the motivation for them joining and that they would help ensure Romania's future in a new Europe. He spoke with pride as he talked of Romanian history and the future his country must have to sustain its part and the existence of its people. His mood lightened and became gentler when he spoke of Petru and his family. That they were so welcoming to him, he felt as a member of the family, regularly being invited for meals, drinks and to play and assist with the children. That this was what he was fighting for.

Tatu's determination and passion seemed to energise the group a little, providing extra motivation and understanding for the others.

Meino had spoken next, advising the soldiers he was the son of an innkeeper from Sinj. He was from Croatia and a member of the 369th Infantry Regiment. He had volunteered for the unit when Germany had asked for soldiers and his country had been wary of Italian expansion. He had left his young wife and father to run the Inn whilst he fought for his country and believed that his suffering would bring a better future. That if he volunteered he would save others from being selected to fight.

Nicu had volunteered to speak next, his determination to involve himself apparent. He spoke in a low emotionless voice, his eyes fixed on the terrain to his front. His occasional, even startled glance at Hausser and Tatu interrupted his stare, a sign he was keen for acceptance, even reassurance after the loss of virtually all his comrades. He explained he was originally from Hotin on the Polish border and had seen the desperation of his country on the loss of Bessarabia to the Russians. That his relatives in Odessa had come to stay with them upon the Russian invasion and he had learnt from his uncle of the cruelty that had occurred in the southern city. His father had wanted him to work in the market with him, but that when the Germans and Romanians had retaken the historical city he had joined up to help defeat the Russians and end any threat to Romania once and for all.

Tatu had patted Nicu on the shoulder in encouragement when he finished, the younger man clearly struggling to complete his contribution, the emotions stirring within him creating a lump in his throat and distorting his voice, youthfully dismissed as the cold.

Hase watched as Hausser spoke to the group. Explaining he had joined up as his father had been in the army before him and that he had been around soldiers all his life. He had been born in Dusseldorf, but had moved to Potsdam at the age of 14 where he had originally joined the 76th Infantry Division. His mother was Romanian and he had learnt the language from an early age, this had provided the opportunity for him to be transferred to units serving in southern Russia. After a spell before Moscow, he had fought in the Crimea with the 11th Army and had then been transferred back to the 76th as the 11th Army was transferred north towards Leningrad. Upon the movement into Stalingrad, he had been transferred to the southern front once again as a result of his language knowledge. He had concluded that it was ironic he was now in Russia as this was where his father had fought during the previous war.

Hausser encouraged Petru to talk, and the 'older man' of the group as the officer fondly called him, began by describing his family and children back in his beloved Bucharest. He described the first time he had met Tatu at the furniture makers they had worked at for 6 years before the war. The group had grinned at some of the antics that he had described they had accomplished in the workshops behind the furniture store. He continued, explaining that over time they had begun to invite Tatu more and more to the house he shared with his parents and that soon they felt his friend was part of the family, that his children called him uncle.

Petru continued and started to talk about the lavish meals his wife would prepare when Udet interrupted him abruptly, stating that he was in no mood to listen to talk of food in this situation and that he had been hungry all day. This drew coughs and splutters from the soldiers as they chuckled in the extreme temperatures, the condensed air clouding around them as all of them exhaled.

Meino slapped the young soldier's shoulder and demanded he explained himself for interrupting his elder. Udet grinned sheepishly beneath his scarf, realising it was now his turn to talk. He described his love of Falkensee, the town he had been born in. It lay near Potsdam and was very beautiful with parks and its close location to the Havel River and waterways. He explained that as a young teenager he had been fortunate that the Olympics had occurred so near his home and that his parents had taken him to see the many parades and ceremonies that had occurred at that time. He continued, stating all should visit his home when the war was concluded, and that his mother was a wonderful host. Observing his father was always able to source extra rations to provide a splendid party, much to the surprise of his brother and him.

Udet had fallen silent in mid-sentence as he glanced something in the distance, the light from the moon illuminating the distortions in the snow at the foot of the slope they had come upon. The other soldiers following his gaze as he slowly pointed.

As they had begun to approach the frozen lake, the temperature had gradually dropped even further, the close proximity to the large expanse of water chilling the air. A light breeze enveloped them as they negotiated a slope and passed through some bushes in their approach to the water, some 50 metres away. The breeze enveloped each man like a cold wave as they descended the decline, seeming to pull them forward, embracing them, their eyes strained to make out the images before them. The freezing air seemed to now cling to their bodies, attempting to seep through every seam, every opening, in their thickly layered clothing.

It was then they came across several bodies in the frozen snow. The retreating Romanian soldiers had been ambushed in the open in broad daylight by a Russian patrol, their attempts to surrender ignored as the initially concealed Russians had opened fire with machine guns. The seven Romanians, having fled the initial breakthrough in haste, had only rifles which offered little defence. They had survived undiscovered as the initial advance waves had passed by, but with limited food and warm clothing, they tried to move north in an attempt to locate a friendly unit. The route was predictable and they were encouraged to see a small number of tracks in the snow crossing the many Russian tracks heading east to west. They had considered that these tracks were potential allied soldiers that had preceded them, men that they would perhaps meet further north. They had followed these tracks.

Despite the tracks, their movement had still been restricted by the deep snow and they had offered virtually stationary targets to the Russians waiting for them in nearby bushes. The Russian penal soldiers, realising their foe offered little resistance, had opened fire and most targets had received several wounds. The Russian patrol had then proceeded to loot the helpless men of any personal belongings as they lay, begging for help. Any individuals that attempted to resist were shot, the Russians jeering at their victims as they pleaded for mercy, their weakened body temperatures already dropping in the cold. Their mission accomplished, the victors had departed leaving the surviving wounded to their obvious fate in the snow. The moans and frustrated weeping of the wounded Romanians granting them chilling satisfaction as the Russians slowly walked away. Heading north to their predetermined rest point for the night, they had walked amongst a number of similar scenes, of further images of butchery. The bodies of the dead they had ambushed earlier, bodies of the survivors that had preceded this group.

Hase observed that their group was crossing the tracks that were in the snow heading north, not joining or following this route. The men were spaced protectively across the area and passed through the grouping of corpses in the snow, their steps deliberate and cautious as to not to tread on the fallen, their eyes scrutinising and scanning the surroundings for any threat.

The contortions of death on the bodies' faces frozen in these temperatures instilled in the men the certainty of death in these surroundings if they were discovered. A morbid curiosity or simply horror at what could occur imprinting snapped visions of frozen curled fingers, of men reaching for life from a cold embrace of death as they succumbed to their wounds. Unable to rise, their fate sealed as the snow and wind sucked the warmth from their bodies.

Hase had become quite shaken by one corpse that seemed to stare through him as he passed. He could just make out that the eyes were open as he approached in the gloom. The life in the eyes extinguished, but still seeming to stare directly at him. The temperature had frozen the man's eyes some hours earlier, but they still seemed to be pleading, to be begging for assistance. His mouth open, his last struggles for breath as blood filled his lungs, the escaping liquid frozen to his cheeks. The darkness in the snow indicated the man had sustained several wounds and that he had been shot at close range at least once. From his expression he may have been pleading for his life, for mercy...and this was what he sensed now, observing the corpse's last expression. It would be a gruesome vision in his memory that would stay with him for some time to come.

Hausser distracted the men from their thoughts, wary the scene had broken their progress. He determined to keep them moving, to prevent them from losing body temperature if they stopped. Moving to the brow of the final slope before the lake's edge, he turned to beckon the hesitating soldiers. 'Come on. There is nothing we can do here. Once we are at the lake's edge we will make better progress. Keep alert.'

The men responded as Hausser indicated for them to continue, ushering them forward with his outstretched gloved right hand. They passed him individually, grim determination in their bloodshot eyes. Tatu had pushed Petru forward from the scene initially and was the last to pass Hausser, glancing over his shoulder at his dead countrymen as they departed the scene, the officer's gloved hand comfortably placed on Tatu's shoulder.

Hase waited for them at the banks of the lake, Meino and the two younger soldiers some feet away to the north. The two Romanians and Hausser approached slowly, stepping cautiously down the frozen bank, their boots unable to break the surface of the snow for leverage. Hausser placed his right hand on Hase's shoulder to guide himself down the last few feet of the steeper part of the slope, then turned to assist his two Romanian comrades. Once they were all at the same level, Hausser indicated for the men to close in around him with his gloved hands.

The officer addressed the group in a low voice, the condensed air escaping from his lips as he spoke, 'I think we shall continue along the lake for a while...we will be safe from the Russkies in this cold. I think they will not venture out or if they do, not to the lake's edge where it is colder.' He paused, coughing slightly, the cold catching in his throat, 'Tatu has told me of a fishing lodge some distance away and I think it best we rest there for the day ahead. This is colder than I imagined and draining our strength.'

Hausser looked slowly round the group, his eyes red from the frost. In response, the men slowly nodded, realising they had now a limited time in these elements before exposure began to set in.

The young commander continued, 'It will be dangerous staying in the fishing lodge for the day, but I think we have no choice...if we stay out in the cold we will be finished. We will continue northwards at late afternoon or dusk. Come...let's move before we freeze to death here.'

The group of soldiers turned and began to trudge slowly northwards. Hausser hesitated, indicating to Hase to wait with his hand. Turning to him, the officer's voice was now a whisper, 'Young Hase, keep a watch from the rear...if someone looks unsteady call me. They will be very cold now so I will try and keep their pace up. Time is short.'

He nodded grimly in response to the instruction, knowing the commander was becoming concerned for their safety. Hausser nodded once, acknowledging his acceptance and turned to join the soldiers, both men joining the group a small distance away.

As commanded, he fell to the back of the group, his rifle in his gloved hands across his chest. He sensed the light breeze from the lake, realising he could no longer feel the lower temperature, his body was already too cold to acknowledge any change.

The view over the lake was distorted, a low mist forming above the ice...it would be thicker by dawn and he considered they must have perhaps three hours of darkness left. Across the lake he could hear a faint cracking as the ice shifted with the temperature, the noise initially unnerving as if existence itself was being strained to breaking point in these temperatures. To him the sheer beauty of the sky was now eclipsed by its vicious and lethal clarity in this cold.

As they trudged along the bank, he realised the soldiers were now like deep shadows against the snow and landscape in the moonlight, the bitter cold and their experiences seeming to have sapped their resolve. They seemed slower, more hunched in stature than before. The exposure to the elements and the attrition of the previous day had taken its toll, they were now physically and mentally exhausted.

Chapter Seven: The Frozen Embankment

They had been progressing north for almost 45 minutes along the embankment. The cracking and splintering of the ice as it settled in the severe temperatures the only sounds to accompany their trek. The pace of the soldiers had now reduced considerably in the severe conditions and each man's body core temperature was now slowly slipping in the bleak environment.

A slight breeze swept across the men from right to left as they progressed, carrying with it the chill off the ice, the low temperature from the lake dropping even further with this wind chill. Occasionally this would move the looser flakes of ice on the surface as they moved slowly through the terrain, the surplus dancing across the lifeless surface.

The temperature was now so crisp that the soldiers' exhaled breath hung in the air, swirling as Hase walked through it as he followed the main group. The rasps of the men's breathing through their frozen scarves and thickening layer of frozen condensation on their uniforms now evident under the moonlight and breathtakingly sharp lights from the stars. The group having now gradually drifted closer together as if for collective warmth or emotional support in the bitter temperature.

The landscape was only interrupted by the occasional frozen bush or tree, with the terrain offering no cover from the elements other than the slight decline down to the lake. Some distance to their left was the side of a ravine dropping to the decline, but this did nothing other than capture the colder air within it, creating an insurmountable barrier for the cold air around the lake.

Hausser had initially attempted to sustain conversation along the frozen water's edge, but this had proven ineffective as each man began to withdraw mentally into their own individual solitary world. The answers to the young commander's questions becoming shorter and shorter until individual men simply did not comprehend that the question was targeted at them.

The young officer had therefore resorted to a different approach, spurring the men on collectively with promises of the 'buildings not being far', 'the group stopping to rest for a day', 'that they could light a fire and become warm' and that 'that would cook warm food when they arrived.' This produced no external response, but he knew the men would perhaps acknowledge his words and gain some resilience from the encouragement in the short term.

Inwardly, Hausser was becoming increasingly concerned. He pushed himself to observe each man individually and all the signs he had experienced the previous winter before Moscow were returning. The solemn, withdrawn emotionless faces, the slowing and then negligible responses, the seemingly glazed expressions in the men's eyes all lead him to believe they were slowly beginning to lose body temperature. This, coupled with their exhaustion, would slow their progress and expose them further to the elements as it took longer to reach their destination.

The commander observed that even the Romanian quartermaster was beginning to struggle. He had initially assisted by declaring the stores of smoked fish and bread at the Fishing Lodge would be more than sufficient to fill their stomachs for days. That there would be a warm fire and alcohol for their enjoyment. But now he too had become withdrawn, concentrating on supporting Petru who seemed to have developed a slight limp, dragging his right foot. Hausser hoped this impediment was in the Romanian's mind and not the onset of frostbite.

As the small group struggled northwards, Hausser realised that if they were attacked now they could offer little resistance as the men would struggle to react immediately, their withdrawn minds in their frozen bodies unwilling or unable to process the danger until it was too late. He consoled himself that if his men were in this physical state due to the elements it would take a brave Russian commander to attempt to spur his men out into these temperatures, let alone order them to sweep the side of a lake where the temperature would be even lower.

The commander considered his men, determining, from his previous years' experience, that at this time his stronger men seemed to be Hase and Udet. The younger body of Udet and experience of Hase providing a resilience able to recover more rapidly from the extremes placed upon them. The rest of the group were now just following on with Udet leading and Hase trudging behind them. Both soldiers were also showing the signs of exposure, but seemed more able to display signs of resisting the elements than the others.

The other four soldiers were walking together, beginning to draw closer to each other as a sign of combined comfort. Petru and the younger Romanian, Nicu, had both emotionally struggled the most with the previous day's events and this had bound them together spiritually, but weakened them in these temperatures. Tatu had become attached to his countrymen's plight and Meino was simply inexperienced to these temperatures and resisting them mentally.

Hausser dropped back to walk alongside Hase as the group slowly began to ascend a gradual slope, the frozen expanse of water slowly dropping away to their right as they progressed. As he drew close, he could see that the man's gaze was firmly upon the group in front of him, the signs of an internal distance from events becoming evident. Keen to re-establish the soldier's alertness, he prodded his right shoulder with his gloved left fist, 'Hase?'

Hase had watched the young commander gradually fall back to walk next to him, but this had been slow to register in his mind, his vision set on the four men walking to his front. Their repetitive trudging drawing him into himself, a mental escape from the cold. The air around him seemed still, occasionally disrupted by a breeze off the frozen lake, the extreme cold no longer registering in his mind, his body numb to the elements.

He stumbled to his left, the action disrupting his line of thought, the pressure on his right shoulder almost causing him to lose his balance. He turned to his right, his mind confused, looking onto the covered face of Hausser. The man's helmet was frozen white, with crystalized condensation all over his uniform. The scarf covering the commander's mouth seemed frozen and the condensed air that pushed through it was disrupted as the man spoke to him. Then he heard him speak his name, 'Hase! Wake up!'

'S-Sorry?' He hissed back, the words seeming distant, as if someone else spoke them.

'Think hard…it's me, Hausser. Come on man, focus.' The commander seemed irritated with him, his eyes narrowing. He felt the officer grasp the front of his jacket with his gloved left hand, shaking him.

'Y-yes I know.' He stammered, 'I was confused.' He felt the cold sweep through his body as if jabbing him sharply. He looked into the eyes of Hausser, the commander seeming concerned for him. He could now see the officer blinking frequently, his eyes focused on him, his exhaled breath hanging in the air between them.

'Good.' Hausser retorted, 'We need to get to the fishing lodge or some cover…or these men are finished.' There was concern in the young officer's eyes as he continued, the exhaled air being forcibly pushed through his scarf, his teeth gritted beneath the frozen cloth. 'I made a mistake…I never thought it would be this cold. I-I should never have tried for so far at night.'

Hase shook his head, reality now seeping back into his mind, the cold intensifying in his body. His reactions sharpening briefly in the freezing air as the officer's frustration and warning pierced his almost mesmerised state. He felt the commander drop his hand from his chest, observing him half turn from him, looking forward, to the north.

He followed his eyes, seeing the group had stopped a short distance ahead, with Udet beyond them, his outstretched arm indicating for them not to proceed further. Udet turned to face the group, and he could hear him hiss, 'Hausser, kommen sie.' The younger soldier's outstretched hand indicating for them to join him, Udet then sank down on one knee in the snow, his gloved hands raising his rifle in readiness.

He followed Hausser as he trudged past the group of four other soldiers, observing the small group as they slowly turned to look at him passing, their expressions confused, reactions abnormally slow. The young commander lowered himself to a crouch as he approached Udet, responding to the soldier's caution. He followed likewise, feeling the cold in his joints resist the action, complaining painfully of the strains placed on them.

Udet acknowledged them as they drew alongside. The young soldier's breathing visibly more rapid from the rate of exhaled air surrounding him. He turned to Hausser, 'Just ahead, sir. There are some buildings in the depression.' Udet's eyes were wide with excitement as he spoke, his demeanour seeming apologetic, 'Sorry, I got nearly to the edge of the drop before it registered.....I think I must have been distracted or something. There are lights in the main building, do you think the Russians are there?'

Hausser nodded, clutching his MP40 in his right glove tighter. 'Let me take a look...you did well.'

As the officer moved forward carefully, half crouched, then lowered himself to a crawl, Udet turned to look at him, 'Do you think they saw me, Hase?'

Hase shook his head, his eyes strained in incomprehension as Hausser replied on his behalf, 'We would hear them if they had.' Aware the young soldier had also probably displayed the same signs as himself, slow to react as he walked aimlessly northwards in this repetitive terrain. Startled, he realised that Tatu was now approaching from behind him, also half crouched, the quartermaster's reactions gradually returning, his mental resistance rising.

Hausser was now lying on the edge of the depression, looking over at the collection of buildings that comprised the fishing lodge. The commander turned, looking back, indicating with his left hand for them to join him, but to keep low. The three men responded, moving a short distance crouched and then crawling the remainder of the distance to be alongside their officer.

As they drew alongside Hausser, they looked over the edge of the drop in front of them. They had now ascended a gradual slope and to the front of them lay the sides to another depression, within it the fishing lodge. The lights from the main building windows illuminating the landscape for some distance around the depression and out onto the lake, almost to the end of a small wooden pier. The other buildings surrounding the main dwelling lay in darkness with the exception of one smaller wooden outbuilding, smoke rising from its side chimney. Smoke also rose from a bigger chimney on the main building and they could clearly see movement within, with the distant noise of muffled voices emanating from the solid structure.

A thin mist was now slowly creeping in from the lake and beginning to seemingly grasp at the sides of the pier, a further cold embracing the wooden structure frozen firmly in the ice of the solidified water. A number of small wooden boats lay discarded around the large building and in the road that led off to the north where a number of discarded boxes indicated a hasty retreat by the previous occupants.

Hase squinted further, seeing light casting shadows across some other distortions in the snow. He strained his eyes until it dawned on him, there were also bodies around the building, the prone figures frozen in distorted death's embrace in the bitter temperatures.

Tatu noticed these bodies also, his teeth gritting beneath his scarf at the sight. The quartermaster realised these bodies were probably his countrymen, ones he had spoken to just a few days earlier as he had scoured the area for some additional supplies for the 'party' with his German neighbours. The experience now seeming distant history of perhaps another world after their recent exploits and change of fortunes.

The four men watched, the silhouette of a man in the window facing their direction moved as he changed positions, the sentry's attention now fully on the conversation around the open fire in the main hall. Hausser indicated as he observed a figure leaving the main building from the doors facing the lake, and they watched as the silhouette disappeared behind the structure before reappearing on the left side, heading in the direction of the outbuilding with smoke rising from its small chimney.

It was then Hausser spoke, his voice hissed through the frozen scarf, 'Udet, go after the lone man, try not to shoot unless you have to, and not before we do.' He studied the young soldier, observing him nod, 'Go around the depression and come in from behind that building.' He indicated to one of the outhouses to the left.

Udet nodded again and then crawled off to the left until he was sure he was away from the edge of the depression, then he rose to a crouched position and ran off half-crouched into the darkness.

Hausser turned to Tatu, 'Make your way down the lakeside and cover the door to the water, Hase and I will make our way in where the sentry is. They do not seem to expect company in these temperatures.'

Tatu nodded and whispered in reply, his voice almost a sneer. 'We are cold, they are in the warmth, that is their weakness...they will not escape from me.' With this he turned and crawled away to the right, then rose to a crouched position, running back down the slope they had just climbed to enable himself to advance towards the lodge along the frozen lake's surface.

Hausser turned to Hase, 'Wait here, I will get the others to cover.' With this, the young commander pushed himself slowly back from the edge and turned, crawling a short distance before rising and walking to the group of three soldiers, standing some distance away.

Hase watched as the commander spoke to them all and each man nodding slowly in response, their actions seeming lethargic and confused. He bit his lip, looking down he carefully pulled the bolt back in his rifle, checking there was a bullet in the chamber. The weapon seemed different from what he remembered before, but he realised this was due to the time he had been carrying it and his emotional detachment from events. The metal seemed darker than before, the extreme temperatures and contrast with the snow enhancing his perception. He considered the stories he had heard of weapons jamming in extreme cold, of firing pins breaking at crucial moments...all of these factors a possibility in the current situation.

Hausser patted him on the shoulder, breaking his line of thought, 'Time to move!'

He watched as the officer crawled to the edge of the depression and searched for something to hold before swinging himself over the edge, dangling briefly and then dropping to the ground a metre below, the landing sound muffled in the thick snow. He followed Hausser's lead as the three other soldiers slowly took up position on the edge of the walls of the depression, spacing themselves a couple of metres apart, their instructions to cover a retreat should the enemy be too powerful.

He swung himself over the edge of the drop to the ground below, feeling the weakness in his arms as he dangled in mid-air, the cold of the temperature in his muscles fighting him. Letting go of the frozen overhang, he dropped into the depression below, a dull thud as he landed in the deep frozen snow. He moved swiftly a couple of steps, propelled by the drop and then crouched, joining Hausser concealed behind a large stacked pile of chopped logs to their front. The snow covered stacked wood a welcome concealment from any potential observers.

The officer considered that there could be no retreat, that these buildings were their survival. There was probably nowhere else for them to shelter and no energy remaining for them to make any journey if there was. This added to his determination, his mouth stiffening.

Hausser turned to look at Hase, his eyes raised expectedly. The soldier nodded, indicating he was ready, his rifle now held out in front of him. Hausser nodded once, looked down at his MP40 and pulled the bolt back. Hase noticed as the young commander took a sharp intake of breath, the rasp as the air was sucked through his scarf followed by a wheeze as the cold air entered the man. Then the officer nudged forward, glanced round the log pile in a final check of his path to the main building and ran out half crouched across the snow towards the exterior corner wall of the lodge.

Hausser reached the corner and concealed himself out of view of the window occupied by the sentry. Composing himself, he turned and indicated for Hase to wait before following him.

He watched as Hausser breathed heavily, the short run in the extreme temperatures having proved very taxing. Then the commander glanced around the corner, observed no movement from the sentry and indicated for him to follow.

He looked round, making sure there were no observers, then back to the window. The sentry's silhouette clearly visible off to the right side of the window, but his attention in the other direction, into the room. Over to the left he noticed a movement, he tensed, holding his breath. Then he exhaled, quickly recognising Udet slipping from his cover behind the outhouse and beginning to approach his target building. Checking the surroundings again, he tensed, considering someone may be about to open fire. Dismissing this, he thrust himself from the woodpile, running at a crouch across the short distance to the exterior wall, slipping next to Hausser. His back against the building and rifle held upright in front of him.

Hausser nudged him with his left shoulder, both of them out of breath from exerting themselves in the extreme cold. As the commander nudged, Hase leant out, looking to the left and seeing Tatu approaching the building across the side of the lake, his PPSH41 held menacingly, the large fur overcoat now open to permit greater movement.

'Ready?' the commander whispered quietly, his breath still laboured.

Hase nodded, his grip tensing on his weapon, his finger extending towards the trigger.

'Now!' The commander pushed his back from the wall and disappeared round the corner, the distance to the lodge's main entrance now only some 5 metres. He followed, keeping low below the window and reaching the side of the doorway, looking across the entry point at Hausser. Both realising they were now less than a metre from the sentry on the other side of the door.

Their eyes met and Hausser seemed to smile at him. He nodded in return and the commander raised his submachine gun, stepping away from the side of the door, turned and lifted his foot as a splintering noise came from the direction of the outbuilding behind him. With this, Hausser kicked forward and the doors gave way under the impact, swinging inwards with him advancing into the room. Twisting his MP40 upwards and hitting the surprised Russian in the mouth, knocking the sentry backwards as the Russian dropped his rifle, the officer lowering his weapon to fire a short burst into the roof of the room.

Hase stepped out, his rifle at the ready, gripped tightly in his hands. Turning to advance into the light of the building through the open doors, he stepped over the threshold. He felt a wave of warm air engulf his face, the reaction making him slightly dizzy. Shaking off the distracting feeling, he advanced, hearing Tatu's deep voice barking a command in Russian from the other side of the building, 'Don't move! Surrender or we shoot!'

Chapter Eight: Blood and Ice

The Russians in the wide main hall were caught completely by surprise, their astonishment at figures emerging from the bitter cold evident on their faces. Their weapons, out of reach against the wall were a reflection of the complacency that had overcome them. The alcohol dulling their reactions, they simply remained sitting on the floor, their faces twisting to meet the new arrivals, disbelief evident in their expressions. Slowly a number raised their hands in front of them, their eyes vacant and empty, the shock evident on their faces.

Hausser advanced into the centre of the room, his submachine gun pointing at the assembled audience, the plaster and dust dislodged from his gunfire dropping onto his helmet and shoulders. He stood legs apart, facing his enemy, a look of grim determination on his face.

Tatu moved along the wall, his PPSH41 held tightly, pointing menacingly in front of him at shoulder height at the group of Russians…the weapon's magazine contained over 70 rounds, more than sufficient to destroy his foe should they react unfavourably. He stopped as he came to the collection of Russian weapons, ensuring he stood between the captives and the guns, sending a clear message to undermine any attempt to gain access to them.

Hausser glanced across at the Russian sentry, now cradling his face in his hands, the blood seeping through his fingers. He hesitated seeming to consider the situation, then calmly looked towards the door, 'Hase!' He commanded, indicating with the sway of his submachine gun for his comrade to move the injured man across the room to the others.

Stood just inside the door, Hase lowered his rifle, moving the weapon into his left hand and nudging the sentry's leg with his right boot. He interjected in a low but firm tone to the prone man, 'Davai!' Gesturing an indication with his right hand for the soldier to join his countrymen.

The Russian dropped his hands abruptly, staring up at him, his eyes moist from the blow to his lower face that had connected with his nose, the blood oozing from both nostrils. Their eyes met, and he saw a look of uncertainty, even puzzlement in the Russian's blue eyes. Then the gaze was broken as the injured man realised the importance of compliance, the soldier purposefully crawling across the floor to join the nearest section of the seated group.

Hase watched as the man adopted a place amongst the others, assuming a cross legged seated position with his countrymen, his expression blank, but glancing at him once more with a puzzled expression.

Hausser moved slowly towards the open doors facing the lake, closing them as he did so. He turned to Tatu, the Romanian's weapon still pointing menacingly at the group, 'Move them across the room…to the far side from the fire. I will get the others…they need warmth.'

The young commander strode confidently across the room towards the main entrance, nodding at Hase as he approached, a smirk of reassurance on his face. He continued past his shoulder, stepping back into the cold and turning to the left, moving out of sight.

Tatu turned to the seated audience, 'Move over there.' He exclaimed, indicating to the back of the hall, the furthest from the fire, 'Slowly now.' His eyes narrowing as the Russians hesitated.

Slowly the Russian soldiers complied with the instruction, initially only two men slowly rising and walked cautiously across the room. But as initial fear subsided at the action, more and more of the group made the short distance to sit against the far wall. Their eyes glancing with distrust from the Romanian to his weapon and back again, occasionally glancing at the soldier next to the main doorway. The sentry displayed slightly different behaviour, the young man staring only at Hase, his eyes the only sign of confusion, seeming to study him unnervingly.

Tatu was keen to gain control, and indicated for the men to sit side by side, all facing into the room. Thus allowing him to observe each man's actions with ease, reducing any eye contact between the Russians without him noticing. He instructed they all sat cross legged, reducing their ability to react or rise quickly from their seated position and then he personally assumed a seat to the right of the open fire, next to the discarded weapons, his own weapon never straying from the Russian soldiers.

Tatu nodded approval across to Hase, the young soldier covering the movement with his rifle from the main entrance. Hase observed the quartermaster with some respect, noting the Romanian's attention to detail in covering the captives and reducing their ability to react. He saw the steam now rising from the quartermaster's large leather overcoat and uniform as the heat from the fire thawed the frozen clothing. He soon realised that the steam was also rising from his own uniform, the cold beginning to dissipate from his body as the temperature around him gradually rose. Aware the scarf across his mouth was becoming moist as the frost melted, he pulled it down to around his throat.

He slowly observed the Russian captives seated cross legged against the wall. Most were expressionless, their faces displaying the effects of shock at being overcome with such ease, their fate uncertain. Most were watching the Romanian quartermaster, seated observing them, his weapon targeting them directly. A few displayed the signs of worry, the knowledge of their previous day's exploits against the countrymen of the soldiers that now held them prisoner playing heavily on their minds. The sentry was the only soldier showing differing signs, his demeanour conflicted, his younger mind distracted from the situation with a different array of thoughts. The Russian's eyes moving from the floor to the soldier at the doorway, him.

There was a shuffling noise behind him and he spun round, his rifle at the ready. Hausser stood in the opening, his face deeply concerned, the frost on his helmet glinting in the light spilling from the room.

Petru stood behind him, his rifle strung over his shoulder, arms supporting Nicu. On the other side of the younger Romanian was Meino, also half carrying Nicu. He looked at the young soldier between them, his face very sullen and colourless, his eyes closed, his body shaking uncontrollably. The group pushed past him, with Hausser turning to face the seated Russians, his MP40 submachine gun pointing menacingly.

Meino and Petru half carried Nicu to the front of the fire, laying him gently before the blaze, their faces solemn. The young Romanian groaned as his body was laid on the floor, his mind drifting in and out of consciousness, the cold having lowered his core body temperature significantly. He lay on his side facing the fire, shivering uncontrollably before the open heat.

Seeing a couple of the Russians smile unsympathetically, Hausser grasped his submachine gun and raised it, returning their facial expressions back to concern, the commander aware that their captives could use the opportunity of the distraction to their advantage.

Hausser turned his head to speak over his shoulder, 'Don't give him any food until he warms up, the shock could kill him.' He returned his eyes to the seated captives, studying their expressions for signs of any enjoyment of the young Romanian's plight.

Petru knelt next to the younger soldier, Nicu, removing his own overcoat to cover the shivering countryman, gently pulling the young man's scarf down from his face. The older Romanian's face was solemn with concern, emotions for the young man overcoming his own physical reactions to the warmth in the room as he carefully placed the overcoat over his prone countryman.

Meino removed his frozen helmet and sat dejected next to the pair, his stare on the young suffering soldier and his plight. Despondent, he slowly started to unwrap the scarf from around his mouth, pulling the felt balaclava down.

Nicu was shivering uncontrollably, the warmth from the fire causing steam to rise from his clothing. The young Romanian was barely conscious, with little knowledge of his surroundings or the captives behind him. Petru leant over and retrieved a discarded Russian jacket, rolling it methodically and placing it gently beneath the young Romanian's head for comfort, also pulling the soldier's balaclava down over his chin to aid his breathing.

As Hausser turned to Hase, Udet entered through the main doors beside him, his rifle held at waist height. Udet nodded to him as he entered turning to beckon the men behind him into the building. Hase followed Udet's gaze and saw a wounded Russian stumble into the room, his bearded face covered in blood, his nose broken. Behind him walked a soldier in German uniform, the trouser legs torn and stained with blood. In his right hand he held a pistol, pointed determinedly at the Russian's back, only some inches in front of him.

The German soldier glanced at him and his uniform and gave a slight smile of recognition before the seriousness returned to his face, a deep look of distress etched across his forehead.

Hausser stepped back, his eyes still on the seated captives, 'Put the new prisoner with them.' He indicated to the seated audience with a tilt of his head. Briefly studying the new German arrival, he nodded to him, 'Which unit are you?' The young commander requested, turning his gaze back to the seated prisoners.

The despatch rider pushed the Russian forward brutally with his free hand, the man stumbling and falling to the floor to the right of Udet, landing half way to the seated Russians. None of the prisoners moved to help him, but slowly shuffled aside to allow him a place, their solemn faces studying the man suspiciously. Udet watched the man fall, a look of contempt on his face, then slowly turned and moved exhaustedly towards the fire, quietly removing his helmet and dropping it to the floor.

'4th Panzer Army,' the young German retorted. 'Private Albrecht sir. Despatch rider.' He attempted to present a more formalised stance to the officer, but his emotional exhaustion was clear by the shaking of his voice. 'This animal…' He indicated with a sneer at the Russian on the floor with his pistol, '…was going to cut me up.'

Hausser looked at the prone Russian, the man slowly crawling across the floor to his countryman. The commander considered the situation for a second, 'Very well, we are secure. Hase, close the doors properly and stand guard. Be alert, I think these are all of them but we cannot be too careful.' He looked across at him as he spoke, indicating for him to close the doors. Nodding in return, Hase turned to the half open doors and began to push them together.

The officer turned to Albrecht, 'Go sit by the fire, and check the food the Russian's were eating…perhaps we will have a meal after all once we have all warmed through.'

Private Albrecht nodded, 'Yes sir!' He turned and approached the prone Romanian, leaning over to inspect the ration boxes to the left of the fire, noting a number of unopened tins to his satisfaction.

The young commander continued, 'Petru, how is Nicu? Is he recovering?' The concern was evident in a lower, more gentle tone to his voice.

Petru turned his gaze from the young Romanian on the floor, 'He's not good, Hausser. He kept quiet until we realised he had passed out in the snow. Hopefully in a couple of hours we will know whether he will survive…he is young, so that may help.' The Romanian's concern for the younger man was clear, his eyes moist with the heat and emotion.

Tatu stood up, a deep grunt of dissatisfaction emanating from him, 'Give me their officers and the piece of shit that just came in.' He indicated to the older Russian with the blood soaked beard, 'I will take them for a walk…the others will not trouble us then.'

Hausser shook his head, 'We are German soldiers that is not what we do.' His annoyance at the quartermaster's demands evident in his tone.

'Nonsense!' Tatu interjected, 'The men I want are scum! They murdered my countrymen outside and in the snow in cold blood, we deal with them now! The others will survive, the officers and that older one are evil, and the other men will be free of them. They will not give us any trouble then.'

Hausser sighed, his face troubled. He realised that the quartermaster was telling the truth, but could not condone the 'murder' of his prisoners. He shook his head, 'No…'

A Russian prisoner stood up abruptly, 'I can speak Romanian...what he says is true. We murdered the men in the snow, they had no defence...' His voice tailed off as Hausser reacted to his movement by grasping his submachine gun more tightly, pointing it menacingly in his direction.

Hausser spoke calmly and with a determined tone. 'Stay where you are...don't move closer...'

The Russian held his hands out in front of him in subservience, backing up to the wall, 'I understand, I won't be trouble. I just wanted to state that he is right. We were ordered to ambush any escaping troops, but not slaughter them. They made us do it!' He slowly pointed to five of the seated Russians, his face exasperated, the fear creeping into it. Two of the men he indicated shook their heads in disbelief, their expressions displaying a deep anguish.

One of the men he pointed to, a sergeant in his thirties, turned his face to him, 'Shut Up, you fool...they will shoot us all.'

Hausser was becoming frustrated and directed his next comment to the Russian sergeant, moving his submachine gun to point at him, 'Be quiet, let him speak! The rest of you stay still!' The officer was aware the prisoners were becoming agitated, their head movement increasing as each man looked around the others concerning him. 'Tatu cover them!' He instructed, hearing the Romanian quartermaster raise his weapon.

The young Russian soldier continued, 'The army wanted us to capture the troops that escaped, but they ordered us to ambush them. Some pleaded for their lives, but we left them in the snow. Some were shot, the others we left to freeze to death.' The young man was becoming upset, the tears forming in his eyes and his voice shaking, 'They ordered us to murder them...even when they surrendered. They said it would make us stronger...make us hate you more, make you afraid of us...they are evil.' His voice tailed off as he suddenly realised what he was doing.

The young Russian prisoner looked around his captors seeking assurance, the Romanian quartermaster watching their side of the room with his weapon raised, the German officer also alert, his submachine gun held tightly pointing towards them. The older Romanian knelt by his shivering countryman and the three other Germans next to the fire, all staring at him. Next to the closed doors to his left was the German that puzzled him, also observing him, his face and eyes showing concern at the escalating situation.

As he looked silently at his captors, he realised their mood was changing with what he had said, the emotion he had displayed betraying his countrymen. He slowly lowered himself on his knees, his back against the wall. His emotions reeling, but understanding he had told them the truth, no matter how dangerous this was. The Russian next to him placed his hand on his leg, a small gesture of reassurance.

The German despatch rider spoke up, his voice shaking but directed at Hausser, 'The Russian in the smoke shed was going to cut me to pieces.' The tears began to form in his eyes once more, 'Not only kill me…but torture me until I died. Udet saved me.' His voice became more determined, his eyes tightening. He placed his hand on Udet's arm in a thankful gesture, 'Take him and the leaders outside, let them stand on the lake…it won't take long. We free the others then.'

Hausser took a deep breath, sighing in part disbelief, turning to look at Hase, seeing the young man's confusion. The young commander cleared his throat and sighed, his words in a slow dismissive tone, 'Tatu…take the six outside to the lake.'

Tatu moved forward, indicting to the six men with his submachine gun, 'Get up you scum, we are going out.' His face grim with determination, 'Take your uniforms off.'

Hausser spun round. 'Wh…what?'

The Romanian quartermaster looked across at him, 'We will need them to get through the Russian lines…and they don't need them anymore.' He glared at Hausser, his determination clear.

Hausser considered briefly then slowly nodded, his face grim. 'Do it.'

The selected Russians slowly rose from their positions, their demeanour defiant but resigned, the submachine guns pointing at them overriding their urge to attack their captors. Hesitantly, one by one they removed their tunics and trousers, revealing their felt body length underwear. One by one they followed Tatu's indication, slowly shuffling towards the door to the lake, aware he was covering them with his weapon.

Petru rose from his position, picked up his rifle and joined Tatu, his weapon pointing at waist height towards the prisoners. His face filled with hatred, he indicated for the first Russian to open the door.

As the six prisoners slowly filed out of the hall onto the lakeside, Hausser turned to face Hase, stretching his hand out to indicate for his comrade to remain calm, the commander seeing that the man was struggling to comprehend what was happening.

The door closed behind Petru as the men walked out towards the pier, the older bearded Russian turning briefly and solemnly to observe the soldiers inside. As they walked slowly, their heads dropped, the realisation there was nowhere to run, their fate sealed. The men felt the intense cold bite at their bodies, the frost beneath their feet sucking at their body heat.

Back inside, Udet stepped forward to cover the remaining prisoners, noticing they were all looking at the floor, avoiding any eye contact, each individual captive struggling with his personal thoughts.

Hausser's gaze slowly moved from his comrade to the group, then twisted back surprised as he heard Hase cough, take a sharp intake of breath then begin to speak. He slowly shook his head looking despondently at the young commander, his voice trembling, disbelief and tears in his eyes, 'What are we doing here?'

The burst of submachine gun fire outside broke the silence, the men in the room instinctively 'jumping' at the abrupt noise and the dark meaning it conveyed.

A stillness descended on the room as they all slowly and purposefully turned to look at the lone soldier that had just spoken, Hase standing with head bowed next to the main entrance.

Hase noticed their wide eyes and the surprise on their facial expressions, some stared at him with open mouths. The prisoners shifting in their positions all looking at him, with Udet and Hausser responding by tightening their grips nervously on their weapons, taking a step forward menacingly, their stance indicating for the prisoners to become calmer.

The young Russian sentry was wide eyed, his bloodied mouth open. He slowly raised his hand, pointing towards Hase, the soldier standing in German uniform next to the main doorway.

The young Russian shook his head in disbelief, stuttering briefly, the remaining prisoners' gaze all following his outstretched hand, their faces stunned, voices silent. The sentry's incriminating finger pointed straight at Hase's face. 'Y-you...You are Russian!'

Chapter Nine: Der Hilfswillinger

Some distance to the north of the lodge, the Russian captain sat relaxed in the small personnel carrier, his left boot resting on the front metal cupola of the tracked vehicle. He watched as one of his men unloaded a box of supplies from the other carrier and trudged with the heavy wooden container towards the artillery emplacement through the deep snow. Observing the gunners delicately move shells from a covered emplacement, he smiled comfortably to himself. The emplacement had been dug the day before and the heavy guns pushed into their new home earlier that morning. A clearing made in a small wood to provide extra cover should German planes take to the sky in search of ground targets.

The heavy artillery pieces faced north and were soon to commence firing into the lower suburbs of Stalingrad. His smile portrayed his thoughts that the Germans were now on the 'back foot' with the Russian army sweeping round their flanks. The morning briefing had indicated that resistance to the offensive after initial fighting had seemed weak, with the two prongs of the attack now heading towards Kalach in the German rear.

He looked down at the box of cigarettes in his lap, nestling in the curves of his thick overcoat. The red circle and strange writing on the packet indicating a definite improvement on the cigarettes he had received from army stores in war to date. The American branded tobacco was apparently 'Lucky' and he considered this complimented the British vehicle he was currently relaxing in. He contemplated these cigarettes were indeed lucky for him, the war supplies from America supplemented by considerable quantities of food for the Red Army. The British, keen to demonstrate their own support, providing him with a vehicle where horses would have previously been normality. He was also grateful for some personal comfort through the bitterness of war in the form of enhanced rations. Taking a cigarette from the packet, he lit it and closed his eyes as the warm smoke drifted into his lungs, enhancing his body's battle against the elements.

'We are nearly finished here, sir...where to next?' He was startled from his thoughts as the carrier's driver climbed over the right side of the vehicle and turned to speak to him.

'Oh, erm...we go to the fishing lodge. Further south past Dubovyy Ovrag, we drop more supplies there.' He retorted, irritated the man had distracted his line of thought. He grasped the collar of his overcoat, pulling it closer around his neck as a brief breeze swept over them, slowly drifting in from the frozen lake to their east and turned back to the driver, 'Let's go when they start up.'

The man nodded, his bushy moustache and furtive eyes just visible under his felt and fur cap, the exposure from driving permitting him additional clothing for warmth. 'We will head there shortly then sir; the men are just dropping the last cases off for the artillerymen now.'

The officer nodded, taking another draw on his American cigarette and drifting into his thoughts once more, thinking back to the conversation he had had at the end of the morning's briefing. He had approached the commissar and asked for a personal word, the situation he was presented with requiring further guidance. He explained to the young political officer his concerns regarding one of the soldiers he had met, the suspicion of butchery of enemy wounded and killing of prisoners. His concerns that this soldier was, in fact, torturing enemy soldiers.

The young political officer had seemed concerned at first, then his interest had seemed to wander, advising the captain that he was spending too much time thinking of one man when there was an ongoing conflict affecting the entire southern flank of the front.

The captain had argued that this would affect other men's confidence and a unit's efficient function if this went unchecked, that he would not allow this from one of the men under his command.

The political officer had considered this briefly, then stated that the 'party' could not condone such actions by individual troops, but that the man was killing the enemy after all. Dismissing the officer, he had simply advised, 'If you don't like it, ask him to stop or take him for a walk...we are not wasting time on such a thing.'

The officer had not needed an explanation of what 'taking for a walk' had meant, but had been irritated by the lack of direction he had received, the lack of responsibility taken for the problem. It was therefore up to him what to do, and as yet he was undecided.

He was distracted as one of his soldiers mounted the personnel carrier and sat alongside him, their bodies separated by the central storage containers on the vehicle. 'That's all the supplies offloaded, sir.' The man reported, moving his submachine gun across his lap. The young soldier then pulled the ear flaps of his cap down and began attaching them under his chin, wary of the cold that would soon surround them as the vehicles progressed.

The captain looked round, surveying the surroundings. The emplacement was now busy with artillerymen moving shells across from their storage bunker. As he watched, a gunner on the first artillery piece placed a shell into the breach and closed it with a dull metallic thud that resonated across the landscape. The officer in charge of the emplacement glanced across at him, gesturing a brief wave, then holding his arm in the air as he turned to face the on looking artillerymen, their faces fresh with anticipation.

The artillery sergeant nodded to his men, searching their faces for readiness. He received expectant and understanding nods in return, with this he was satisfied. Stepping slightly forward in the snow his hand dropped swiftly, his shout energising his men, 'Fire!'

In reaction, the gunner pulled the firing cord and the artillery piece shuddered backwards, the roar of the gun breaking the calmness of the snow covered landscape scene around them. The gunners, all with their hands over their ears, watched as a plume of smoke rose from the gun barrel into the crisp air. The thunderous sound wave enveloping them as they stood, a hoarse cheer from the emplacement gunners following the gun's bark. The 152mm shell flew across the landscape, its journey taking seconds before landing in the lower housing district of Stalingrad.

The captain leant forward, tapping the driver's shoulder with his left hand. The engine of the tracked vehicle roaring into life, the carrier jumping forward slightly in the rough terrain. The tracks threw up churned snow in its wake as the small vehicle with its three passengers began to negotiate the slope away from the guns. Joining it, the second vehicle laden with supplies jolted after it, the tracks slipping in the frozen terrain until gaining the tracked grooves in the snow from the preceding vehicle. Both vehicles being carefully coordinated to avoid stumps and the roots of the trees as they exited the copse.

Behind them, the second artillery piece fired, then the third, the plumes of smoke rising from the guns as they propelled shells into the lower parts of the distant city. The smell of cordite swept across the artillery placement as the gunners feverishly reloaded their weapons.

The two small personnel carriers continued their journey southwards, joining the rough track now completely obscured by a blanket of frozen snow, their departure signalled by the deep thumps as the guns fired behind them again.

The small vehicles negotiated the makeshift exit from the copse and turned east, descending the gradual slope leading to the main north/south thoroughfare. Joining the main road, they turned to the south, heading towards the village in the distance.

The captain leant back again in the carrier, a rolled up spare overcoat behind him to add extra comfort. He lit another American cigarette, dropping his head back as he did so to look at the bleak grey cloudless sky. He drew deeply on the cigarette and blew smoke into the air, relishing the taste of the American brand in comparison to the rough Russian tobacco he had experienced before. Either side of the track lay iced bodies, contorted in frozen death, evidence of another failed attempt from enemy survivors to escape the Russian army's advance.

The personnel carriers continued for nearly two hours in the snow, occasionally having to stop as one vehicle or the other struggled in the unforgiving terrain. The scenes of scattered bodies and discarded equipment lay all around the wide track as many of the enemy had considered this the road north to use in desperate attempts to escape their attackers. Some had been units determined to resist the attacks from the east, but these acts of bravery had been overcome by determined Russian tank attacks knowing their foe had little anti-tank equipment.

Having exited the village, they proceeded to a crossroads and turned to the east onto a rougher track leading down to the banks of Lake Sarpa. The journey was unforgiving with the track rutted and barely used by vehicles due to the remote destination at the lakes edge. The journey took over an hour as the men struggled to free their vehicles numerous times when the carriers occasionally failed to overcome snow drifts or the frozen rutted ground beneath.

At one point, they had had to slow to negotiate a destroyed lorry, stopping briefly to loot any remaining abandoned supplies from the back of the disabled vehicle. The frozen corpses of the Romanian forward command unit strewn around their destroyed transport, the vehicle and bodies having been overcome by carefully concealed machine guns. The ambushers understanding fully that this would be one of the main escape routes the enemy would take.

It was mid-afternoon when the small two vehicle convoy began to approach the banks of the lake, the light across the Russian Steppe now beginning to fade. The rutted track descended a steep decline to the frozen water's edge as the drivers reduced their speed and lowered the gears on the personnel carriers to ensure they did not lose control, the danger of skidding on such an incline a risk to their precious cargo.

As the captain looked over the frozen lake to his left, he noted to himself that they would inevitably now have to spend the night at the fishing lodge. In the dimming light, he realised his eagerness to avoid exposing his unit to the bleak and bitter night time temperatures on a return journey through the snow was a high determining factor in this decision.

As the first personnel carrier ground over a small rise, the track split to the north and south before the lake's edge. The carriers turned south and began to descend the gradual slope down to the Fishing buildings which now came into view, a low cold mist clinging to their structures. The captain sat up, smiling to himself as he noted a soldier walk out from the lodge to stand between the buildings and meet them. He considered he would scold the sentry for staying in the buildings, but decided to relent when he felt the freezing air of the lower depression envelope the small convoy as it proceeded towards the buildings.

There was smoke rising from the chimney of the main building and as his vehicle approached, the captain just being able to smell the faint aroma of food being cooked in the large hall. His stomach welcoming the thought of a freshly cooked meal and perhaps adding some American tinned meat to the supper taken from his supplies.

The first vehicle pulled into the small yard in front of the lodge and stopped with a brief jolt to the side of the sentry. The captain noted the soldier had some thick layers of clothing to protect him from the cold and nodded as the man stood to attention next to the vehicle, his rifle by his side, saluting him formally.

Saluting back, the captain rose from his seat and stepped over the side of the carrier, turning to face the sentry, greeting him with a warm, 'Hello...at ease soldier.'

The sentry stiffened slightly, 'Welcome to the lodge, sir.' He retorted, eyeing the captain's red epaulettes respectfully.

'From Kiev?' The captain stated recognising a slight accent.

'Yes sir.' The sentry replied, his eyes never leaving the captain's.

'Good.' The captain replied, 'Did not realise we had many from Kiev on this front now.' He looked into the blue eyes of the sentry, his unshaven, but quite direct features interesting him. The man was perhaps mid-twenties and was obviously quite tired from the darkened lines under his eyes, 'Which unit are you from?'

'47th Army initially Sir...but now this unit, I fell asleep on guard duty sir.' The sentry retorted.

The captain's eyes narrowed, his mind quizzical, 'You are a long way from home and your unit...how did you end up here?' He watched as the sentry shifted on his feet, seeming uncomfortable at the scrutiny.

'I was wounded in the Crimea, sir, shipped across the Kerch Straits and ended up here.' The young sentry returned the captain's stare as if to reassure him.

'Well, you may not be in this unit long if you perform well.' The captain replied, his demeanour softening at the sentry's certainty and seeming determination. The officer knew full well that most penal soldiers were desperate to return to ordinary units...avoiding the considerable extra dangers of the penal squads they had been assigned to due to mistakes.

The captain continued, his thoughts drifting, 'Tell me, do you have a soldier here with a grey beard...maybe mid-forties?'

The sentry seemed to consider his question and then replied slowly, 'Yes sir...I think he is out near the lake.'

The soldier's eyes seemed saddened by the question and the captain wondered if the young man could comprehend what behaviour the older soldier was capable of, 'I will need to speak with him later...anyway, for now, let us unload the supplies assigned to you. I will need a full report of the last day's events from your commander.'

The sentry nodded, seeming more comfortable, 'Yes sir, he is in the main hall awaiting you.'

The captain smiled, 'We will stay the night here...have you plenty to eat?'

A brief flicker of a smile crossed the sentry's face, 'Yes sir, any other rations will be welcome though, we have only Romanian food left now.' The sentry seemed to then think of something as his eyes widened, 'However, we do have some Romanian brandy too sir…perhaps you will enjoy this with us?'

'Ah, I see!' The captain was warming to the younger soldier, a smirk forming on his face, 'Perhaps the food is not restaurant quality…but we have some American supplies to supplement the cooking.' The captain placed his left hand on the soldier's shoulder, 'I would be happy to join you in a drink, come…show us inside into the warmth.'

'Yes sir.' The sentry replied, 'Please follow me.' With this, the younger man turned on his heels and walked back towards the main doors of the building, hesitating at the entrance to await the captain, he dropped his rifle from his shoulder and held it in his left hand indicating with his right for the captain to proceed inside.

The captain turned to the crews of the two personnel carriers, 'Unload all the supplies and cover the vehicles for the night. I think we are about to have a welcoming party.'

The smiles of the crews did not go unnoticed by the sentry as the captain completed issuing his orders and glanced inside the building, seeing Hausser looking cautiously out at him, the young commander concealed from sight to the left of the main doors. Hase's eyes then returned to the captain approaching him, his driver directly behind carrying a box of supplies. Behind them the crews were picking up supply boxes, their weapons left in the personnel carriers.

The sentry's eyes moved back to the captain, now standing before him. The man was smiling, in his hand a large box of cigarettes, his pistol holstered, the light from the building now spilling out onto the approaching figures, the sky darkening further. The sentry smiled warmly and welcomingly, opening the door and extending his hand for the captain to proceed inside.

The Russian captain stepped into the light of the room, his eyes reacting to the brightness, glancing to the right as a man coughed, observing a Russian sergeant stood nearby. As his eyes became accustomed to the light he noticed the steaming cooking pot by the fire, then the tall broader soldier stood opposite him, a reassuring smile on his face beneath his broad moustache. He noticed the man was holding a submachine gun pointing at waist height to his right and followed the direction the gun was pointing in. Looking round, he froze, the hairs on the back of his neck tingling as his mouth went dry. A small group of soldiers were sat cross legged on the floor, their hands behind their heads, their glazed eyes looking up at him. All were sat in their felt underwear, their Russian uniforms piled in the right corner. Empty brandy bottles lay amongst the seated men, none of whom were wearing boots.

'Guten Abend, Herr Kapitan.' He heard behind him and spun round in horror. The sergeant was staring at him, a slight smile on his face. In the man's hands he held a German MP40 submachine gun pointed at his waist, then speaking in fluent hushed Russian, 'Don't move or we shoot you all...now call your men inside...*carefully*.'

The Russian captain's stomach turned, his eyes drifting down to the man's neck, his tunic now open at the top. A German uniform beneath the Russian brown colours, the dark cross around his neck outlined in white...the captain shook his head and slowly raised his hands to shoulder height with a reluctant sigh.

The personnel carrier crew members filed into the main hall one by one, each carrying a supply crate, their weapons discarded in the vehicles outside...they were followed by two armed men in Russian uniforms. Each soldier slowly formed a look of amazement and shock on their face as they realised the situation, one by one obediently grouping in the centre of the room. The Russian captain stood amongst his men, a look of dejection and defiance on his face.

The smiling sergeant cautiously approached him, gently removing the captain's side arm whilst keeping his free hand on the trigger of his submachine gun, the weapon supported by the strap over his right shoulder. As the sergeant stepped back, the side arm retrieved, he spoke firmly again in

Russian, indicating to the men seated behind them with a nod, 'Now please remove your uniforms and boots and join the others.'

The captain addressed the armed sergeant as his men began slowly and reluctantly removing their uniforms. The grim expression of the taller broader man pointing his Russian PPSH41 at the group reducing the motivation to protest. Clearing his throat, he attempted to impose an impression of seniority, 'I will give you the opportunity to surrender now...I will guarantee your safety and the safety of your men if you give up.'

Hausser cheekily lowered his head to one side, studying the Russian, his eyes seeming to become sad, then a sly grin began forming on his lips, 'I don't think so, captain. We have come through too much to just give it up now. After seeing what your army has done to others, I do not hold much faith in your promise of safety. Perhaps from you personally...but not from others in your army.'

The Russian captain nodded reluctantly, 'I had to offer you this way out...there are thousands of my countrymen between you and your goal to the north, you will not make it to safety. Even if you do, what then? Your Sixth Army is virtually cut off on the Volga...where will you go then? You will lose this war...the seeds are already sown. You are an officer and your responsibility is the safety of your men...as is mine.'

A brief smile formed on the German soldier's face, 'Perhaps so, captain, but we will see. You are correct in assuming my responsibility is my men and that will keep us fighting. This position is a setback only I think...the Russian Bear is not yet dead, but mortally wounded I think.'

Hausser turned to the German soldier standing next to him, the man's rifle pointing at the group, 'Udet, collect their uniforms and boots and place them in the carriers...we leave in one hour.'

Udet nodded, his body straightening, wary of the on-looking Russians, raising his rifle to place over his shoulder, 'Jawohl, Herr Leutnant.' He stepped forward, beginning to collect the discarded uniforms from one of the Russian captives. The other armed Germans and their allies in the room seeming to emphasise their weapons to the startled prisoners.

The burly Romanian man with the bushy moustache now addressed the Russian captain, his gun never leaving his targets further across the room, his eyes stern, 'Your friends here have killed a lot of our countrymen in the last couple of days captain, think yourself lucky today that this German officer...' He indicated to Hausser with a jerk of his head, continuing, '...has more restraint. If it was just me...you would all be dead now.'

The Russian captain looked across at him, surprised by the outburst, 'We were instructed to intercept escaping troops...'

'Intercept!' The Romanian quartermaster interrupted him, his voice becoming raised with contempt, 'What does that mean captain? Murder? I see no prisoners you 'intercepted'.' The Romanians voice was becoming filled with contempt.

Hausser interjected, 'Not now, Tatu.'

The quartermaster glanced at Hausser, his eyes narrowing then moving his stare back onto the prisoners, his voice firm and dismissive, 'Join your friends at the back of the room, captain. Sit cross legged and no sudden movements...all I need is the excuse...'

The Russian captain nodded in defeat, indicating for his men to withdraw to the back of the room with his right hand. Slowly the men followed his lead and cautiously lowered themselves amongst their countrymen on the floor.

The captain observed that all the previous captives were drunk, the smell of alcohol strong amongst the group, his realisation the Germans had contributed to the prisoners rations to reduce resistance and movement. He watched as the Germans and Romanians moved the uniforms and weapons outside, taking some of the recently arrived American ration boxes with them. Noting that one younger man seemed weaker than the rest, his face drawn and colourless, his body covered in additional clothing and a large padded overcoat, one of the Germans assisting him to walk outside.

The captain then studied the sentry he had first met, the German commander addressing him individually and quietly in Russian. Noticing the younger man seemed uncomfortable with his stare, he adjusted his vision to the floor of the room, realising this man was a Russian volunteer. He wondered what could have caused such a change of heart, eventually dismissing the thoughts and simply summarising this man was now also his enemy, if not even more of a target.

As the German preparations for departure became more conclusive, a growing fear rose within him. Would they shoot their captives? Just throw grenades into the room as they departed? He began to realise the same thoughts were beginning to surface amongst his fellow captives, their uneasiness reflected on changing seating positions and concerned eye contact.

The Russian captain watched as the Germans slowly exited the room, leaving just the burly Romanian guarding them, making his stomach turn. He considered the larger man had enough rounds to finish them all off before they could get even half way across the room towards him. He also seemed to have the motive to kill them all due to his previous outburst.

His line of thought was broken as the German Leutnant re-entered the hall, his exhaled breath indicating the temperature outside was already quite low. The German officer walked confidently into the centre of the room, ensuring the Romanian still had a good line of fire should anyone rise to confront him.

The German Leutnant stood defiantly, surveying the group, then addressed them all, his eyes moving from man to man, 'We will be leaving now…there are sufficient supplies for you for a number of days and ample firewood outside for cooking.' He hesitated, watching the group of captives relax slightly as their worst thoughts were addressed, 'Do not try to follow us as I fear you will get lost in the dark and cold…your winter is oblivious to which country its victims come from.'

Hausser paused again, letting his message be digested by the captive audience, 'Your captain will look after you as I believe he is a good officer.

The men who previously commanded you are all gone now…I wish you good luck gentlemen.' With this, the German officer clicked his heels together and saluted the seated Russians formally, drawing a surprised wide-eyed response from his audience.

Hausser turned smiling faintly, 'Tatu, let's go…I think you have become too settled here by the fire, old man. You will miss all the adventure.' He grinned at the Romanian quartermaster's exasperated glance at him in response. As the Romanian responded and passed him, the young German commander slapped his shoulder playfully, the quartermaster returning a forced smile. With that the two exited the building, leaving the relieved yet exasperated audience to consider their situation.

The Russian captain smiled in relief, his stomach settling on hearing the engines of the personnel carriers roar outside and the sound beginning to recede as his enemy slowly moved away in the darkness. He slowly turned to see the Russian soldiers as relief spread across their faces, cautious smiles beginning to form across their faces.

The captain waited for about a minute, his caution finally overcome when he considered they must try and secure the buildings once more. Turning to the men, he instructed certain individuals to gather the food and check the surroundings, posting sentries although unarmed at each doorway and window. Once this was achieved he moved the remaining men near the open fire.

Once they were assembled, the Russian captain indicated for the men to help themselves to the pot of stew next to the burning logs, the soldiers greedily ladling the steaming portions into mess tins and consuming the contents ravenously, their relief at safety motivating their hunger further.

Slowly the scavenging men returned producing some more rations and some firewood, all complaining of their cold feet without the benefit of boots.

One younger soldier returned from the wooden pier, in his hands a pair of boots, the cheeky smile at his confidence of the find evident on his face as he handed them to the captain, 'Sir…we can now send someone out to get help.'

The captain took the boots from the smiling soldier, turning them over in his hands and inspecting them, a wry smile slowly forming on his face, 'Perhaps not soldier...the boots are of different size and for the same foot. It seems our Romanian and German captors have a sense of humour...these boots are so we can get firewood without catching frostbite, no one will be able to go long distances in them.'

The soldier's dampened demeanour amused the captain further and he attempted to lighten the young man's mood, 'Good find though. I think the enemy had thought this through, if we get news of them out they will be hunted down. For now, they have escaped.'

The captain's thoughts became more serious as he considered another issue, addressing the group, 'What of your commanders...what happened to them?'

The soldier that had produced the boots slowly responded, his eyes downcast, 'They took them outside sir, their bodies are next to the pier. They blamed them for us killing their countrymen.'

The Russian captain nodded grimly, knowing the characters of the men that had been killed and that there was a degree of truth in the Germans line of thought. He noticed some furtive glances around the group and considered questioning this, but rejected it, 'Was there an older soldier amongst them? One with a beard?'

The young man looked him in the eyes, his stare dark with suspicion, 'They took him also...he is out there too...it seems they shot him several times. He is some distance from the others, I think he tried to run. He was a strange man though...perhaps he deserved it sir.'

The captain nodded slowly, relieved his troublesome mission had been accomplished without a decision that had formed confliction within him, 'I think you may be right there.'

He turned to the talkative soldier, 'As for the Russian amongst them, do we know anything about him?'

The man hesitated, uncomfortable at the question, 'He seemed troubled by what happened when they took them outside. When he went out to meet you, I asked the big Romanian about him and he said that the young Russian apparently owes his life to the officer after what happened in the Crimea...so he is bound to him through loyalty.'

The Russian captain nodded thoughtfully, wondering what could have happened in the battles around the Sevastopol peninsula to provoke such service. Dismissing the thoughts, he ate a spoonful of stew hungrily.

In the cold freezing dusk outside, about a half a mile away to the north, the personnel carriers slowly and cautiously drove through the night, their speed minimal to avoid hitting obstacles. All men had now several layers of clothing to protect them and their scarves and felt balaclavas protecting their faces against the extreme temperature.

Hausser slowly turned to Tatu, wary of the older Romanian's grim mood, 'We did a good thing tonight Tatu...those men did not need to die.'

The Romanian turned to him, his exhaled breath hanging in the air, 'Perhaps you are right Hausser, they were following orders at a difficult time...they still deserve some discomfort though.'

The young German commander looked quizzically at the quartermaster, 'What do you mean?'

The Romanian quartermaster grinned under his scarf, staring mischievously at the German officer, 'When you were not looking...I took the stew outside and pissed in it.'

Chapter Ten: Understanding

As the personnel carriers lumbered slowly northwards, Hase surveyed the surroundings. The evening was not as cold as the previous night, with a high cloud cover preventing the temperature from plummeting. To his right, the frozen lake had a light mist across its surface, the lower temperature of the ice mixing with the air temperatures about a metre from the surface creating the distorted view as the contrasting levels of cold mixed. Occasionally some light from the moon would penetrate a gap in the clouds and provide further dim light to the surroundings, but the clouds were thick and all were aware that it may only be a matter of time before it began to snow heavily again.

The snow was deep either side of the track, concealing the potential horrors beneath of frozen corpses and discarded equipment. Half submerged bushes and small trees lined the left side of the rutted track with the right side of the track fully exposed allowing a freezing breeze to drift in off the lake.

The front personnel carrier was being driven by Meino with Albrecht sitting beside him, his eyes scanning the surroundings for any potential threat, a newly acquired Russian submachine gun resting on the front of the vehicle's metal plate. Behind them sat Hausser and Tatu, both engaged in sporadic conversation, their moods seeming light with both men occasionally seen to laugh.

In the second personnel carrier, Udet had been nominated to drive and was accompanied by Petru next to him, his rifle also held at the ready. Next to Hase was Nicu, virtually covered completely in blankets and thick padded clothing to ward against the cold, his body yet to fully recover from the exposure he had suffered. Occasionally the weakened man would adjust position, or moan as the vehicle jolted over an obstacle or rut under the snow.

At the fork in the track, the vehicles stopped next to each other as Hausser briefed them on his intended plan for the next part of the journey. The young commander explained that the track to the left lead to the main road, but that this would probably have Russian vehicles and patrols along it as they were now behind Russian lines. Hausser explained that his plan was to continue up the coast track, which from inspection showed no evidence of traffic since the last snowfall...that this track would lead into the village to their north, Dubovyy Ovrag...that this route entering the town would probably be not as well guarded as the main road to their west.

The commander advised his intention was to pass through the town innocently, presenting themselves as a returning patrol as they were all now dressed in Russian uniforms. In the confusion of the offensive that seemed to be ongoing, there would be many disorientated units moving about and they were to pass themselves off as a patrolling unit searching the area for stragglers and deserters.

After checking his map briefly, Hausser advised that only the Russian speakers should converse when they neared the town, indicating to himself and Tatu. He advised that if they were to be challenged, they should say they were returning to their unit in the next town to the north, Chapurniki. They would then repeat this in Chapurniki stating they were from Dubovyy Ovrag if questioned. He continued, advising if they were successful in the first town, they would join the main road and make better progress northwards towards safety.

The commander had then smiled briefly, stating that once they were beyond these villages or towns, they would be approaching the Volga bend, near the outskirts of Stalingrad and then would hopefully re-join with German units there if not before.

Realising at that point the men were becoming apprehensive of the journey ahead, Hausser had explained that if they were fortunate, this was the last part of their journey and once past the towns they would be very near German lines if indeed the Russians actually held both towns. He continued that they may be lucky and German and Romanian forces may not be much further north, advising he had explained the most challenging option first. This seemed to alleviate some concerns and the young commander ensured he made eye contact and addressed each man individually as he spoke to bolster their personal moods.

Then the young commander then indicated to Hase to come and talk to him and they had walked a short distance down towards the banks of the frozen lake whilst the others discussed their views, the conversation encouraged by Tatu.

As they stood on the bank of the lake in silence, Hausser opened a packet of the American cigarettes and offered them to Hase, smiling as he gingerly took one. As the young commander lit his cigarette, he turned towards him and seemed to survey him for some seconds. The cold breeze from the lake enveloped them as they stood there initially in silence, both men tightening their overcoats against the colder air.

Hausser blew smoke out over the lake, his face becoming serious, 'I realise you may be troubled, Hase. The last couple of days have been taxing on us all…are you still comfortable to be with us?'

Hase looked at his commander, his eyes moistening as he realised the officer was requesting a reassurance from him of his loyalty. He cleared his throat, 'Hausser, this is difficult for me. I am wearing my country's uniform, but underneath it is a German one. Yes, I have doubts, but Stalin has committed immense crimes against us Ukrainians, starving our population and his secret police taking people from their families in the night. My father used to speak of the hatred he had for the communists…I hold his beliefs after what I saw in Kiev and the brutality of the army towards our own people.' He raised the cigarette to his mouth and drew on it, watching the end of the Lucky Strike glow, realising his gloved hand was shaking, 'You did a good thing for myself and my men in the Crimea…probably saving our lives. My loyalty therefore lies with you and with your country now…or until my country is at least free of the communists.'

Hausser nodded, seeming to understand his confliction, 'It is difficult for you and this war is becoming very bitter. I cannot say your country will be free after the war is over as I do not know the answer...but you are now one of my men. Regardless of your country of origin or the insanity that is occurring around us, I am very grateful for your loyalty. If we work together I am confident we will survive this. I thought perhaps the further we were from the Ukraine and the Crimea the more doubts you would have...but now I realise I was wrong. For me, you are a German soldier now, and perhaps a good one.'

Hase grinned, surprised by the officer's comments, taking another draw on his cigarette. He slowly turned to the young commander, 'I am not sure I will ever be a German soldier in my heart, but maybe a free Russian? Yes, perhaps...I would also like to add one other comment if possible, sir?'

Hausser's eyes darkened, concerned for what was to come, 'Please do...'

He drew breath and looked the officer up and down, 'You look ridiculous in a Russian uniform.' His mouth formed a cautious smile.

Hausser's eyes widened in surprise and he threw his head back and laughed, 'You are a cheeky dog, Hase. But I am proud to have you with me and call you a friend.' The young officer placed his gloved right hand on his shoulder, 'Come, let's get going before it snows...let us see if we can get through the Russian lines safely.' With this, the officer patted his shoulder twice, turned and slowly walked back up the slope towards the other men.

Hase stood there for some seconds thinking and looking out over the lake. He knew now what he was, what he had become...he was now, as the commander had stated, a soldier in the German army. His loyalty was now to his commander and the men in his unit, the men behind him.

Dismissing his thoughts as if concluded, he turned, throwing the unfinished American cigarette away, hearing the singe as it hit the iced snow. As his mood lightened, he began to ascend the slope back towards the personnel carriers.

Chapter Eleven: He Who Dares.......

The personnel carrier lurched into a rut in the track, concealed by the snow. The engine whined as Udet applied pressure to the accelerator, the metal tracks momentarily skidding on the concealed root before ripping from the grip of the frozen plant.

On the horizon, across a bleak and frozen landscape, he could just make out the lights of the distant town. Hase realised there was a slight incline rising to the outskirts of the town dwellings as they cautiously approached, the track gradually rising to the left.

The vehicles slowed in the snow as Hausser glanced round from the first personnel carrier to check the readiness of his men, noticing with satisfaction that all the men had removed their overcoats. Hase's and Hausser's eyes met and he could just make out a fleeting smile on the young commander's face as he turned back towards the village, the excitement and adrenalin rising within them.

The small vehicles began to ascend the slope, their engine tones rising as the tracks began to struggle to gain a grip in the snow, the ice beneath challenging their progress. He could smell the exhaust of the leading carrier as the greyish warm smoke rose from the revving engine, the bluish grey cloud then hanging in the air as its temperature dropped, the following carrier then swirling the plumes of exhaust around as it progressed through the still freezing air.

As they got some 100 metres from the first building, he could see the door open, with the light from within the dwelling cascading out into the night, casting shadows across the landscape. Four Russian soldiers walked slowly out into the track, their silhouettes indicating weapons held provocatively, their senses sharpened by the approaching vehicles. The uncertainty of the chosen route of approach initiating some suspicion.

Hase tightened his grip on his rifle as the personnel carriers approached the Russian soldiers who stood in the middle of the track at the entrance to the town. His stomach seemed to twist as Hausser raised his right hand, indicating for the carriers to stop before the sentries, licking his lips beneath the scarf placed across his lips, his mouth dry in nervous anticipation of the forthcoming encounter.

The lead personnel carrier jolted to a halt before the two soldiers blocking the track, with the second carrier skidding slightly as it came to rest behind the first. Hase could feel his heart beating loudly in his chest as the first Russian soldier cautiously approached the side of the lead vehicle next to Hausser. The Russian held a lantern in his left hand and this swayed slightly as he walked, casting a wavering light across the snow.

'Where have you come from?' The Russian soldier addressed the young commander as he sat slouched in the vehicle.

Hausser saluted nonchalantly, clearing his throat, 'From the fishing lodge, we were dropping off supplies.'

The sentry eyed the seated sergeant indifferently, slowly returning the salute, 'Have you your papers?' He requested, stretching out his hand.

He watched as Hausser retrieved the documents taken from the Russian captain from his chest pocket and hand them to the soldier, who unfolded them to allow further inspection, raising the lantern with his left arm to enable him to read the papers.

The Russian sentry perused the documents then slowly looked back at the young commander, his eyes narrowing, 'Where is Captain Medvedev? Your papers say he is in command.'

Hausser straightened himself in the carrier, as if becoming frustrated with the private's scrutiny, 'He remained at the lodge for the night. There was an incident there he wished to investigate. We are heading for Chapurniki for more supplies.'

The sentry nodded slowly, seeming satisfied by the explanation, 'Did you find any enemy stragglers?'

Hausser shook his head, 'No, they are all dead now I think. No one can survive outside for long in these temperatures.'

The Russian sentry nodded, a large cloud of exhaled air escaping from his mouth, a grin forming on his face, 'Yes…I think the Romanians and Germans are done here now. They are putting up quite a fight to the west though and we are struggling to the north, they have dug in well.'

Hausser leant forward inquisitively, stretching his hand out to the sentry as an indication to hand back the papers, 'How far north are the lines?'

The sentry passed the papers back to him and stretched, scratching the right side of his forehead, 'Near the Volga bend. The Germans are putting up quite a fight there I think. Every now and again you can hear the artillery fire, but we are moving up heavy guns now to blast them out.'

He watched as Hausser nodded, seeming to absorb the information, 'Good, perhaps they will think twice before attacking the namesake of Stalin again, eh…comrade?'

The sentry nodded, lowering the lantern, 'You must take care on the roads…I think there are still some enemy units ahead. We hear gunfire every now and again to the north. The locals are also mostly Kalmyk's, some of which may have had more allegiance to the previous occupants than us. We have been hanging most of the collaborators along the main road this evening to show the locals what the Red Army thinks of traitors.'

Hase's grip on his rifle tightened further as he heard the sentry talk of the executions…these were Russians like him that had chosen a different allegiance. Next to him, Nicu moaned in his sleep, a fever sweeping through him due to the exposure.

The sentry looked back, seeing the heavily wrapped body lying in the back of the personal carrier, 'What is the matter with him? Is he wounded?' The Russian called across to the second vehicle.

Hase swallowed hard, noticing Hausser turn round to look at him, 'Er...just unwell, we think he has exposure. He was outside in the cold for too long.'

The sentry nodded, turning back to Hausser, 'Perhaps you should stay here tonight captain...one of your men is not too good I think?'

The young commander shook his head slowly, 'No we must continue, we need to deliver our last supplies to the units ahead.'

An explosion in the village ahead made all the men jump, with all ducking instinctively. The immediate buildings obscuring any view, but Hase could see a plume of flame rise into the air some two hundred metres ahead of them in the town, with smoke billowing around it into the night sky.

Hausser watched as the Russian soldiers tightened their grips on their weapons and turned to face into the town. Their stances alarmed, they moved to aim their weapons at any potential threat, the sentry next to Hausser gritted his teeth, turning to run back towards his men he shouted contemptuously, 'Fucking Kalmyk dogs!'

An approaching wave of sound engulfed him as Hase sat up in the second personnel carrier, the engine noise screaming as he gulped, the adrenalin surging through his body in response. He could hear heavy machine gun fire now as the landscape filled with the deep scream of the engines, but he could see nothing due to the close proximity of the buildings.

They all instinctively ducked as the twin engine plane swept out above them from the obscurity of the buildings, the engines screaming as the pilot opened up the throttle. Flying directly above them the engine noise engulfed them as the plane passed overhead, seeming to be only metres above the soldiers, the pilot flying dangerously low.

As he watched the plane rose into the air and banked steeply left over the lake. He caught a glimpse of yellow wing tips and black crosses on the wings as the pilot pulled back on the stick of the ME110 and accelerated across the lake, continuing to bank north.

As the men shook themselves from their shock, Hase became aware of another plane to the west, the pilot of this other ME110 mirroring the manoeuvre of his leader, to circle the town. As he glanced back, the plane over the lake passed through a ray of light from the moon through the clouds, a glint from the reflection on the glass canopy catching his eye.

Two of the Russian sentries raised their weapons and fired frustrated shots after the departing aircraft over the lake, the cracks of the rifles as they fired loud in the cold air around them.

Hausser grinned beneath his scarf, leaning forward he patted Meino's helmet, 'Go! Go!' Realising the air raid was a perfect cover for them to pass through the town, the noises of rifle and machine gun fire ahead of them now loud in their ears.

The engines on the personnel carriers roared and the first vehicle jumped forward, startling one of the Russian sentries who turned to face it. Albrecht fired a burst from his submachine gun leant on the vehicle's front metal plate and the man fell backwards, blood pouring from his face as it imploded, the snow splattered dark beyond him. The other Russians, surprised, turned to face the new threat, but Tatu and Hausser were ready and opened fire with their submachine guns as they turned, with two more of the Russians slumping backwards into the snow. The last, the sentry that had approached the vehicle dropped the lantern, turned and ran for the house the sentries had exited earlier. As he got to the doorway, his body spun around, sinking to his knees, then falling face forward into the snow, the bullet from Petru's smoking rifle having hit him in the middle of his back, shattering his spine.

The first personnel carrier churned snow as it searched for traction and then jolted forwards, making a cracking sound as the vehicle passed over the legs of one of the fallen sentries. The vehicle then leapt forward once more and entered the town, turning left round the first building as Hausser hastily indicated to Meino. The second personnel carrier lumbered forward, following the preceding vehicle, a further dull cracking sound being heard as the metal tracks ground over the broken bones of the dying sentry.

Chapter Twelve: Attack of the Zerstorer

As the second personnel carrier negotiated the corner, turning left, Hase glanced around him, his rifle now raised and gripped tightly. The adrenalin was pumping through his body as he saw the narrow side street they had entered was littered with supplies and bodies in the snow. As they advanced, the buildings to either side were beginning to burn ferociously having been lit by explosions and tracer bullets.

The heat from the fires on either side drifted across their faces as they drove forward cautiously. To their right, further into the town he could hear frantic shouts in Russian as soldiers attempted to calm frightened horses. He glanced right, looking through a window as it cracked and shattered, the inside of the building an inferno as the wooden structure was consumed by flame.

He heard the chatter from a heavy machine gun further to his right and glanced between the burning buildings, briefly spotting the burst of tracer bullets rising into the sky at an angle from him to the north.

Hase closed his eyes as the vehicle shuddered, then jolted forward again, grinding its tracks across the torso of a body hidden in the snow. The sound of the cracking of a crushed ribcage echoing off the side buildings.

Next to him, Nicu rose from his lying position, confusion and horror on his face as if awoken from a deep dream. Hase swiftly leant across the central section of the carrier and pushed the bewildered soldier back down into the foot well of the carrier, indicating for him to stay low. In response, Nicu lowered himself further and pulled a greatcoat over his head, as if to conceal himself from the horror of the sights around him.

The carriers bounced over bodies and discarded boxes as they negotiated the small lane between the houses, the stench of burning flesh catching in the soldiers' nostrils. As they reached the end of the lane it exited onto a wider road running to their left and right, 'North and South' he noted to himself. He saw Hausser raise his hand and the vehicles stopped just before they reached the main highway.

Bullets spattered across the iced road and they all instinctively ducked slightly as the scream of another engine sped past from right to left, the ME109 escort for the twin engine planes now completing its own strafing run of the town.

He watched as the pilot pulled back on the stick and the plane rose rapidly from its low level attack and soared vertically into the air, peeling right to turn to the west and then bank sharply round to the north, the V12 engine roaring as the sound wave swept over them. Behind the ME109, tracer bullets flew sporadically after the plane from inexperienced Russian machine gunners in the town.

Hase saw Hausser turn to Udet and indicate for the vehicles to continue and they lurched forward once more, the cracking of wood in the burning buildings to their right startling the men further.

As they turned right onto the main road, his eyes widened in awe at the sight of sheer destruction before them. On either side of the highway buildings were burning out of control, casting flickering light from the flames onto the street. Abandoned vehicles and discarded equipment boxes lay along the sides of the road, dropped by Russian soldiers as the air raid began. Several Russians were hurriedly attempting to offload equipment from a burning lorry to their left, but as he watched the petrol tank exploded. The flames shooting outwards from the vehicle as it rose from the ground, engulfing the soldiers around it. He watched in horror as they fell backwards, their uniforms burning intensely with the petrol fuelled flames.

The personnel carriers accelerated in the wide street, Hausser frantically indicating to the drivers to stay in the middle of the road. The small vehicles began to gain speed on the better road and their engines roared as if to spur the men to safety.

Hase glanced at Udet, a grim determination on the young soldier's face as he drove, the lines of concentration etched on his temples as he struggled with the vehicle's steering, the small carrier bouncing and scraping off the many obstacles in the road.

On the telegraph poles on either side of the street hung the bodies of the local inhabitants accused of 'collaborating with the enemy'. He was aghast that the whole street seemed to be filled with them, with some poles hosting two bodies hung from the neck with signs pinned to their chest. Several bodies were on fire due to their close proximity to the burning buildings and the stench of burning flesh was now becoming overpowering.

The vehicles slowed to negotiate the bodies of dead horses in the road, the narrow gap between the recently deceased animals an indication of the surprise the Luftwaffe had achieved as the Russian livery sergeant had dragged his animals across the road. The Russian sergeant had also been killed attempting to save his animals, his body lying contorted across one of the horses, his lifeless eyes staring blankly at the passing soldiers as their vehicles slowed to negotiate the blood soaked gap between the deceased animals.

As the personnel carriers gathered speed again, Hausser's vehicle swerved to avoid three terrified dogs running across the street. The young commander staring as they passed them, their small frightened thin bodies propelling them quickly into another side street to his left.

As they neared the centre of the town, the fires on either side seemed to increase, Russian soldiers running either side of the street to get to cover and potential safety. He could see a couple of heavy machine guns being mounted on makeshift platforms as a defence in preparation for any further attack.

Some local inhabitants, their clothes worn and ragged, huddled next to buildings that were not alight and he noticed several furtive glances in their direction as they passed. The local population obviously distrusting of the new occupants due to history and the many recent executions.

The sounds of war echoed through his ears, the moaning and crying of the local residents at the further carnage inflicted upon their lives, the Russian soldiers' shouts of alarm or orders to move men or equipment, the sporadic firing of small arms and machine guns into the air. Hase's senses seemed overwhelmed at the sights, sounds and smells he was witnessing and he forced himself to look ahead, to close out the visions around him.

Hase fixed his eyes on the horizon into the darkness ahead, leading out of the town. He was aware of the tears on his cheeks, the sorrow of human suffering. Then he stiffened, attempting to distinguish something he had seen in the distance, a glint in the sky. The hairs on the back of his neck stiffened, his mouth becoming dry as he swallowed hard, realising the planes were about to start another run.

'Hausser! Hausser!' He uttered a forced shout.

The young commander turned and saw his outstretched hand pointing. Hausser's eyes widened, his mind needing no explanation for what the young 'Hiwi' had seen, the angle of the soldier's outstretched arm enough explanation.

The young commander turned desperately to Meino, shouting, 'Get off the road, NOW!'

Meino glanced upwards, seeing the ME110 in the distance now swooping down to begin a low pass across the town, a low pass directly down the main road...straight towards them. He pushed his right foot down on the pedal and the small carrier turned sharply to the left, the right track briefly leaving the ground due to the steep turn at speed. As the track hit the snow once more, it skidded, then propelled the small vehicle forwards towards a side street.

In the second vehicle, Udet performed a similar turn...following the first carrier. Hase looked out to his right as the ME110 began to fly level with the road, its guns now flashing as it approached. Some 100 metres in front of him a Russian squad was caught in the street and he watched mesmerised as the figures turned and tried to open fire on the approaching aircraft. In an instant, they disappeared in a flurry of bullets from the twin engine plane, tearing their bodies to pieces and peppering the snow around them as they fell.

Bullets spattered across the road behind them as Udet desperately steered the second carrier into the side street, the roar of the plane's engines as it passed just behind them deafening the soldiers momentarily. To the rear, Hase heard some further explosions as the fighter bomber dropped some of its deadly cargo and rose into the air, banking away to the right. Russian machine gun fire accompanied the explosions as the gunners desperately attempted to drive off the planes.

As they slowly and cautiously progressed down the side street, he became aware of the number of inhabitants sheltering in the lane, this part of the town seemed to have yet escaped the attentions of the Luftwaffe. Many of the townsfolk were sitting to the sides of the lane awaiting the end of the air raid, the people either elderly men, women or children looking defiantly at the men in the carriers as they passed them by. He considered the majority of the residents of the town were Kalmyks and mostly anti-communist, their reaction to the men in the carriers in Russian uniforms therefore understandable.

Behind them, he could hear another plane completing a strafing run along the main street, with Russian machine gun fire in response becoming louder and more organised, a sign the enemy had deployed more weapons against the 'Destroyers from above'. There were some further explosions and then he could hear the aircraft engines become more distant to the west as the pilots banked back north towards Stalingrad, their attempts at destroying or disrupting enemy lines of supply potentially a success.

As they neared the end of the lane, he saw Hausser indicate for them to turn right from his hand actions, the two carriers entered another smaller side street that ran parallel with the main road. They proceeded along this lane cautiously to the end and then turned back to join the main road at the northern edge of the town.

As they turned left to face north onto the main highway, Hase looked briefly back down the main street, the burning buildings and vehicles an indication of the success of the air raid. Bodies of Russian soldiers and the town's inhabitants lay scattered across the road and next to the buildings grimly overseen by the corpses hanging from the telegraph poles. With this last glance, he realised the full extent of this war now had no boundaries, that potentially the human soul was now lost to hatred and madness.

With his mood now fully despondent, he turned and slumped back in his seat in the carrier as both vehicles lumbered north into the darkness.

Chapter Thirteen: With the Compliments of the Enemy

They continued north for some time, the snow on the road compacted and frozen assisting the speed the personnel carriers could perform. In the darkness the evidence of war and destruction was barely visible apart for the occasional abandoned or destroyed vehicle pushed to the side of the highway, the wide road deserted in the winter gloom. The only sign of life since leaving the town behind them had been a lorry slowly moving south, its driver and guard waving solemnly to them as they passed.

The soldiers in the two personnel carriers travelled in grim silence, fully aware that any investigation of the ditches and slopes to the side of the road would reveal more bodies, frozen and contorted in death. To a couple of the soldiers the irony did not lack consideration, that these corpses were finally at peace with one another, the German, Russian and Romanian bodies now lying next to each other, or even in indiscriminate groupings.

Hase sat slumped in his seat, his greatcoat collar pulled up under his helmet as protection against the cold. The scarf that had been round his mouth was now wrapped tightly round his neck as he smoked the American cigarettes Hausser had given him one after another. He observed the beauty of the sky with the rays of the moon shining through cracks in the almost continuous ceiling of heavy snow cloud. The air was relatively still apart from the disturbance of the carrier in front of them and cold air drifting in from the right. He could see the condensed breath of the men in the front and in his own carrier as they drove, the exhaled breath hanging in the air like mist as if suspended by imaginary lines from the sky, then the small condensed air clouds swirling as the vehicles and men passed through them.

The slight breeze from the lakes to their right was now continuous and the colder air from the iced expanse of water nipped at the men's noses and exposed flesh as the vehicles proceeded northwards. As he threw his forth cigarette into the road, he noticed the lead vehicle slowing and beginning to turn off the road to the left, joining a small track that lead into a field.

Hase squinted into the darkened expanse as the lead vehicle left the road, seeing the outline of three destroyed Romanian R2 tanks in the field. One of the burnt out tanks was off to the left, its turret missing and the rest of the vehicle lying at an angle from where it had received a hit to its tracks. He watched as Hausser's vehicle lumbered slowly behind the two remaining destroyed tanks to sit behind an improvised defensive snow wall.

As his vehicle slowed to negotiate the slope of the track leaving the road, he observed the nearest tank had been hit on its weakened flank, just below the turret. The gaping hole punctured in its side sealing the fates of the crew inside as the splinters of heated metal caused by the impact had imploded into the vehicle. He considered the ends of the lives of the tank crewmen to have been virtually instant, but in extreme terror as they must have desperately tried to stop the advance of Russian tanks the day before.

Behind the destroyed tanks, the land rose in a gradual incline, and he could just make out a grouping of trees further to the north at the top of the slope. As his vehicle jolted to a halt next to the lead carrier, he noticed they were now just off the track and concealed behind the destroyed and abandoned defensive position. Next to his vehicle, the track continued up the hill, winding its way along gradual inclines as it rose into the distant trees.

Hase lifted himself up from his seat, placing his gloved hands on the side of the carrier and stepping over the metal plate into the snow, feeling his boots break through the first thin layer of upper ice. The crunch of the iced snow was mirrored by the others as they all climbed out of the vehicle, with Udet assisting Nicu clamber over the side of the carrier. Hase reached inside his greatcoat pocket and retrieved the American cigarettes he had placed there earlier. Lighting one, he turned back and leant into the vehicle to retrieve his rifle which had been lying next to him in his seating position, blowing smoke into the air as he turned to walk the short distance to the others.

The soldiers were gathered between the two tanks, sitting either side in the snow, or crouched against the vehicles. Hausser was leaning against the tank on the right and smiled as he approached, indicating for him to sit next to Tatu. As Hase lowered himself next to the Romanian quartermaster, using the side of the tank as support, Tatu slapped his shoulder playfully, 'Still with us young Hase, Eh? If you keep this up there will be a place for you in the Romanian army I think.'

He looked round, seeing the smiles and grins on the faces of the other men, feeling the heat on his face as he flushed, slightly embarrassed. As he assumed his seating position, the stout Romanian placed a firm arm round his shoulder, 'No need for shyness here, young Hase. You are our friend and comrade. Together we will all come through this no matter what comrade Stalin has planned for us!'

He smiled sheepishly, feeling more at ease now. Petru leant forward and offered him a handful of biscuits, 'Here Hase, have some rations from our new American friends. Eat my friend, keep your strength up.'

Hase reached out and took two biscuits from Petru's outstretched hand, smiling and nodding his thanks to him. Having the food in his hand made him realise just how ravenous he was, having not eaten in nearly twelve hours, he bit greedily into the first biscuit. The flavours of sugar, chocolate and oatmeal filled his mouth and throat, tantalising his senses and inviting him to look more closely at the tasty biscuit. He could just make out the word 'Hershey' on the darkened surface of the second biscuit as he pushed the remains of the first biscuit clumsily and greedily into his mouth.

He watched the seven men closely between the two tanks as he chewed the second biscuit, Petru turning to Udet and indicating for him to pass one of the ration boxes he had taken from the personnel carriers. Udet obliged, cheekily demanding a biscuit for his task which he received upon delivery of the box. Petru busied himself opening the carton and passing out the tins that had lain within until nearly all soldiers present had one.

He watched as Albrecht surveyed the rectangular tin, turning it over in his hands, seeming puzzled. Petru smiled and nudged Udet, who grinned widely, cleared his throat loudly and proceeded to hold his tin out into the middle of the group, a wry smile on his face. They all watched as the younger infantryman pulled a strange looking key from the side of his can and proceeded to wrap this round a rough part of the exterior of the container. As he twisted, a strip of metal from the can opened and Udet began to wind this round the key until the base of the container was almost removed.

Udet smiled at the reaction of the other soldiers, 'American beef for all!' He declared triumphantly, 'This will lift our spirits for the journey north.' He nodded across to Hase and winked, a grin forming on his face as Petru tossed cans across to him and Tatu.

Hase smiled briefly as he moved the tin around in his own hands, surprisingly feeling warmth on the canister. Looking up he saw Petru smile at his obvious surprise, 'I left the box of tins next to the engine.' The Romanian explained as the grins on the faces of the group widened.

Hase moved the tin around in his hands trying to determine a similar approach to opening the sturdy fist sized canister as Udet had. Once he had realised the best approach, he duplicated Udet's actions and opened the tin successfully, tasting the corned beef cautiously at first before eating more readily once he determined the delights from the flavour.

He watched as the men ate from their tins using their knives and bayonets to retrieve the remaining scraps of meat from the containers. Most ate the contents of two tins and some biscuits driven by their hunger and he observed with some relief that Nicu was eating with them, the colour seeming to slowly return to his features as he sat wrapped tightly in his thick coat with blankets around his shoulders.

Once the meal was consumed, Hausser tossed a packet of American cigarettes to each man and they all smoked, their moods lighter than in the previous hours due to the sustenance and camaraderie. Hausser left the men to their thoughts for a couple of moments before beginning to speak of the journey ahead, his scarf now around his neck and the outline of a stubble beard showing round his chin. His eyes flashed as he began to speak, the cold of the night and atmosphere seeming to brighten his blue eyes making them quite piercing in the gloom of the night air.

Hausser drew breath, looking across to his men, 'We need to consider how we will make the last few kilometres.' He waited until all the men had turned to look at him before continuing, 'We have come about half way I think, but there is still some distance to go through enemy territory.'

The commander shifted on his seated position and produced a map from inside his tunic, laying it in the centre of the group. Pointing to the road north of Dubovyy Ovrag on the worn paper he looked around the men, all intently viewing the page where his gloved finger was., 'We are about here, with Chapurniki about four kilometres further north. We will have to go through that town to get across the river in its centre, then we have a short distance to Krasnoarmeyskiy Rayon, a lower suburb of Stalingrad. It is there I think the lines are at present according to the information from the sentry back in the town.'

The men all nodded solemnly, realising the distance they still had to travel and the dangers they faced.

Hausser continued, 'If we keep moving now, we should get to the town just before dawn. If challenged we are heading north from Dubovyy Ovrag to deliver orders and some supplies to a unit just south of the Stalingrad suburbs, that should hopefully get us through. There is one problem however...we have insufficient fuel to make the whole journey in our vehicles I fear.' The commander paused, wary the group's mood was becoming more subdued.

He smiled to alleviate concerns, his voice becoming softer, 'If we stay calm and together we will get through this...we will move from here in twenty minutes. Meino, fill the vehicle tanks with the reminder of the fuel from the spare cans and leave anything we don't need. Once we get going then it is just twelve more hours my friends and we will reach safety. Now are there any questions?'

Hausser glanced around the group slowly, giving each man a chance to ask anything. Satisfied, he folded the map and placed it back into his tunic.

Nicu spoke softly from his right, his huddled figure leaning against the tank slightly behind the commander. 'I have a question.'

The men all turned to look inquisitively at the young Romanian as he moved the blankets from his left shoulder. He lifted an empty beef tin with his left hand, pointing at the small writing near the base of the can, 'Where or what is Uruguay?'

Chapter Fourteen: Firefight

Hase stared down from over the makeshift emplacement snow wall, seeing the road some 120 metres away, the moon glinting against the iced parts of the surface. Next to him on his right, Udet slowly raised his head to the same height as his, with just his eyes looking over the snow obstacle.

A thin mist was slowly moving in off the lakes beyond the road, but even with the poor light of the moon reflecting across the snow, he was able to vaguely make out the far edge of the highway. As per Hausser's instructions, he was to keep watch over the thoroughfare whilst the others unloaded the carriers of any unnecessary items and emptied the spare fuel cans into the vehicle tanks.

Udet patted his shoulder softy, whispering, 'Sehen sie, Hase?' His right hand rose to point at the truck on the road in the distance. 'Da!'

Hase turned his head to the right and saw the distant lorry slowly and methodically moving north up the road, the vehicle's cautious driver wary of the limited control he had over his vehicle with only tyres and no tracks on the iced snow.

Pushing himself from the snow emplacement, he moved at a crouch back between the destroyed tanks to the personnel carriers where the rest of the men were grouped. Approaching Hausser, he gently placed his hand on the young commander's arm to gain his attention.

Hausser was looking at the map, placed across one of the stowage bins on the carrier and turned as he felt the contact on his arm, 'Yes Hase, what is it? What have you seen?'

Hase rose to a standing position, aware they were concealed from any view from the road by the destroyed tank hulks, 'There is a vehicle on the road

Hausser, he is heading north slowly. We will probably overtake him when we set off.'

Hausser nodded solemnly, 'We will head off in 5 minutes...we may stop him to see if he has fuel...that is now my major concern. If we have to resort to movement on foot, I am worried it will take a lot longer and expose us to extra risk.'

Turning to Meino, who was sorting through the contents of the stowage bins in the snow next to the carriers, Hausser drew breath, 'How is it coming along, Meino? Are we nearly done? I want to leave soon.'

Meino looked up from the assortment of supplies on the ground. 'I am nearly finished; all the fuel is spread equally between the carriers...but it is not enough I think. I have removed all the supplies we do not need, leaving ammunition, food for 2 days and the water. We should be re-packed in a couple of minutes.'

Hausser nodded, addressing all the men around him, 'Good...then we leave shortly.'

Meino interjected, 'What shall I do with our helmets, Herr Leutnant? We have them stacked in one of the cars.'

Hausser considered for a moment, 'Take them, I don't want a German...' He hesitated, looking across at Tatu, '...or indeed a Romanian sniper taking our heads off from a distance because we have the wrong helmet on.' He grinned, seeing Tatu 'tut' and raise his eyes in response.

Meino started handing items from the pile of equipment in the snow to the men around him, indicating for them to be placed in the carriers. As the stowage bins on the personnel carriers were opened and the items dropped inside, a distant 'crump' noise echoed across the landscape.

Hausser flinched and stiffened, dropping to a crouch, indicating for the men around him to do the same.

Another sound similar to the first drifted across the snow as the soldiers moved silently behind the carriers, facing up the hill, their weapons at the ready.

'What was….?' Albrecht whispered, his eyes wide with fear. His right hand pulling the catch on his PPSH submachine gun, the loud metallic click seeming to break the silence further.

'Shhh!' Hausser interrupted him, 'Quiet.' The young commander scanned the ridge above them, his eyes squinting to try and pierce through the gloom. In the darkness he could only see the snow continuing up to the top of the hill, there were no shapes or movement he could make out in the white expanse before him.

Then another 'crump', but this time he glimpsed a slight flash of light off to his right, in the trees at the top of the hill, some three hundred metres away. Hausser exhaled slowly, his breath held as he had scanned the snow in front of them…he now knew the source of the noise.

'Hausser, what is it?' Udet had crept to join the others and was now behind the commander.

Hausser looked over his shoulder slightly to acknowledge the infantryman, his voice a whisper, 'Artillery battery in the trees, firing north I think…into Stalingrad.'

The soldiers crouched behind the personnel carriers all cautiously turned to look up the hill towards the trees, their adrenalin rising as they realised how close they were to an enemy artillery battery.

Hausser paused, straining his ears to listen, then spoke, turning his head to address the others to his left, 'Probably three guns I think, they are reloading now…perhaps.'

Tatu leant forward past Petru who was between him and the commander, 'Hausser, let's take them…they will have fuel. We destroy the guns and take the fuel…simple.'

The commander's eyes narrowed, his expression grim, 'We don't know how many they are. Until we do, we stay put. If we start the engines now, they may hear us.'

Tatu shook his head, 'Let Petru and I go and take a look...we are in Russian uniforms and we need the fuel...what do you say?'

Hausser hesitated, his mind seeming conflicted between escaping and gaining the fuel they needed. After several seconds, he turned to face Tatu, their eyes meeting, 'Go then. No shooting, just find out how many they have, their sentries. See if they have any vehicles, that's where the fuel will be.'

Tatu nodded once, running his tongue over his lips and right hand nervously over his moustache, 'Very well...we will be back in ten minutes.' The Romanian slapped Petru's left shoulder with the outside of his right hand and both men pushed themselves from the carriers, running half-crouched off to the right.

Hausser turned to the remaining men, indicating for them to close in around him. As they did so, he became aware that they were breathing heavily, their eyes wide and pupils dilated, the signs of excitement and adrenalin. He drew breath, 'If we attack, I want to come in from two sides. That will confuse them as to how many we are. We will attack along the hill and from the right, hopefully disrupting any defence.'

The soldiers nodded in response, their faces grim.

The young commander continued, 'Meino, you go with Tatu and take Udet with you. Hase, you and Petru come with me. Albrecht, you will stay with Nicu. Now, do you all understand?'

Albrecht interjected, 'I can come...I know what to do.'

Hausser turned to look at the young dispatch rider, his voice firm, 'You will do what you are told...you are not a front line soldier yet. You stay here with Nicu.'

Albrecht nodded slowly, his face flushed after the embarrassing contradiction, the realisation he should not question his orders, 'Yes sir.' He whispered slowly, 'I am sorry.'

The commander's eyes lightened, 'That's alright…there will be plenty of opportunity for you to prove yourself later I think.' Pointing at the young German's weapon, he paused, then continued. 'Take a rifle instead of that submachine gun, you will be more use to us with a different weapon.' He leant forward and patted the young soldier's shoulder to reassure him.

Leaning back, Hausser looked round the other soldiers, 'Now, remove your Russian uniforms. We have too much clothing on to move quickly. We attack dressed as Germans, then we have the chance of being prisoners if it goes wrong.'

The men nodded grimly, slowly beginning to remove the Russian grey felt tunics.

The commander turned to Hase, his face downcast, 'Hase, if we fail…you run. Do you understand?'

Hase swallowed hard, wary of Hausser's scrutinising eyes upon him. Nodding, he whispered cautiously, 'I understand.'

'Good.' The commander stated, 'Then let's get ready.' With that he turned and began unbuttoning his Russian tunic.

Albrecht stopped and stared at the young commander, his eyes fixed on the commander's neck, 'You have the iron cross, Hausser?' His eyes examining the black cross outlined in white.

Meino prodded Albrecht with his right hand, 'Yes he has…but he does not talk about it. Concentrate on what we have to do.'

Albrecht shook his head, 'Y-yes, sorry, I just saw it and….'

Hausser interjected, 'It was a long time ago.' Pushing the metal cross back inside his German tunic, he leant over into one of the stowage bins and picked up his MP40, collecting some extra magazines from the bin and pushing them into his belt. Picking up his steel helmet, he placed it carefully on his head and grinned thoughtfully, turning to face them, 'It feels like a distant dream now.'

They turned as Petru approached from the left, running half crouched towards them in the snow. As he came to a stop, breathless in front of Hausser, his eyes widened as he realised they were all in German uniforms. Gulping air, he began to speak, 'They have three guns in a clearing in the trees, heavy artillery.' He exhaled a cloud of air, 'There is a machine gun position to the left covering that approach, but I do not think they expect trouble, there seems to be only two guards. The rest are firing the guns, or trying to sleep I think.'

Hausser nodded, indicating for him to continue, 'How many men?'

Petru continued, his breathing becoming more relaxed, 'Maybe twenty?'

The young commander pursed his lips, 'That many? We are six...where is Tatu?'

Petru smiled slightly, the corners of his mouth rising, 'The old fool is already near or in the trees...he said he wants the perfect position.'

Hausser shook his head slowly in disbelief, a frustrated smile forming on his lips, 'Blood thirsty fool, we have to attack now just to get him back!'

Petru continued, 'Tatu is going to try and stop them organising a defence against us, he will create a diversion.' He paused looking around the soldiers watching him, 'They have a carrier like ours I think, so there should be fuel there.'

The commander hesitated for a moment, thinking through the situation. Turning to the others, he observed they had all removed any excess clothing or equipment they did not require, 'Very well...change of plan slightly. Meino, go with Petru and Udet. Hase, stay close to me.' He indicated with his free hand, 'We set off up the slope and then move to the flanks after about 100 metres, I will give the signal. Meino, take your group in along the ridge. Hase and I will come in from the right. Do you all understand?'

The soldiers nodded in grim silence, the colour draining from their faces, their adrenalin rising once more.

Hausser continued, 'They have more men than us...so we go in shooting, we do not have any other option.' He looked into each man's face to determine their individual resolve, 'Spread out and keep low until we are near the trees, then follow me in.' He hesitated, waiting for the information to sink in, then continued, 'Let's go!'

They moved out from the cover of the personnel carriers into the field, all half crouched, their boots slipping in the snow as they began to ascend the slope. Hausser assumed a position on the right with Hase some eight metres from him, equally spaced from Udet, then Meino, with Petru on the far left, heading for the top of the crest...and the trees.

Hase looked to his right, wary Hausser was ahead of him on the incline. His heart was beating loudly in his chest, the excitement and adrenalin spurring him forward as he propelled himself up the incline. His breathing became sharp and heavy as the exertion on the slope began to become tiring against the freezing air, his calf muscles aching as they struggled against the terrain.

He gripped his rifle tightly as he felt the cool breeze from the lakes across his face, his realisation of sweat running down his face as the warm liquid chilled quickly upon coming into contact with the cold air. The hairs on the back of his neck tingled as he pushed himself up the incline, his arms aching with the weight of his rifle and the exertion.

As he moved to the right following Hausser, he looked up at their objective. The trees were now becoming larger as they approached, their branches heavily weighted down with snow. Beyond the trees he heard a thump as one of the Russian guns fired again into the distance, the flash of light through the branches causing him to duck his head instinctively.

The distance to the trees narrowed to fifty metres and he could hear another artillery piece fire, the smoke from the blast rising from the trees before him. The distance was now thirty metres and his breathing was now very heavy, the sweat pouring down his face and into his scarf. As he neared the first group of trees he heard a shout of alarm from within the bushes to his right, cut short by the flashes from Hausser's MP40, the Russian sentry falling backwards into the branches.

He crashed into the first tree trunk, his body heaving from the exertion as he glanced round the large trunk, branches concealing a full view. From the flickering lights of three small fires behind the guns, he saw the Russian gunners momentarily freeze in their positions at the shots then turn towards them, reaching down for their weapons next to the artillery pieces.

Hase leant round the tree and raised his rifle to his eye, seeing a gunner raise a pistol towards Hausser's direction in the trees to his right. The rifle jerked upwards as he fired, the Russian artillery gunner twisting left as the bullet entered his shoulder at high speed, the pistol falling from his grasp.

To the left, he heard an explosion and his back was hit with debris from the blast, the shock wave pushing past him round the tree, the air filled with twigs and dirt, distracting his view. He closed his eyes quickly in reaction and then opened them, pulling the bolt back on his rifle.

Submachine gun bursts from the right and left felled several gunners and he saw Tatu dart out from the trees far to the right, his PPSH submachine gun held at waist height flashing indiscriminately into the Russian positions. Hausser advanced more cautiously, half crouched from the bushes nearer him, firing controlled bursts from his MP40 before him as the Russians desperately tried to defend themselves.

Squinting through the branches, he saw a Russian crouched behind one of the artillery pieces, his felt cap moving rapidly from side to side. He noticed him playing an object in his hands and realised his intention, raising his rifle again and firing, the weapon kicking back into his shoulder as he forcibly gained more control.

The Russian jerked as the bullet hit him in the thigh, blood spurting across the snow. As the soldier slid backwards across the side of the artillery piece, the grenade in his hand dropped next to him, the Russian next to him screaming in panic. There was a flash and the artillerymen were blown backwards from the grenade, the fragmentations and blast killing them instantly.

Hase pushed himself from the trunk, advancing through the trees, the branches scratching and clawing at his uniform and face. He frantically pulled the bolt back on his rifle and raised it again, biting his lip hard as he fired at a Russian soldier at the doorway of his tent. The bullet entered centrally through the soldier's chest, the man's legs buckling as he sank to his knees, falling forward into the snow with blood soaking across his full length grey felt underwear.

As Hase entered the clearing, he saw Tatu turn and fire into the tent he had just shot at, the burst from his submachine gun killing the four occupants almost instantly as they struggled with their equipment and to free themselves from their sleeping bags.

Hausser was reloading in front of him, tossing his spent magazine onto the ground and replacing it with a fresh one. Pulling the bolt back, the commander turned to make eye contact, nodding as Hase emerged from the trees, his rifle before him.

Another explosion to the left followed, and he ducked his head as the frozen earth and snow hit him on his left side, the blast of air dirty and foul smelling. He staggered, spitting earth from his mouth and lips, turning determinedly to the left to advance further.

Sporadic gunfire from in front of him and further back in the small camp echoed across the clearing as the three other Germans and Romanians fought for control of the tented section. As Hase advanced further, he became aware of Hausser to his right side, his submachine gun at waist height.

He flinched as a Russian ran screaming out towards him from the trees on the left, a bayonet in his hand. Hausser turned and fired a burst from his submachine gun and the soldier spun backwards, the bayonet falling into the snow, blood splattering across Hase's face as he advanced further.

As they turned slightly into a bend in the clearing, Hase saw Meino on the ground fighting with a larger and broader Russian, the Croatian grappling with the man above him as the Russian tried to stab him with his bayonet. Meino was holding the Russians wrists and desperately trying to hold back the blade, the sharpened tip dipping downwards towards his chest as they fought.

Hase raised his rifle quickly, sucking in his breath and holding it as he fired. The rifle butt kicked backwards into his shoulder as the Russian fell sideways, the bullet entering his right temple. Hase looked down at his weapon, pulling back the bolt and loading another bullet into the chamber. Raising it again he fired and hit another gunner bearing down on Udet who was half crouched, his rifle held in defence above him with both hands, the German's weapon empty. The Russian fell sideways as the bullet hit his left side.

Hase pulled back on the bolt once more, looking down briefly, realising he had one last bullet. As he looked up, he saw another Russian kick Udet in the chest and jump forward on top of him as the young Berliner fell backwards. The Russian soldier was grasping for his knife as he fell forwards onto the young soldier, a frustrated whine coming from the Germans lips as he hit the ground awkwardly, his hands attempting to rise above him in defence.

A scream of hatred and frustration emanated from Hase's lips as he charged forward, the adrenalin surging through him. As he neared the pair on the ground, he brought his rifle swiftly up, hitting the Russian on the left shoulder, unbalancing him and knocking him off the young soldier, the knife landing innocently on Udet's chest as he fell.

Hase jumped over Udet's body and stood above the Russian, looking down into his face as the man twisted on the ground, his arm broken. The Russian stared up at him, terror in his eyes as he saw the man in the German uniform above him lower his rifle to point at his face. The Russian soldier started shaking desperately, his lips moving uncontrollably, 'Nein! Bitte! Bitte!' The subdued man pleading as he looked up at him, his eyes wide in fear.

Hase stared down, the realisation the begging man was his countryman surging through him. He hesitated, startled by the man's pleading eyes and outstretched hand desperately begging him not to shoot. Then he twisted the weapon round in his hands, dealing the prone man a swift blow to the left temple, knocking him unconscious.

As Hase straightened up, he became aware the shooting had stopped. Turning slowly, he saw Hausser standing over four kneeling Russians, their hands behind their heads, his submachine gun pointing at them menacingly. Two were weeping and must have been no older than eighteen.

'Please don't Hausser!' He called across as he saw the commander pull back on the bolt on his weapon.

Hausser glanced across at him briefly, making eye contact and nodding slowly, his breathing heavy.

Behind the commander, Tatu sat breathless on a stool outside one of the Russian tents, the body of a Russian artilleryman half in and half out of the tent doorway, the remaining occupants all dead inside.

Petru was further back, inspecting the personnel carrier parked behind the tents. Next to it was the main supply emplacement for the guns with boxes of food and ammunition strewn across the area.

Udet painfully rose to a seated position and began coughing to his right, falling and rolling on the ground clutching his chest. As Hase looked down, he saw the young German had blood on his lips and was now beginning to moan loudly.

Further back, Meino was sat dejected, his helmet lying on the ground between his legs. His head in his hands, his shoulders shaking as he cried.

Hausser broke the silence, 'Tatu, keep an eye on these,' The officer indicated to the four prisoners.

Tatu nodded, turning on his stool to face the four Russians knelt in the snow, his gun lowered.

The commander then walked over to Udet, kneeling next to him and inspecting him. Udet was sobbing uncontrollably and shaking as Hausser ran his hand down the young German's chest, then looked in his mouth, 'Hase! Help Udet back to the carriers...I think he has broken ribs and he has bitten his tongue during the fight. Take Meino with you, and some fuel cans if Petru has found any.'

Hase moved next to the young commander and leant down towards Udet. As he and Hausser helped Udet to his feet, the young German spat blood and started clutching his side painfully, his face white with shock. Udet placed his arm on his shoulder and they slowly turned to walk away, Hase turned slightly to face the commander, his voice pleading, 'What of the prisoners?'

Hausser looked him straight in the eye, 'They will live long lives I think, young Hase.' A brief smile flickered across his face, then the commander's features became serious and turned back as Petru passed him, four fuel cans in his hands.

As they started back down the slope, Hase was aware that Udet was leaning quite heavily on him, his body hunched in pain, his footing challenged in the snow. Udet was dragging his rifle with his left hand, his right hand across his chest. The young soldier was moaning and occasionally spitting blood into the snow. Meino walked slowly behind them, his rifle slung over his shoulder as petrol cans weighed heavily on his arms.

Halfway down the slope, his heart sank as he heard five single shots ring out across the snow...the fate of the prisoners sealed. Anger and frustration rose within him as he realised the young commander had lied to him...that they had probably murdered the Russian prisoners in cold blood.

As they continued slowly, he considered that Hausser had perhaps no option, the Russians were too close to the road and would call for help as soon as they departed, that they could also shoot at them as they walked slowly in the snow. Perhaps there was no other way, despite the callousness of the situation. Despondency and disillusionment set into his mind as they neared the personnel carriers.

Then four explosions rang out as dull thumps as the breaches of the guns were blown up, the last explosion being far louder, signalling the destruction of the ammunition.

Hase helped Udet gently into the back of one of the carriers, ignoring Albrecht as he questioned Meino repeatedly of what had happened. Having given Udet some extra blankets and water, he went and sat alone between the destroyed tanks, listening to the excited chatter of Albrecht as he questioned the solemn Meino of the action that had occurred. Meino emptied two of the fuel cans into the personnel carriers' tanks and packed the rest of the equipment that he had selected to take into the stowage bins.

Nicu handed him another biscuit bar in comfort and sat down next to him in silence until Tatu, Petru and Hausser descending the slope to join them. The commander slumped next to him exhausted and greedily swigged from a water bottle, his face covered in dried sweat and dirt from the action.

Slowly Hase turned to the commander, his eyes filling with tears, 'Did you shoot the prisoners?'

Hausser sipped from the bottle and slowly lowered it from his mouth, turning to him and clearing his throat as he sighed, 'As I said before Hase, they will live long lives...they will. If we leave them unharmed they will be placed in a penal battalion for losing a position, they will die within weeks. We shot them in the feet and legs, one bullet each...none will see frontline action again I hope. They also will not be able to get to the road without help...so we are safe for now.' The young commander sighed, removing his helmet and dropping it to the ground, his hair now matted with sweat to his head, 'They have enough supplies and medical equipment to last until they get help. We also left them their Vodka, only now its twenty rations amongst five.' Hausser hesitated, a determined but frustrated expression forming on his face, 'We can't take them with us Hase! We need to survive this!' The commander picked up his helmet and rose to his feet, shaking his head as he turned and walked despondently to the carriers.

Hausser addressed the men, his face tired and drawn, 'Get your kit and get redressed in the Russian uniforms…we leave in ten minutes.'

As they prepared to get into the personnel carriers, Hausser stopped them, his face solemn. 'Hase, you drive the lead vehicle with Udet, myself and Meino. Petru, you drive the second vehicle with Tatu, Albrecht and Nicu.'

The soldiers nodded, confused by the new arrangement. Slowly, they mounted their vehicles. As Hase started the carrier's engine, Hausser got into the seat next to him and offered some brief instructions of how to drive the vehicle.

Slowly the vehicles pulled out of the makeshift position and descended the slope to join the main road. As they turned left onto the highway, he glanced at Hausser, 'Were you going to shoot the prisoners when I asked you not to?'

The young commander smiled briefly before answering, his composure returning, 'Not really, young Hase…I had no bullets in the gun.'

As the personnel carriers accelerated northwards on the highway, heavy snowflakes began to fall, drifting down to earth and settling on the frozen landscape, the air becoming crisp as the temperature dropped further.

On the hill behind them, amongst the trees, sitting in the last remaining upright tent, seven very relieved, wounded and bandaged Russians were getting drunk.

Chapter Fifteen: Into the Darkest Hour of the Night.

As the snow fell softly onto the landscape, the visibility decreased dramatically. The personnel carriers slowed to a crawl, the thickness of the snowfall limiting vision to just a few yards.

Hase sat attentively in the driving seat of the vehicle, straining his eyes into the blizzard before them. The pace of the vehicles had now dropped to minimal speed and he was struggling to see the road in front of them. He could feel the vehicle tracks slipping on the snow above the ice on the road and made gradual changes to the controls to ensure they remained in what he considered to be the middle of the highway.

The soldiers were gradually becoming covered in the falling snow, the large snowflakes resting upon their uniforms and helmets in the freezing temperature.

Hausser turned and addressed the two soldiers behind him in the lead carrier as they moved cautiously northwards, advising them of what was required in the village ahead. Udet coughed violently, spitting blood from his mouth over the side of the carrier.

'How are you feeling now, Udet?' Hausser asked.

Udet clutched his chest, his face covered by his scarf, but eyes presenting a man in intense pain, 'I should be alright in a couple of hours...the Russian just knocked the wind out of me, Herr Leutnant.' He replied, his voice strained in agony.

'Just keep your spirits up.' Hausser retorted, 'We should be in Stalingrad later today if all goes well.'

Meino grinned beneath his scarf, 'Perhaps the Russkies may wish to delay us longer, Hausser...how will we get through the lines?'

Hausser nodded, his face grim beneath his own scarf, 'I understand your concerns Meino, but we will deal with that when we get further north, the next challenge is the town ahead. Once we get through that, then we will worry about trigger happy Germans and Romanians.'

Meino nodded, 'Yes Herr Leutnant. Hopefully the snow will continue, that may help us.'

Hausser nodded and turned back to look into the blizzard, his eyes squinting to try and see through the wall of white falling before them, 'If this snow keeps up, we will arrive in the town in daylight, something I was hoping to avoid.'

Behind him, Meino and Udet stole a glance at each other, their concern for the dangers ahead growing.

Hausser turned to him, 'Hase, you seem to have mastered the Russian vehicle I think, how do you feel about driving us into Stalingrad?'

He glanced across at the commander, 'I would be happy to, the controls are quite straight forward once you get used to them.' He smiled, 'Perhaps its best I drive.'

Hausser studied him, his consideration that the young man may have a number of conflicts on his mind due to the situation. The commander considered that although he felt this man as one of his unit now after all that had happened over the last year, he was still not a German soldier, however he trusted him.

Seeing a shape in the falling snow before him, Hase braked hard...too late, the personnel carrier hitting the obstacle with its right wing and skidding sideways. The men jolted forward as the vehicle came to an abrupt halt.

'Achtung, Aus!' Hausser shouted with alarm, grabbing his submachine gun and jumping over the side of the carrier.

Behind them, Petru braked and the second carrier skidded to a halt at an angle to the first, Tatu already half way out of the vehicle.

Meino jumped over the other side of the vehicle behind him, grasping his MP40. Hase turned, seeing Udet wince as he tried to climb over the side of the carrier, slipping on the metal plate and falling heavily into the snow, a pained grunt indicating his landing.

He clambered over to the passenger side and climbed out, kneeling down to help Udet, the young soldier lying groaning in the snow. Udet forced a smile as he saw Hase bending down above him, swearing in pain as he was helped to his feet, his left hand grasping Hase's upper arm for support, his rifle in his right hand.

As Udet looked round, he saw the silhouette of Hausser kneeling in the snow to the front side of the carrier before a shadow on the road. Next to him, the upright silhouette of Tatu, his PPSH 41 held pointing forward, into the darkened falling snow. Meino was on the other side of the carrier, also pointing his MP40 into the gloom, moving it sporadically from side to side as he attempted to see through the thick virtually impenetrable snowfall. The others were behind the second carrier, their weapons covering the approaches to the vehicles from all sides, their heads jerking nervously from side to side in attempts to see through the darkness.

Udet leant heavily on Hase as they slowly moved towards Hausser, becoming aware that the snow was beginning to lie thick on the ice covered road beneath. As they approached, he realised the young commander was kneeling before a body lying almost motionless in front of him.

Udet looked down as they drew alongside Tatu, seeing a badly wounded Russian soldier lying on his back before the young commander, his right leg shattered due to the impact with the carrier, the white of a bone visible through bloodied flesh and a tear in his uniform. On his left side, blood seeped through a hand pressed firmly on a fresh bullet wound.

The wounded man was coughing as he strained to talk to Hausser, blood in his mouth preventing him from conversing too much. As he watched, Udet became aware the man was close to death, the blood seeping out onto the snow beneath him from his wounds as he struggled to talk.

Udet observed that the wounded man was now beginning to shiver, his voice becoming strained as he coughed some more, the exertion bringing more blood into his mouth. Then suddenly, his eyes rolled upwards and his head fell back into the snow as he died.

Hausser slowly rose from his kneeling position, turning to face them, his eyes saddened. Swallowing, the commander spoke softly, 'He was from the lorry you saw...they were ambushed up ahead. He believed they were shot at by Kalmyk partisans...escaped from the town behind us.'

Udet looked into the commander's eyes, seeing his sorrow, 'Do you think any Russians are left ahead of us?'

The young commander shook his head, 'No, there was just him and two others...they were killed in the ambush. He was trying to make it back down the road to Dubovyy Ovrag.'

Hausser looked across at Hase, seeing the soldier was staring morosely at the body behind him, aware the man had understood what the dead Russian had told him, 'You didn't kill him Hase, he would never have made it back...he was too badly wounded. He would have died on the road in the snow, alone. You couldn't see him through this.'

Udet felt the soldier next to him tense, his body straightening up to face the young commander. He looked at Hase, seeing the man nod determinedly back at the commander, sadness in his eyes.

Hausser maintained eye contact for a second, making sure Hase seemed controlled and then turned to face Udet again, raising his voice to ensure the men on the second carrier heard him, 'Get back in the carriers. I want to get through the town ahead in this blizzard, its perfect cover. Keep your eyes open, the Kalmyk ambush could be waiting for us ahead, but they probably will have looted the lorry and gone.'

With this he looked back at Udet, 'Get yourself covered up in the carrier, the next part of our journey will probably be the trickiest.' The young commander winked at him, then turned to his right, 'Meino, can you take the

Russian off the road please, I don't want him being hit by any traffic. He doesn't deserve that.'

Meino glanced over his shoulder, nodding, 'Yes, Herr Leutnant.'

Udet paused, glancing down at the Russian soldier lying in the road. Noticing he seemed relaxed now, the intense pain and fear he had experienced seconds earlier now gone. He was aware Hase was also looking down at the corpse, his breath being forced through his scarf, tears visible in his eyes. Udet turned to look at the commander, 'Did he say anything else, Hausser?'

Hausser sighed, turning slowly and directing his attention back to him, sadness in his eyes, a grim expression on his face as he pulled the scarf down from around his mouth, 'Yes he did, Udet. He said he loved his wife and child just before he died.'

Chapter Sixteen: The Kalmyk Rifleman

Hase gunned the engine of the personnel carrier, revving the machine to keep it warm. Seeing Meino climb in behind him, he engaged gear and the vehicle skidded forward in the snow, its tracks struggling for grip.

Behind them the other engine roared into life as Petru followed and they slowly progressed northwards. The snowfall was now thickening further and visibility reduced to just in front of the carriers as the flakes swirled around them.

The soldiers sat in grim silence as the snow slowly settled across their helmets and arms, the vehicles speed inadequate to unsettle the white blanket that slowly began to cover them in the carriers. The anticipation of the struggle ahead immersed each man in pensive thought, their minds filled with a mixture of determination and fear of the unknown. Each man struggling with thoughts of what lay ahead, what a mistake could lead to or even of what lay in store for them if they successfully passed through the Russian lines.

The drivers sat hunched over their controls, straining their eyes into the darkness and thick snowfall for obstacles. The snow now settling on the iced surface of the road causing the tracks on the vehicles to slip occasionally, pumping adrenalin into the men as they felt the vehicles slide or shudder. In each man's mind the thought of breaking a track or a vehicle becoming unusable was an additional fear, reducing them once more to walking and potential further dangers this would bring.

As a cold ground breeze slipped in from lake and enveloped them from the right, the pungent aroma of burning gripped their nostrils briefly, causing the men to raise their weapons in caution. The settled snow falling from their arms and helmets as they raised their arms, the weapons pointing out to each side of the carriers.

Within seconds the smell was gone, the men peering into the wall of falling snow around them for signs of the aroma's source or potential attack, but unable to glimpse anything. The thick snowfall concealing the burning lorry some 30 metres to their right, the bodies of the ambushed crew lying on in the cab and out on the iced lake.

The ammunition lorry's cab was burning slowly in the falling snow, the two ambushers having cautiously stopped unloading the back of the truck as they heard the engines approach in the blizzard. Concealing themselves hastily on the bank, they pushed their faces into the broken ice, overburdened lorry tyres having slewed across the frosted terrain, the figures ducked as a new potential enemy passed, wary the arrivals may be looking for the crashed vehicle, or them.

As the engine noise subsided to the north the ambushers stood up, embracing each other in relief, the Kalmyk mother and fourteen-year-old boy thankful for the snow's concealment. They slowly picked up the boxes they had chosen from the lorry and trudged off across the road to the west into the blizzard.

The boy hung his head as he remembered his father's last words to him earlier that day. To take his mother and flee to the west, to stay with relatives further to the southwest for safety. The Russian soldiers had then come hunting, taking his father away, striking the lad when he tried to resist and knocking him to the floor of their small house.

He and his mother had collected his father's rifle, pistol and some food and left within minutes, resigned to proceeding in the bitter cold to endure survival. Trudging through the town and witnessing the Russian soldiers' brutality to their neighbours, seeing the hatred in their eyes as they taunted people they believed had assisted the German invaders.

On the outskirts of Dubovyy Ovrag he had come upon his father one last time. His body lifeless, hanging limply above them from a telegraph pole, a message crudely nailed into his chest. 'The German collaborator'. His father had been beaten before being executed, and it was then the fourteen-year-old boy's emotions twisted from desperate sorrow to hatred as he consoled his grief stricken mother...at that point he vowed to avenge his dead father. The years of his father's teachings on hunting for food...only killing for what they needed and sparing animals that were young or female if possible came to fruition. He vowed to hunt in revenge from that moment forth.

He was a proficient marksman and the driver's death had been a simple shot. As the vehicle had slewed across the road and down the slight bank, he had momentarily lost sight of his next target, but had fired again as he saw the Russian soldier run away, smiling inside himself at the man's fear. He scolded himself for the emotion when he realised he had only wounded him and that he had escaped, using the bank as cover. The last Russian soldier had stayed in the cab of the lorry, initially laughing in relief at the small youth that appeared with the rifle, his size disproportionate to the length of the weapon. The soldier's mocking quickly transformed to fear and desperate pleading for his life to both the boy and his mother when he glimpsed the hatred within the youth's eyes and realised the teenager was motivated by revenge. He had slowly trudged miserably in front of the youth as he was forced down to the lake's edge, tears flowing down his face as he realised the boy had no intention of showing mercy. As he reached the water's edge, he had turned to face the youth dressed in bedraggled clothing, 'please' the only word to pass his lips before he was shot in the face, his body crumpling backwards onto the frozen lakes edge. The blood seeping out across the ice, the soldier dying instantly.

The boy returned to his grief stricken mother, a grim look of satisfaction on his face. The youth then lit a fire in the cab of the lorry with the assistance of a fuel can and the couple had begun to trudge away when they heard the engines approach. In nervousness, they instinctively dropped down on the side of the road whilst the vehicles passed, the shadows of the personnel carriers above them on the road seemed close enough to touch. Realising there was more than one engine, the boy considered this potential foe to be too powerful to engage at this time, vowing he would always try to use the element of surprise in a future attacks. He was learning...and quickly.

As the couple trudged through the snow, now turning slightly to the south west, he smiled briefly as he heard the crump of the lorry exploding some distance behind him. The knowledge the Russians in the next village would now have less ammunition pleasing him...then reality returned, a brief tear rolling down his cheek for the loss of his father, before he placed his arm round his mother's shoulder for comfort. He realised he needed to be strong now for both of them, this would ensure their survival and the continuation of his new purpose.

Half a kilometre to the north, the personnel carriers accelerated slightly as the snowfall lightened, visibility increasing. They were now less than two kilometres from the outskirts of Bolshiye Chapurniki as dim light filtered through the falling snow. A new day had begun.

Chapter Seventeen: Passage into the Storm.

Hausser blew smoke from his cigarette into the cold air and turned to face the three soldiers in his personnel carrier, his eyes narrowing, 'The town ahead is only a short distance away now, so check your weapons and remember that only the Russian speakers should talk...no matter what happens.'

The soldiers nodded grimly, their adrenalin rising within them. The metals cracks of bolts being pulled to check rifles and submachine guns echoed around them, indicating for the soldiers in the second carrier to replicate the action.

Tatu turned and addressed Nicu and Albrecht, his hand resting on Petru's shoulder, 'Be alert the two of you, do not speak from now on, I will do all the talking if we are challenged...understand?'

Both young soldiers nodded quietly in the back of the second carrier, their faces solemn and eyes wide with anticipation for the road and challenges ahead.

In the front carrier, Hausser turned to face the direction of travel, peering over the front metal plate of the vehicle. He could see the lights of the town before them in the distance with the lake to the right and a snow covered expanse to the left. The tracks of the carrier rolled over the ice, buildings and lights becoming larger as they began their final approach to Bolshiye Chapurniki.

Hase slowly reduced the throttle of the engine as they approached to within two hundred metres of the entry to the town. He observed the burning upright oil drums to either side of the road at the first houses, the crude heating arrangement surrounded by three Russian sentries. As they approached further the sentries turned to face them. To their right, a machine gun behind a sandbagged position was pointing directly towards them.

He swallowed hard as the first carrier slowed further, watching a Russian sentry walk slowly into the middle of the road before them, raising his left hand in indication for them to stop, a PPSH submachine gun in his right hand. The three other soldiers took their rifles from their shoulders and walked slowly out from the cover of the buildings and the warmth to join their sergeant in the road, their bayonets glinting in the morning light.

The last few snowflakes fell across them as the carriers came to a halt before the Russian sentries, their engines idling as the Russian sergeant approached, his felt cloth headwear excellent insulation against the cold.

Hausser smiled a greeting to the man, raising his hand to offer two packets of American cigarettes to the sergeant, 'Good to see the snow has stopped.' He smiled widely at the sergeant, dusting his shoulders of the settled snow.

The sergeant smiled briefly back, 'Yes, quite a snowfall we had...where are you heading?' He took the cigarette packets from Hausser's outstretched hand, nodding in gratitude.

Hausser saluted the man casually, 'We are carrying supplies and despatches for some forward units near the Volga.' He indicated behind to the empty sealed boxes in the carriers. His smile widening to a grin, 'We also have a bottle of Romanian brandy for one of the commanders at the front. A 'special' delivery.'

'Which commander?' The sergeant retorted, his tone questioning.

'Captain Markov of the NKVD.' Hausser replied defiantly, his eyes remaining fixed on the sergeant.

'I see. Have you your papers?' The sergeant seemed reluctant to challenge further when the gift was for a high ranking political officer at the front.

Hausser reached into his pocket and produced the creased and stained papers, handing them to the sergeant.

The Russian looked down at the paperwork, reading the worn writing slowly, then looking back at the young commander, his eye brows raised, 'Is Captain Medvedev with you?' He glanced back at the second carrier.

Hausser shifted slightly in his seat, trying not to display his frustration at the Russian sergeant's scrutiny. Looking him directly in the eyes, he replied solemnly, 'No, he remained in Dubovyy Ovrag due to an injury he sustained there in the air raid last night.'

The sergeant eyed him for a couple of seconds more, then nodded, handing Hausser back his papers, 'That's fine, please pull over to the left there.' He indicated with his outstretched hand, 'I think my officer would like to talk to you.'

As the sergeant stepped back, Hausser indicated to Hase where to park the personnel carrier some twenty metres further just past the first building on the left.

As the vehicles moved slowly forward, the Russian sergeant turned on his heels and strode back towards the wooden building on his right. Hesitating and glancing back at the carriers, he knocked and entered. Hausser tossed a cigarette packet to each sentry as they slowly passed them, the gesture greeted by welcoming smiles from the Russian soldiers as they caught the Lucky Strike packets.

Once they had passed the sentries, Hausser turned slightly to look at Hase, seeing the fear in his expression, then whispered, 'Stay calm everyone.'

The personnel carriers pulled slowly over to the left and stopped at the side of the road just behind a crudely built wooden house. There were logs lying around the building and smoke gradually rising from its stone chimney. The disinterested sentries slowly re-shouldered their weapons and walked back to the burning fuel drums they were originally using for warmth, resuming their conversation which drifted across the road.

As they sat pensively in the personnel carriers, a lorry slowly approached from the town and passed through the improvised checkpoint, heading south. Udet's gaze followed the truck, seeing blood spattered across the tailgate and an arm protruding limply from the covers on the side. The realisation the truck was carrying the wounded and dying chilling him to their own potential fate.

Seeing the door to the hut open, Udet leant forward and touched Hausser's shoulder to alert him. The young commander turned and saw the Russian officer talking at the doorway to the men inside, feeling the caution within him dissipate as he realised the officer was bidding the occupants of the hut farewell.

The officer turned, seeing the carriers, and placing his cap on his head carefully with both hands as he walked across the road towards them smiling. The Russian commander was in his mid-forties and well dressed, his face reddened from the warmth of the hut and the alcohol rations he had consumed as a 'precaution against the cold.' As he reached the carrier, he saluted Hausser, 'How are you men today? Hopefully you will soon be out of the cold, eh, Comrades?' He smiled broadly, noting the fleeting smiles and nods from the men in the carriers. Looking at Hausser, he cleared his throat. 'Now sergeant, if you wouldn't mind giving me a lift to the bridge up ahead, my transport is delayed it seems.'

Hausser nodded cautiously, 'Yes sir, would you like to sit in the vehicle?'

The officer shook his head, 'Not necessary, I am used to these, I will just sit on the centre panel as you men all look tired.' He clambered over the side of the carrier, apologising to Udet as he stepped clumsily over him. Placing his legs either side of the central stowage bins on the carrier, he gingerly lowered himself onto a blanket Udet had placed over the boxes.

The officer laughed slightly, 'Well I may look silly up here, but I will be able to see what everyone is up to at least.'

Hausser grinned in response, turning to the others to ensure they understood to smile also. Looking back at Hase, the young commander tapped him on the shoulder, 'Let's go then, don't drive too quickly as we do not want to lose our special cargo.'

The officer laughed, slapping Meino's arm in jest, noticing the men grin back. 'Yes, let's not make me look more of an ass than I already do.' He declared, 'Carefully onwards please.'

As the personnel carriers moved slowly forward, the officer grasped the metal centre console either side of his thighs to steady himself, 'So sergeant, where are you from?'

Hausser half turned to eye the officer behind him, 'Cholm, sir.'

The officer thought for a second, his demeanour becoming stern, 'Ah yes, currently in enemy territory I think...you are a long way from home, sergeant.'

'Yes Sir, but one day I will return, once we have pushed the fascists back,' Hausser retorted.

The officer smiled again, 'That's the spirit. We will return once we push them back, then overall victory will follow shortly afterwards I think. Don't you all agree?' He looked around the carrier observing the smiling faces, 'Your men are very quiet, sergeant, are they ill or hungry?'

'Yes sir, just very tired I think...we have been on the move for days.' Hausser replied, becoming cautious should the officer direct a question to one of the others.

'I understand, perhaps some rest when you get to your destination will be in order.' The officer leant back against the box behind him, a comforting smile on his face.

Udet adjusted the blankets around his shoulders, attempting to conceal his unease at the closeness of the Russian officer. Looking around, he started to observe the early morning movements in the town. The buildings were mostly wooden huts of varying sizes with a scattering of stone built houses. Small gardens bordered the buildings and some had a variety of belongings strewn about the front of the dwellings. There were a number of small side lanes leading from the main highway towards unseen huts and buildings behind. In several of the side lanes he saw the bedraggled local inhabitants grouped together or gathering snow to heat for water for the day.

As they drove slowly northwards, he saw the parked American made trucks to the sides of the road, the Russian infantry sleepily beginning to exit buildings to either side encouraged by their officers and sergeants. The dull hangovers of the billeted soldiers evident in their bleary eyes and bewildered expressions, their unsteady stances indicative of the previous night's revelry.

After about two hundred metres, they crossed a small town square and Udet counted five white Russian camouflaged tanks parked on the right side of the square, their crews busily attending to their vehicles, a couple making tea over a burning oil drum.

The Russian officer addressed Hausser again, 'You have a number of fascist weapons with you, sergeant, where did you get them?' He indicated to Udet's rifle and Hausser's MP40 lying in the foot well.

Hausser turned slightly, 'There was insufficient weapons for the front line soldiers, sir, so we gave them ours and took weapons from the enemy fallen.' He studied the officer, hoping his explanation did not arouse suspicion.

The officer nodded, 'Very good of you and your men sergeant, we must all show our willingness for sacrifice to ensure victory.' He paused, retrieving a cigarette from his pocket, 'Anyway, between us...' Lighting the cigarette, he drew deeply, '...I prefer the Kar 98 German rifle to our own Mosin Nagant, better aim I think.' He withdrew the cigarette from his lips, holding it between his fingers and indicating to the MP40, 'Not as good as our PPSH, not enough in the magazine and exposes the user to enemy fire if he's not careful.'

Hausser smiled reassuringly, 'I agree, sir, a useful weapon, but not as good as our own submachine guns.'

The Russian officer nodded, 'Yes, the submachine gun and our resolve will drive the fascists back for our final victory I think.'

The personnel carrier slowed as it approached the bridge in front of them. Hausser looked round and saw the sandbagged emplacements either side of the waterway and a number of Russian soldiers standing around the start of the bridge. All the Russian soldiers wore white padded camouflage uniforms and seemed well armed.

The officer leant forward, 'Ah, here we are...my command post for the day.' He saw the Russian soldiers at the bridge begin to remove their rifles from their shoulders as they approached. Noticing the sergeant tense in front of him, he laid a hand on his shoulder, 'Don't worry about them, sergeant, they are just very cautious. Mostly from the east, some virtually oriental, they are vicious soldiers, but they can't understand a word I say and I have no idea what they say to me most of the time.' The officer laughed, waving to the Russian soldiers at the bridge to alleviate their concerns, 'They can all drink more than me too!' He laughed aloud, 'And they don't seem to feel the cold at all.'

Hausser nodded cautiously, 'They look fearsome enough.' He quickly glanced round to reassure the other men in the carrier with his eyes, 'I don't think the fascists will be able to resist them when they attack.'

As the carriers came to a stop before the bridge, the Russian officer clambered out, once again apologising to Udet for leaning on him as he exited the vehicle. Udet nodded in return, smiling reassuringly at the man.

The Russian officer turned and leant across the carrier, extending his hand to Hausser, 'Thank you for the lift sergeant...I hope we will meet again.'

The young commander grasped his hand smiling, 'I hope so too, sir. Is there anything you can tell us about the road ahead?'

The officer straightened up, smiling, 'Yes, be careful on the road from now on. The fascists are shelling the northern part of the town at times, but hopefully our aircraft will take out their guns soon.' The officer saluted Hausser, smiling as the salute was returned. He turned and indicated to the nearest guard on the bridge, shouting, 'Let them through to the other side...they are on special orders.'

As the guards began to move slowly to the side, the carrier advanced forward cautiously, jolting to a halt as the officer turned back to face them, the lead vehicle nearly stalling until Hase revved the engine.

Smiling, the Russian officer leant forward slightly, 'One more thing that should cheer you men up that I heard on the radio earlier. The Russian armies have just closed the ring around Stalingrad this morning at Kalach. The fascists are now cut off in the city ahead. It's only a matter of time now.' He glanced at the smiling soldiers in the back of the carrier and turned, walking away towards the soldiers on the right side of the bridge.

Hausser turned to face the front, his expression rapidly becoming grave as he considered the Russian officer's statement, 'Drive on!'

Chapter Eighteen: Malye Chapurniki

Both personnel carriers passed over the bridge slowly, the occupants eyeing the Siberian soldiers with controlled caution, intrigued by the differing facial features and the fact these men were well equipped with grenades and new rifles. The Russians returned their stares as they passed, used to the attention their presence brought and presuming this was a similar behaviour. Udet noticed some with faces indicating Mongolian descent, their high cheek bones and differing eye contours puzzling him.

The lead personnel carrier rattled over the bridge, the steel tracks squealing as they gained contact with the road again and skidding for a second as the ground surface changed. Hase accelerated, passing the remaining Siberian guards on the road northwards and passing into Malye Chapurniki.

As they gained distance from the Russians, Udet groaned, his voice deliberately subdued, 'Bloody clumsy oaf, he stood on me twice.'

Meino grinned at Udet's discomfort, leaning forward, he whispered between the two front passengers, 'We had better make good progress through here...I think the Russian bear is awakening and we are in the middle of their reinforcements.'

Hausser nodded, turning his head slightly, 'I agree, but no speaking please you two, any hint of a German voice here and we are all dead, understand?'

Meino nodded, 'Yes, sorry.' Leaning back in his seat, he swallowed, trying to alleviate the nervous lump in his throat. Turning to Udet, he put his finger to his lips indicating for the younger soldier to remain quiet.

Hausser leant over to Hase whispering, 'I think we will not tell the others about what the Russian said.' He looked at the soldier sat in the driver's seat next to him, seeking his agreement.

Hase nodded, his eyes fixed on the road ahead, 'I understand, sir.' A grin forming on his face, 'I don't think the others will understand me anyway.'

Hausser nodded, a smirk on his face, 'Cheeky dog...you know what I meant.'

Hase nodded, smiling at the exchange, then he stiffened as he began to take in the surroundings as they drove further. The buildings north of the river were similar to the south, of wooden and stone construction, but severely damaged. A crudely painted sign hung to their left, daubed in red on the side of an ammunition box. He read the Russian wording slowly as they passed, the sign an ominous warning to those advancing northwards, 'Enemy shelling on the road ahead.'

Fires raged unchecked through a considerable number of the structures with sparks and smoke blowing across the road around them. This part of the town was virtually deserted, with the occasional Russian soldier to be seen down the side lanes. An unnerving, almost disconcerting silence settled around them, the northern part of the town seeming virtually deserted.

As they drove further they began to see frozen bodies along the sides of the road, half buried in snowfall. Hase considering the frozen limbs protruding from the white embracing blanket covering the most gruesome of visions and offering the dead some degree of respect. The evidence of a heavy desperate battle was everywhere and Hase imagined the frantic fighting that must have occurred as the Germans and their allies attempted to stop the Russian advance. He considered there seemed to be a considerable number of Russian dead to either side of the highway, their brown uniforms frozen to their extended limbs. Occasionally he could spot a German or Romanian uniform amongst the corpses, but these were far less frequent indicating a defensive battle as the Germans and their allies retreated northwards.

Glancing into the many side streets, he observed the occasional Russian soldier searching the streets or looting the dead, their faces covered in scarves from the heat and smoke. Glancing left, he saw two wolves in an empty lane, both tugging on a concealed item in the rubble, beneath the snow. The hair on the back of his neck rising as he realised they were feeding on a half-buried corpse, blood dripping from their mouths.

Hausser sensed his distraction and leant forward, whispering, 'Keep going, Hase, not much further now. You need to keep your eyes on the road, there is a lot of smoke ahead.'

He shook his head, turning his vision back to the highway, noticing two Russian soldiers by the side of the road. They were standing in their greatcoats smoking, their faces flushed with the heat from the fires. Both slowly turned to observe the passing vehicles, their faces expressionless, lines of tiredness beneath their eyes. One slowly rose his hand in a greeting as they passed, with Hausser returning the gesture.

To the right, an aging Russian civilian approached, shuffling along the iced road and pulling behind him a small cart with sparse belongings piled upon it. His thin bearded dishevelled features straining with the weight of his cart, his eyes transfixed on the road behind them, seeming oblivious to their presence and where he was. He imagined the man had suffered great hardship and now he was potentially alone, the last evidence of his life piled on the small cart he dragged down the street.

The vehicle accelerated slightly as they neared the northern part of the town, his eagerness apparent in the lead vehicle to escape this place that caused him concern and uneasiness. Heavy smoke now billowed across the road before them, the buildings on either side burning out of control, their wooden structures being consumed by fire.

As they passed into the billowing smoke, the pungent aroma of the acrid burning wood entered the soldiers' nostrils, causing each man to hold his breath. The dark smoke of the burning timber mixed with an unmistakable smell, the odour of burning flesh, turning the men's stomachs. Sparks and light fragments of wood flew around them, hitting their faces and uniforms and overwhelming their senses.

For a moment they were blinded, the feeling of disorientation virtually overpowering the men as the smoke enveloped the two personnel carriers.

The vehicles slowed dramatically in the severely reduced visibility, then as suddenly as they had entered the billowing mass, they exited on the other side, at the northern outskirts of the village. The brilliance of the snow covered landscape causing them to blink in the sharpening light as their eyes adjusted.

Hausser looked ahead and drew breath sharply, gritting his teeth and whispering, 'Scheisse! They are moving up. There must be hundreds of them!'

Before them on the iced road, some one hundred and fifty metres in front of the lead carrier, marched two long columns of Russian soldiers on either side of the highway. The two columns stretched as far as the eye could see, with officers and commissars between the two lines of soldiers, spurring the marching men along.

The Russians were marching north, towards the lower suburbs of Stalingrad.

Chapter Nineteen: Close Enough to Touch

As the second carrier emerged from the billowing smoke, Tatu's eyes widened when he saw the Russian soldiers marching before them. With a quick intake of breath he turned to the stunned soldiers in his carrier, his voice stern, 'Keep alert. No talking and avoid eye contact as we pass through them.' He glanced around seeing the strain on each man's face as they took in the ominous sight in front of them.

The stout Romanian quartermaster ran his hand down over his bushy moustache nervously, 'I know you are all exhausted, but we cannot make a mistake now.' Glancing at Nicu and Albrecht in the back of the carrier, he indicated to them both, 'Get further down in the carrier, cover yourself with blankets and look as though you are injured or asleep.'

The two men stared back at him, their eyes wide with adrenalin and fear, both slowly taking in the information and nodding. Nicu slipped down in the carrier, moving his body so that only his head was above the metal sides of the vehicle. He forced a smile at Tatu, pulled his greatcoat collar up and wrapped a blanket round his shoulders, moving his rifle to between his legs and covering the weapon with another blanket. Albrecht observed the man next to him and followed suit, lowering himself into the carrier so his knees were nearly in the foot well.

Tatu nodded with a degree of satisfaction, 'Remember, no talking whatever happens.' He checked both men's faces for understanding, satisfied, he turned back to face Petru, 'Are you alright, my old friend?'

Petru nodded, a faint smile forming on his lips, 'The final challenge lies ahead I think…this should be interesting.'

Tatu nodded slowly, his concern rising as the vehicles continued slowly along the highway, observing they were now only one hundred metres from the rear of the advancing columns.

He followed the line of infantry before them as the long line extended off into the distance. Noticing it then snaked to the right and over a slight hill, he wondered how many troops were before them. In the distance, several heavy dark plumes of smoke ascended up into the sky on the horizon, indicating the ferocity of the battle ahead near the Volga.

A thump from the right made him turn to look across the snow covered field that extended towards the lakes. A large Russian artillery position lay across the white expanse, some two hundred metres from the road and interspersed amongst the guns sat American supply lorries, seemingly loaded with shells for the guns. As Tatu watched, another gun fired, jolting backwards with a plume of smoke rising into the crisp air, the shell soaring into the sky and then down into the suburbs, beyond the horizon.

In the field before the guns lay bodies half covered in snow, an indication of the Russian advance towards the city. Surveying the field, he realised there were hundreds of bodies, an indication of the ferocious fighting that had occurred in the preceding days as the Russians had advanced towards German machine guns on the small rise before them.

Several destroyed Romanian R4 tanks lay in the field, some of the broken hulks still smouldering and he observed many bodies around them. Considering that the tanks had driven out to combat the infantry and then been overwhelmed, his eyes fixed on a destroyed Russian T34 in the centre of the field. He realised that the Romanians had then perhaps faced overwhelming numbers of Russian tanks as they tried to drive the Russian soldiers back. His eyes became moist as he considered the frantic battle his countrymen had faced, knowing they were outgunned, but attacking anyway in desperation. Perhaps they had gained some comfort and resolve from delaying the enemy, allowing many to escape into the city behind them.

His eyes withdrew from the scene in the field as he realised the lead carrier was now starting to move between the two columns of Russian infantry. Noticing Hausser in the front car salute a commissar who had moved to the side to let the vehicles past, the Russian officer shouting to his men to be aware of the carriers behind them and to move aside.

Tatu raised his hand and saluted the commissar as they passed him, the carriers proceeding at a cautionary speed to avoid drawing attention. The commissar smiled back, nodding to him, then turned to shout at his men again, encouraging them forward.

The Romanian listened as the commissar shouted words of encouragement, 'kill the fascist invaders', 'drive them from our home city' and two statements that almost made his blood run cold, 'take no prisoners' and 'for each fascist you kill brings victory one step closer for Mother Russia.' His mood darkened as he realised the war was now in a different stage from the one he was accustomed to. As the commissar's raised voice faded behind them, he heard similar words from the next commander they passed and then another commissar.

Slowly the vehicles weaved a path down the highway, the infantry on either side occasionally staring or nodding at them or gesturing friendship. Tatu considered he would just look to the front of the vehicle, wary of turning round to see the expressions of Nicu and Albrecht.

Behind him, Nicu's eyes were closed tightly, his fear driving him to block out the outside world, his hands shaking beneath the blanket. He grasped his weapon tightly, exasperated with how useless it would be if the surrounding Russians suspected their identity.

Albrecht occasionally looked out from the cover of his blanket, his curiosity sporadically overcoming his fear. His stomach was churning, and his hands sweating as he realised the sheer number of Russians around them each time he opened his eyes.

The vehicles slowly turned the gradual bend in the highway to the right. Tatu observing the broken makeshift defences on the right of the road that had been overcome in the preceding days. Several sandbagged emplacements were linked by shallow foxholes and some makeshift barricades, the signs of a hastily prepared defensive line.

Amongst the positions lay the dead, half covered in snow. He observed German and Hungarian uniforms amongst the soldiers that had fallen as well as several Russian dead. He considered there had been desperate hand to hand fighting here as the rear guard Axis forces had tried to hold and push back the Russian attack.

The sandbagged emplacements were all depressed or destroyed and he realised Russian tanks had driven over them in their advance. One emplacement that they passed had a broken German MG42 heavy machine gun twisted and bent against the sandbags that had fallen in on it, the Romanian closing his mind upon seeing a frozen hand reaching out from the snow still grasping the weapon, the soldier's body crushed to pulp by the heavy tank as it rose up over the makeshift emplacement.

Tatu had briefly closed his eyes and then reopened them, wary his reaction was observed by the surrounding Russians. He saluted and smiled at another commissar that turned to observe them, the officer returning his smile with a raised hand.

The Romanian quartermaster looked forward again, seeing the marching columns turned to the left after a further one hundred metres, the road then going over the slight ridge. As he sat there, he felt the deepest sorrow for what had happened, the sheer number of dead and the destruction that had occurred seemed to be now endless, the new normality. They were now so far from home, the thousands of kilometres they had travelled in what he thought initially to be an adventure, seemed now to be an insurmountable distance to return, the return to safety.

A jolt by the carrier as it overcame a small obstacle on the road forced him back to reality as he realised he had half drifted off, his body exhausted. The 'whoosh' that he had heard overhead alerting him to danger. As his senses became fully alert, he saw the Russian infantry all stop and look to the north momentarily, then the nearest Russian officer turned, shouting in alarm, 'Enemy artillery, take cover!'

Tatu glanced back down the slope as the artillery shell exploded just in front of the Russian gun positions, throwing the frozen dead and dismembered bodies that had lain there into the air. The Russian infantry on either side of the road dropped to lie on the verges, their hands sweeping over their heads in a desperate and futile attempt to prevent injury from shrapnel.

Several more 'whooshes' soared overhead and he watched as the artillery fired from southern Stalingrad had now found its range. The first shell landed in the middle of the Russian position, the explosion sending a wall of fire and dirt into the air. He stared mesmerised as the artillery crews caught in the blast were thrown upwards and sideways, their bodies broken in the explosion, the sound wave engulfing them. Then another blast hit one of the artillery lorries, the flames bursting outwards, followed by a larger explosion as the shells near the vehicle blew up, smoke and flame billowing into the air.

Tatu jerked backwards, his body pushed into the wooden seat behind him. He realised Petru was now accelerating and he looked ahead to see the lead carrier turn to the left on the highway and progress over the top of the slight ridge. He stole another glance to his right, his adrenalin racing as he heard the sounds from above with many more shells following the first couple. The shells burst all around the Russian artillery position, tossing bodies, equipment and frozen dirt into the air. The position seemed to disappear in the smoke and explosions as more flames rose rapidly into the air ignited by fuel.

Petru turned the vehicle to the left, his view of the spectacle taking place some three hundred metres further down the ridge was gone behind them, and he turned to see the lead vehicle accelerating down the gradual slope before them. He looked past the vehicle and down the slope, overlooking the bodies covered in snow, the burnt out hulks of vehicles sitting by the sides of the highway and in the fields to either side. He stared further, into the burning buildings in the distance, the plumes of smoke all across the horizon, the explosions he could see as shells rained down on the city suburb before him, the southern suburb of Stalingrad. Beyond which he thought he could just make something out, between the visions of man-made hell, the tall damaged and burning blocks and factories, just a glimpse of what made his heart jump, the wide expanse of the Volga River.

As he stared at the horizon, seeing a large explosion on one of the taller building's sides, the dust and smoke rising into the air, he became aware the sounds above had changed. Now he could hear a distant rumble from their front, the echoes of war hitting them like a wave from the fighting in the city to the north.

He stared seemingly trance like at the devastation, the flashes in the buildings and tracer fire flying across the city landscape as a dust and smoke cloud seemed to hang over the torn city, the scene now just over five hundred metres away.

Tatu was shaken from his vision, his mouth open at what he had seen as Albrecht's hand grasped his upper arm firmly, a desperate tightness in his grip. He turned to the side, he became aware the young despatch rider's head was next to his as their helmets made contact, clunking together.

He felt the young German's breath on his neck and heard his strained whisper, 'Tatu, Stukas!' His senses tensed on hearing the word, his eyes following Albrecht's outstretched arm pointing high above them to their front.

In the distance, high in the sky, he saw six planes flying towards them, the distinctive bends in the wings confirming Albrecht's gasped warning. As he watched, the aircraft to the right seemed to bank sharply, then begin to descend rapidly towards the road in front of them. A mechanical scream began to fill the air as the Stuka pilot switched on his siren as he descended, the noise filling the air and drowning out the sounds of war from the city before them.

The plane descended rapidly, then performed a dramatic turn as it levelled off and immediately started to climb again, a small black object falling to earth as it turned. The following explosion was a direct hit on the road to their front throwing the broken bodies of the infantry that had sheltered on its verges into the air.

Tatu shook himself into action, seeing the intent of the other planes. He attempted to shout to the lead vehicle, his voice hoarse, hardly making a sound. He coughed, then shouted frantically, 'Davai! Davai!' Seeing Hausser glance round, concern on his face, the carriers accelerated once more, the vehicles bouncing on the road's surface as they neared maximum speed.

Tatu glimpsed a Russian soldier lying on the verge and they made eye contact, seeing the terror in the man's eyes before he ducked his head again. He watched as some of the infantry attempted to fire their rifles at the aircraft in a vain attempt to defend themselves. A Russian commissar scrambled to his feet, drawing his pistol to fire at the oncoming aircraft as they accelerated past, the Russian officer raising his weapon in readiness.

The air was now filled with the noise of the mechanical screaming, the Stukas beginning their bombing runs after the first met little ground fire. As the carriers hurtled down the road, Tatu's emotions blurred as the entire world seemed to be screaming, the noise deafening as all five planes dived on their prey.

He stared in awe, his hands over his ears as the first carrier slowed, reaching the point where the first bomb had landed, the carrier bouncing as it traversed the shrapnel and damaged road surface...Tatu did not hear the cracking of bones as the vehicles rode over the dead in the urgency to escape.

The sirens stopped dramatically as the planes levelled and then rose steeply back into the air, the explosions in their wake throwing frozen snow and broken men into the air behind them. Tatu felt the blast wave of the nearest explosion on the back of his head, dirt and debris being thrown into the carrier.

He turned and looked up as the planes began banking to the east, their sirens once again beginning to sound as they turned in a wide circle to the south. Tatu's eyes widened as he saw their intent and shouted once again for the carriers to accelerate, realising the planes intended to fly down the road using their machine guns. As the vehicles jerked forward again, he glanced across at Petru, his friend covered in dirt and sweating profusely.

The Romanian quartermaster turned in his seat to see where the planes were and looked back down the road at the devastation behind them. Smoke was still rising from where the bombs had landed, with several small fires on the road and verges as uniforms and equipment burned. He looked back up the gradual incline, the many bodies of Russian infantry lay across the slope, the snow stained red with the blood of those that had been torn apart or bodies that had disintegrated under the explosive force.

He watched as many of the surviving dazed Russians started moving from the road, fully aware of the intention of the pilots. Seeing several men not moving he presumed them dead or wounded until he realised their inexperience or terror may have kept them there. As he watched the surviving officers and commissars barking orders to move away, he felt an urge to tell them to move, to get the young men to safety, but looking beyond them into the sky he realised it was already too late as one of the Stukas began a strafing run along the road.

The carrier bounced in the tarmac as Petru hit an obstruction and Tatu turned back, grasping the sides of the carrier for support, forcing himself to look away from what was happening behind them. As he did, he realised the carriers were just entering the first set of buildings, some low concrete apartment blocks. The road banked slightly to the right and as the vehicle turned, Petru quickly reducing speed, Tatu glancing back briefly, his view of the hill gone.

He sat back in his seat exhausted, the noises of war now became louder to their front, the muffled machine gun fire behind. As they drove slowly forward, he noticed terrified and relieved Russian soldiers huddled or crouched in large numbers on either side of the street.

Tatu exhaled heavily, running his hand down over his moustache and chin. Realising his mouth was very dry, he looked down into the foot well for his water canteen. Leaning forward he caught the eye of an older Russian soldier observing him from the side of the street, the man smiling and nodding a toothless greeting, 'Welcome to Stalingrad, comrade.'

Chapter Twenty: A Soldier Born

Hausser leant forward and placed his hand on Hase's arm whispering, 'Slowly my friend, we need to understand how to get through.'

The lead personnel carrier's speed dropped to a crawl as it proceeded down the street, the Russian soldiers crouched on either side observing the vehicles as they passed. As the carriers gradually approached a left corner, the speed dropped further, the drivers cautiously aware that this turning meant they would be facing in the direction of the river ahead.

As Hausser removed his hand from his arm, Hase looked around, seeing the Russian soldiers studying them. The sounds of war echoed round the corner, the explosions, rattle of machine gun fire and the occasional shout ringing in his ears. His stomach turned as the small carrier's tracks rattled on the tarmac road as it advanced the last few feet to the bend.

He edged the vehicle past the corner and slowly turned the small tracked carrier into the left bend on the street. The morning sun broke through the clouds as they turned, bathing the street in light and forcing him to narrow his eyes, raising his left hand to shield his vision.

Hase blinked several times before the street in front of him came fully into focus, his eyes widening as he saw the street was almost deserted. Smoke billowed from a housing block on fire on the right side, the ashen air and sparks swirling in the morning sun. Rubble was strewn across the road from numerous explosions on the already damaged buildings that lined the thoroughfare. The damaged and fractured masonry and splintered broken woodwork hanging on the buildings that once provided sturdy residences for factory and river workers.

The street was approximately two hundred metres long, running south to north, with a Russian checkpoint at the end. Two mobile barriers of logs wrapped in barbed wire lay on the tarmac surface. Three soldiers stood uneasily at the sides of the street next to the barriers, their stances nervous and apprehensive, wary of the shellfire overhead. An officer stood with them, smoking a cigarette and talking to one of the men, his right hand gesturing as if to emphasise a point.

In the distance, above the rooftops and housing blocks Hase could see the columns of dark smoke rising into the air. The noise of distant gunfire and explosions echoed across the street, the sounds of bitter fighting and an ongoing battle further to the north seeming to welcome them to their next challenge. As he watched he saw tracer bullets rise into the sky in the distance, between the smoke plumes, the red hot metal projectiles slowly dimming and disappearing over distance.

Udet leant forward slightly, the excitement rising in his whisper, 'I can hear an MG34...they are our guns in the distance.'

Hausser turned his head slightly next to him, his eyes fixed on the Russians at the end of the street, 'Shhh! No talking, Udet. This is more dangerous now!' Udet leant back dejected, his face becoming solemn as he realised they were now slowly approaching the Russian position.

The Russian soldiers turned to observe the carriers as they neared, instinctively ducking their heads as a shell landed on a rooftop a short distance away to the right. The carriers slowly advanced towards the checkpoint, weaving around the rubble strewn across the road. The occupants avoided looking into the broken brick and masonry for fear of observing the charred body protruding from one of the piles of brick.

As they drifted in and out of the dense smoke, the familiar aroma of burnt flesh filled their nostrils, forcing them to hold their breaths. The flames licked upwards from the burning building windows, the heat intense as they slowly passed, the men shielding their faces from the dramatic temperature change.

The Russian officer stepped out into the middle of the street, leaving his three squad members standing by the building corners at the junction of the thoroughfare. Two soldiers on the right corner and one on the left, their duty to police entrants to the forward combat zone. The Russian officer raised his hand as the lead vehicle ground to a halt in front of him, his expression solemn as he confidently stood before them, his greatcoat buttoned up to his chin, the collar pulled up around his ears.

The Russian political officer looked down at Hausser sitting in the carrier and returned his salute officially, 'Where are you going, sergeant?' He asked, a determined look on his face.

Hausser shifted in his seat, uneasy at the man's scrutiny, 'Despatches for the forward command post, sir. We also have some supplies.'

The officer narrowed his eyes, 'Who are you to report to?' His tone becoming more demanding.

Hausser returned his stare, 'We were told to hand the despatches to the commander in the forward command post, I don't know his name. Can you direct us please, sir?'

Next to Hausser, Hase glanced at the young Russian political officer, wary of provoking the man further. The officer was probably in his late twenties and of polished appearance. His boots and uniform were virtually immaculate and visibly out of place in a war zone. He considered that by comparison they must seem like the brushings from the street, unshaven, dirty, dishevelled soldiers attempting to gain access through the officer's checkpoint.

The officer outstretched his hand, his demeanour becoming irritated, 'I will take the despatches…go back and join the other men at the end of the street, the fascists are barricaded in the warehouses on the river. We will need every man to attack and drive them out shortly.'

Hausser shook his head, his voice calm, 'Sorry sir, those are not my orders. My orders are to deliver the despatches to the commander in person. They come from the towns to the south, combat and a situation report on reinforcements and availability I think. Then we have to report back to Bolshiye Chapurniki.'

The officer's face flushed with anger, his voice raised, 'What do you mean, not your orders! I am a superior officer, I am ordering you to hand over your despatches and join the soldiers at the end of the street in preparation for an attack. The command post is just round this corner in the bakery basement, I will deliver your 'despatches'!' He stood staring at Hausser, hand outstretched, his lips pursed in sneering anger.

Behind them, Udet shifted in his seat, moving his hands beneath the blanket across his legs.

The officer glanced round the carrier, a determined look on his face, his stare stopping at Udet, the young soldier's smirk irritating him, 'What are you smiling at?'

Udet shrugged his shoulders, the smile on his face defiant.

The political officer took a determined step towards him, past Hausser, '*I said*...what are you smiling at? What is the matter with you men, do you not understand orders?'

Hausser interjected, 'Sorry sir, our orders are...'

The officer turned his head towards him, 'Silence, I am speaking to this man.' He indicated to Udet, turning back to the young soldier. The officer leant forward, his flushed face drawing close to Udet's face, 'Now I will ask you again...what are you smiling at?'

In the driving seat, Hase noticed the three Russian soldiers at either side of the checkpoint becoming uneasy, their stances now becoming more rigid, their hands reaching slowly for their rifles.

The officer's face was now inches from Udet's, his cheeks flushed red with anger, his right hand began to move to the pistol holster by his waist, 'I will have you all placed in a penal battalion for this behaviour...now I am asking you again, what are you smiling at?'

The officer's spare hand rose slowly from his waist and he prodded Udet in the chest with his finger, his voice menacing, 'Why do you not answer, soldier?' His face now red with anger, spittle splashing onto Udet's face.

Hausser sighed, turning in his seat quickly, 'Sir…'

Udet's left hand shot up from under the blanket, grasping the officer's collar tightly, preventing the man from moving backwards. In a flash, his other hand emerged from the blanket and struck the officer below his jaw, pushing upwards as he did so, a slight crunch the only noise. He pulled the officer's face slightly towards him, the officer's eyes wide with shock, his mouth open, his lips moving but no sound other than a gurgle escaping from his throat. The pistol clattering to the ground at the side of the carrier.

Udet leant forward, his smile turning to gritted teeth as he whispered into the Russian's ear, his eyes sparkling with adrenalin, 'Wir sind Deutsche Soldaten, Russkie schwein!'

He pushed the officer sideways, the man slipping back over the side of the carrier, a gurgling sound coming from his mouth as he gasped for air, his hands rising to his throat, the blood pouring down the side of the vehicle from the wound he had sustained.

Meino's eyes widened as he saw the bloodied knife in Udet's hand, realising it had entered the officer underneath his chin, probably going through his mouth and then puncturing his brain. Seeing the Russian guards initially look inquisitively, then reach for their rifles as they mentally grasped what had happened, he rose up from his seat, the blanket falling into the foot well. He lifted his MP40 with his right hand, firing a burst as he grasped the magazine with his left, the two Russian infantry on the right propelled backwards against the wall, blood splatters extending across the torn brick.

A shell burst overhead, causing all to duck instinctively in response. Meino turned to fire at the Russian on the left to see him disappear round the corner, his rifle discarded in his panic to escape.

Hausser jumped from the carrier, pulling the strap on his MP40 over his shoulder. He spun round to see Nicu run past him to the barrier, the young Romanian determined to clear the obstacle, grasping the wire wrapped round the right log, pushing the barrier slightly. Hausser moved to join him, shouting over his shoulder, 'It seems our luck has finally run out…get ready everyone!'

Shouts could be heard far behind them and Petru turned to see several Russian infantry at the southern end of the street seeming hesitant at the sight before them, trying to understand what was happening. Next to him, Tatu fired a burst from his submachine gun at them, the Russians ducking back behind the corner in the street in response. Tatu then clumsily clambered over the back of his seat and assumed a position in the back of the carrier, next to Albrecht.

Albrecht had originally struggled to comprehend what he had seen around the front vehicle, but now turned quickly in the back of the second carrier, struggling with his rifle, pulling the bolt back and sliding down into the foot well for cover.

Hausser and Nicu were pushing the log to the side, the obstacle scraping across the road, its movement constricted by the scattered debris. Behind them, the engines on the carriers revved, the vehicles slowly moving to the right to proceed through the gap they had created, past the twitching bloodied corpse. Hausser raised his hand to indicate for the vehicles to stop, checking the street to either side.

A shell exploded off to the left as Hausser rolled over the log, coming to rest against the wall, a few inches from the corner. Looking to the left, he could see the burning buildings in the distance and the escaped soldier running down the middle of the street towards a Russian armoured car parked on the right side of the thoroughfare.

He turned to glance to the right, crawling forward to the corner and grasping his MP40 in both hands. A shot rang out and he glanced back to the left, seeing the escaping Russian fall forward, his arms flailing as the bullet entered his arched back. He heard a bolt pulled next to him and looked up. Udet stood next to him, smoke rising from his rifle muzzle.

Udet glanced down at him, a grim smile on his face, 'Enough of this…Hausser, let's teach these Russkies what we can do!'

Hausser blinked, their eyes meeting, then he twisted his head to glance round the corner. Two Russian soldiers stood in the street, their weapons at waist height, looking towards them. Their uncertainty evident in their stances, their confusion clear at what was going on and what they faced. Behind them he could see an open doorway on the left, probably the forward command post he surmised, the soldiers it's sentries.

Hausser glanced back at Udet, seeing Nicu behind him, his rifle also at the ready. Behind them Tatu fired another burst of his submachine gun at the Russians cautiously glancing round the corner of the street some two hundred metres behind.

Leutnant Hausser rose to a crouched position, grasping his weapon tightly, a grim determination overcoming him. He considered walking out and trying to bluff his way through the sentries and discarded this idea quickly, realising they would be ready to shoot before listening to him.

He turned to Udet and Nicu, 'Right, I will run across, you two fire.' He commanded, his voice shaking. Both men nodded resolutely, their determination to escape clear in their expressions.

Hausser nodded at them once, then sprinted across the road, seeing some steps opposite as a potential hiding place. He glanced right as he reached the middle of the road, seeing the Russians raise their weapons towards him. Swallowing hard, his heart beating loudly in his chest, feeling exposed in the middle of the street, he stumbled and fell near the steps as he heard gunfire behind him.

Looking up he saw the Russian on the left spin round and fall face down on the road, the bullet from Nicu's rifle hitting him on the left of his chest and propelling him backwards.

The second Russian fell backwards as Udet's bullet hit him mid chest, shattering his ribcage and killing him instantly.

Hausser looked to the left, seeing a Russian soldier kneeling by the body of the Russian who had tried to escape. Their eyes met, some 50 metres apart and he saw the Russian's alarm, watching him turn and shout for assistance, the engine on the BA-10 armoured car starting abruptly and roaring into life.

The young commander looked back across the street, seeing the carriers negotiate the gap that they had created through the barrier and turn slowly to the right alongside him. He pushed himself upright, and clambered over the side of the first vehicle, glancing back at the armoured car which was attempting to turn round to face them further along the street. Several Russian soldiers were attempting to get past the vehicle as it turned in the road, their weapons raised.

As the engine revved, he saw in front of him both Nicu and Udet fire their rifles into the open doorway, a scream coming from within of injury and surprise. The Russian radio operator sent by the commander to see what was going on outside dying before he could determine what was happening.

As he sat upright in his seat, Meino dropped two Russian grenades over his shoulder and into Hausser's lap as the vehicle surged forward, swerving around Udet who was facing the doorway, his rifle held at eye level pointing inside. They jolted to a halt as Udet backed towards them, then scrambled over the side of the carrier.

Hausser pulled the pins on the grenades and tossed them inside the doorway, hearing them bounce and clatter inside and the frantic shouts of alarm from within. He glimpsed two other objects following his as Meino threw his remaining grenades through the wide doorway, then the vehicle surged forward, its tracks clattering on the now cobbled street.

Behind them, Tatu fired his submachine gun at the Russians near the armoured car, the soldiers ducking instinctively in response. The second carrier passed the doorway as the blast from the explosions inside threw debris and papers out of the entrance. Nicu was several metres ahead of the open door and the carrier slowed to allow him to clamber on board and into the front seat.

Bullets splattered on the walls and flew in the air around them as the vehicles picked up speed, with Albrecht and Tatu firing at the receding Russians over the back of the carrier. Tatu's stomach churned as he saw the Russian armoured car turn to face them, its turret rotating slowly, then suddenly it was out of sight. Both soldiers being thrown slightly to their side as the vehicle lurched abruptly to the left into a side street, accelerating down the narrow lane.

Smoke billowed from the buildings on either side in the narrow lane, obscuring their view and catching in the men's throats. The deafening clatter of the tracks on the cobbled stones echoing across the close walls on either side.

Several shells burst on the rooftops around them as the vehicles swiftly advanced along the cobblestones, the dust and debris falling onto the vehicles below. The soldiers lowered their heads and eyes as they progressed down the declining narrow lane that lead north, north towards the river.

Chapter Twenty One: Close Enough to Touch

The grinding screech that echoed across the walls down the narrow lane drew the attention of Albrecht and Tatu in the back of the second carrier. They stared back up the cobblestones, through the smoke and falling dust and their eyes widened. The Russian BA-10 armoured car had turned into the narrow street, momentarily skidding on the road and hitting the left wall, its metal hull grinding against the brick until coming to an abrupt halt, throwing its three occupants forward in their seats.

Albrecht squeezed the trigger on his Kar 98 as he saw a figure emerge into the lane, the fourth crew member ducking behind his armoured car as the bullet ricochet off the wall next to him. More Russian infantry appeared through the smoke and Tatu fired a burst of his PPSH, the enemy jumping to either side upon glimpsing the muzzle flashes coming from the back of the receding carriers as they bounced down the lane.

Tatu could hear the metallic clunks as his bullets bounced off the front of the armoured car, noticing the vehicle was attempting to reverse. The metal plate on the right side of the armoured car grinding against the wall, showering dust and brick fragments onto the front of the car as it moved slowly backwards.

There was a flash from the armoured car as the turret gun fired, the vehicle's movement preventing effective aim, but still causing the soldiers in the carriers to duck instinctively below their vehicle plate as the 45mm shell flew about a metre over their heads, hitting the buildings at the end of the lane. The armoured car ground against the brick trying to free itself, the engine screaming.

As the carriers bounced down the lane, the buildings burning on either side, Hausser could see light ahead, the lane ending in a small square some twenty metres away. 'Hase, turn left when we get to the square!' The young commander shouted, grasping his MP40.

Hausser saw the grim expression on Hase's face as he nodded slightly, his eyes fixed on the light ahead, the carrier now approaching maximum speed. They could hear Tatu firing behind them as they were suddenly bathed in light, the vehicle lurching sharp left into a compact square, its brakes locking and the vehicle skidding sideways as they realised there was no exit road.

The first carrier came to an abrupt halt, the second carrier skidded into the square behind it, nearly colliding with the first, but drawing alongside with a jolt. As the men jumped out of the carriers, Tatu leapt over the back of his vehicle and ran towards the corner, 'I will hold them off, get into the buildings.' He shouted over his shoulder.

Hausser surveyed the square, a small turning point for vehicles or somewhere to park and unload their cargo, the buildings surrounding them were warehouses and possible factories. Their larger doors and lower windows for loading stock and goods with permanent overhanging wooden pulleys at some of the openings. Some low loading carts lay scattered across the square with a couple of wooden trolleys for individual workers to utilise left discarded by the larger doorways.

To the south of the square was a larger open doorway and he made his way towards this, indicating to the other men to follow, the sound of a burst from Tatu's submachine gun echoing round the square as he fired round the corner to delay the oncoming Russians.

As he walked through the large doorway, a young Russian infantryman emerged from the darkness, approaching him from the back of the building, his rifle at waist height with look of confusion on his face, 'We heard shooting...what's going on, sergeant?'

Hausser wiped his eyes with the back of his hand, considering the situation, then regaining his composure, he looked the young Russian in the face, 'Fascist infantry are chasing us, they are dressed as Russians. Go, help hold them off whilst we get inside.'

The Russian nodded and ran past the other men, confused by their surprised looks as he sprinted towards Tatu's position at the edge of the square. Udet was the last to leave the vehicles, closing the corners of one of the blankets around the stack of German helmets. Noting the blood bathed side of the personnel carrier, he lifted his rifle onto his shoulder, grasped the last ammunition container and turned from the vehicles, lumbering the few metres to the open doorway.

Hausser turned, indicating for the other soldiers to come inside quickly and hearing Russian voices above them through the wooden floor, the scraping of an object across the wooden planks. His voice lowered to a whisper as they gathered around him, 'We have not much time now, so we need to keep moving.' He looked around the large storage room, seeing the staircase the young Russian must have descended. The area was filled with large crates and grain bags, some scattering their contents across the dusty thick wooden floor boards, then he glimpsed a closed double door opposite, facing south...possibly an exit onto the next street.

Machine gun fire echoed through the doorway from the square as Tatu fired another burst of his submachine gun down the lane. Hausser indicated to the barred door, his voice rising in desperation, 'Open it!'

Meino, Albrecht and Nicu immediately moved forward and started to push one of the doors, the light filtering in through the cracks as the door opened slightly outwards with a creek, its progress blocked by a body on the other side.

Tatu ran into the building, gasping, a look of desperation on his face, 'They are coming down the lane, there are too many of them to stop. Hausser...we need to be quick!'

The young commander looked past the Romanian quartermaster out across the square and into the light, seeing the young Russian soldier lying slumped by the corner of the lane, his blood splattered across the wall. The shouts of the advancing Russian infantry echoed through the square, the revving of the armoured car's engine now audible from the narrow street leading to the area.

Udet, Petru and Hase began to take positions next to the opening facing the square, their faces grim with expectation. Udet opened the ammunition container at his feet, retrieving two grenades from within and pulling the pins, tossing them across the square. The grenades bounced across the cobblestones, coming to rest next to the body of the young Russian infantryman.

Hausser could hear disturbances in the room above, the shouts of the Russians as they moved across the small workshop on the next floor. He looked into the eyes of Tatu next to him, the Romanian understanding his intent as he nodded, 'I will watch the stairs Hausser…find us a way out.' The older Romanian's face was stern, his adrenalin rising further.

The young commander turned and moved briskly to the double doors as explosions in the square behind him erupted. Placing his shoulder next to the narrow opening, he realised there was just enough space for a man to get through. Breathing heavily, he cautiously glanced out into the street beyond, looking to the left. The street was relatively wide but empty and stretched some two hundred metres to the left, bending gradually towards the river. Bullet pock marks covered the sides of the buildings, indicating the ferocity of the battle that had taken place as German and their allied troops had retreated northwards. Several bodies and discarded equipment lay in the street, signifying the battle that raged around them. The body of a horse lay some one hundred metres further from him in the middle of the thoroughfare, beyond which a fire was burning in a shop on the other side of the road, the dark smoke billowing across the tarmac. He could hear shellfire and sporadic firing some distance away, perhaps further round the corner at the end of the street, his excitement rising as he realised the sound was from a German made machine gun.

He glanced across, remaining in the narrow opening, seeing an entrance opposite leading into a small residential block some four or five stories high. A dead Russian soldier sat slumped in the doorway, his run across the street ending as the sniper's bullet entered the left side of his head through his helmet. The body sat legs apart in the doorway, the man's head drooped onto his chest, blood covering the tunic of his uniform and a dried pool around his legs on the entrance step.

Hausser hesitated, considering the situation fleetingly, then the gunfire behind him spurred his decision making as Hase and Udet opened fire on the corner, an indication the Russian infantry had now reached the end of the lane. He heard the revving of the engine as the armoured car approached the corner and realised that time was now running out.

He turned to Meino and Nicu, with Albrecht behind them, his face white with shock, 'Get across the road now...cover the rest of us.' Meino nodded once, slipping through the doorway and sprinting across the street before them, skidding into the entrance opposite. He dropped to a crouched position, his MP40 at the ready and glanced from side to side, indicating for the next man to follow with his right hand.

Nicu slipped through the opening and ran across, half crouched, his rifle in his left hand. As he reached the building opposite, he slipped inside, his intent to secure the other side of the apartment block.

The firing behind spurred them on with Albrecht slipping through the doorway and running after Nicu, his sprint to the other side broken as he leapt the last couple of metres, slipping past Meino and into the darkened building opposite.

Hausser turned, hearing the whoosh of shells overhead and explosions to the right, 'Come on, let's go.' He exclaimed, seeing Udet step into the light in the doorway, aim and fire out across the square.

Udet turned with Petru and advanced towards him, their weapons lowered. The young commander watched as Hase reloaded and fired out across the square to the corner. Moving towards him, he realised the soldier was trying to give them time to escape. As he approached, he lowered to a crouch and drew next to him.

Across the square, the Russians were gathering in the lane to rush forward, their shouts just audible above the approaching revving engine of the armoured car. As the front of the metal plate appeared beyond the corner, Hausser drew breath, realising time was becoming very short...perhaps too short.

Glancing round, Hase saw Udet slip through the opening in the double doors and disappear out into the light, the young German struggling with his cumbersome load. Petru hesitated, turning to beckon Tatu who was half way up the stairs, his PPSH submachine gun pointed at waist height.

Hase felt Hausser's hand on his shoulder, the grip tightening, the commander leaning forward, 'Time to go my friend...join the others. It's my job to get you all to safety.'

Hase turned, seeing the friendly smile form on the commander's lips though his heavy stubble, the sadness in his blue eyes. Nodding, he scrambled upwards from a lowered position and ran back through the storage area, the fear and apprehension rising within him.

Hausser raised his MP40 to eye height, glancing back briefly to see Hase reach the door opening as Petru disappeared outside. Tatu jumped from the wooden stairs, raising his left hand in salute to Hausser and turned, striding quickly to the double doors. Glancing outside, he indicated for Hase to go first, his eyes narrowing as the soldier shook his head. Frowning, the older Romanian slapped his shoulder and disappeared out into the light. Hase turned and slowly raised his rifle to cover the wooden staircase, his hands shaking.

The MP40 fired a burst as two eager Russians looked round the corner of the lane, the bullets hitting the wall before them throwing brick and cement fragments across the square entrance. Both Russians ducked back, the shouting in the lane becoming heightened in the preparations to attack, the infantry lacking coordination with no officer present.

Hausser rose from his crouched position, backing slowly from the open doorway, his submachine gun held high, pointing at the corner. The engine of the armoured car revved as it moved forward, the turret emerging into the light of the square, its commander's head visible in the open hatch above the vehicle, pointing frantically to spur the soldiers forward.

The flash from the armoured car's main gun was instant, the shell flying across the square and entering one of the upstairs windows. The explosion rocking the building, the dust cloud billowing down the stairs, filling the storage room. The screams and shouts from the room above indicated several men were wounded or dying from the blast.

Hausser turned to run as bullets from one of the car's machine guns poured into the room, the boxes and bags on the left side exploding as they were hit by the high velocity projectiles. Dust and grain flew through the air engulfing the young commander as he propelled himself across the room, his left arm raising to shield his eyes as he advanced, further dust cascading from the ceiling after the explosion above.

Behind him, Hausser could hear the shouts of the Russian infantry as they skirted the armoured car and advanced around the square, avoiding the line of fire from the vehicle on the corner of the lane.

As he reached Hase, the soldier fired his rifle at a Russian soldier descending the stairway, the soldier's face covered in blood, his ear drums punctured from the explosion. The man fell backwards, slumping against the stairs.

Hausser grabbed Hase's shoulder, pushing him out backwards through the open door, the soldier falling into the street. Bullets whipped around the doorway to the commander's left as he pushed himself through the opening, his shoulder scraping the wooden door as he fell forwards onto the tarmac. There was an explosion in the square behind him as one of the wounded soldiers upstairs tossed a grenade through the window causing the pursuing infantry to hesitate.

Forcing himself upwards, Hausser pushed Hase forward, the soldier half falling again as they scrambled across the road. He could see Meino beckoning them urgently at the doorway opposite as he heard ominous clattering on the road to his right. He roughly grabbed the back of Hase's tunic to steady him and glancing in the direction of the noise, his eyes widened upon seeing the Russian Su-5 Self Propelled Gun approaching them across the tarmac, the exhaust plumes from its large engines rising into the air.

Pushing his comrade before him, the commander lunged forward with a gasp, his tired muscles seeming to scream with the exertion. He tripped on the kerb as the vehicle passing behind them with a roar, feeling Meino's hands roughly grasp him and drag him forward into the building before them, the door being roughly closed behind.

The building shook as shells hit the rooftops, dust falling down onto the men in the dark narrow hallway. Nearby machine gun fire and rifle shots echoed through the building from the open door at the far end of the apartment block. Nicu was further through the building cautiously looking out into the next street through the open doorway with the other soldiers leaning on the walls of the corridor or crouching next to the stairs of the block of flats.

Tatu stooped in front of Hausser, inspecting him for injury, a grim smile forming on his face, 'You didn't tell me we had to dress for dinner…are we going to a party?' He grinned as he viewed the heavily dust clad commander, his face covered in a thick layer of dirt and specks of grain.

Hausser gasped for air, his chest heaving, 'Keep going, we need to keep going!' He pushed himself from the wall and stumbled forwards, brushing Tatu's shoulder, the other soldiers following him towards Nicu. Only Meino remained behind, covering the door they had come through, listening to muffled shots from the buildings opposite as the Russian infantry fought each other in the workshops. His grin widening as he realised the pursuing enemy had mistaken the men on the first floor of the previous building for them.

As Hausser reached the next doorway, Nicu turned, his eyes excited, 'We are nearly there. Just a few hundred metres more, Herr Leutnant.' He proclaimed, pointing out across the cobbled road before them.

Hausser was breathing heavily as he glanced out into the light, standing back from sight. Opposite them, some fifteen metres away were a row of single storey warehouses, stretching to either side, their roofs burning out of control, the smoke forming several wide black dense plumes as they rose into the air.

He realised at ground level it was quite gloomy, as if dusk, the light restricted by the thick smoke. To the left, some two hundred metres from their position rose the high storage buildings and warehouses used for goods sent by boat or barge up and down the river. The nearest heavy dark stone six storey structure pitted with bullet and shell holes, the top floor ablaze, the thick acrid smoke rising in one large plume into the air. In the cobbled street before them lay many bodies, of civilians, Russian and some Romanian soldiers, interspersed with discarded weapons and equipment.

Some twenty metres in the middle of the road to their left sat a smouldering armoured car, the Russian BA-10's engine having been hit by a small anti-tank weapon and knocked out. Around it lay the four crew, killed in their attempt to escape by machine gun fire.

He looked up, the light brighter between the thick smoke plumes. As he squinted, he could just see movement in the high buildings, the soldiers aiming out, out beyond them. He watched as the flashes of a machine gun fired from one of the holes torn in the building side on the fourth floor. The machine gun firing past their position at something further to their right, the hot molten metal zipping through the air above them.

Excitement rose within him as the slightly delayed sound reached his ears, his recognition of the distinctive noise, a German machine gun firing.

Chapter Twenty Two: Gauntlet

Meino grasped Hausser's sleeve, his grip tight, voice trembling with excitement, 'The Russians are outside in the street, Hausser. It's only a matter of time now...we need to go!'

The Croatian turned and raised his weapon along the hallway, cautiously stepping back towards the closed entrance door at the back of the building, his eyes fixed on the door handle and latch he had locked previously. Udet and Tatu also turned, using the protruding staircase as cover, they raised their weapons. Tatu ascended several of the steps, the wood creaking beneath his weight, leaning over the broken bannister, his submachine gun barrel resting on the balustrade.

Hausser looked back out into the gloom, considering their options. The road was a perfect killing zone with the destroyed armoured car as the only cover, yet the distance to the burning warehouses was short. If they could get across the road, then they may reach safety within the burning buildings.

He moved around inside the doorway, from right to left, keeping a metre from the entrance to avoid being spotted. Glancing all around, he sighed, realising the Russians were positioned some distance to their right, the possibility of being fired on by both sides high if they ran out suddenly.

Hausser looked back at the men in the hallway, his face grim, 'We will have to go across...but we have no cover on the other side unless we can get into one of the warehouses. The Germans have a line of fire at us from the left and the Russians from the right...so we need ideas.'

The commander's eyes met with Hase's, realising the man had not understood what he had said. The soldier looking concerned, with dark lines under his eyes, then the contact was broken as Hase looked back out into the street.

Hase had realised the predicament they were in before the commander had spoken, knowing time was short as he recognised the distant voices in the street behind them, the Russian soldiers searching for them. He had felt utterly exhausted in the hallway and had slowly lowered himself to the floor at the foot of the staircase when they had entered. As he looked out into the gloom of the street before them, he could just see beyond the armoured car's rear wheels, the angle of his vision different from Hausser's. Glimpsing something through the smoke filled air, he leant forward, squinting to make out what it was that had aroused his curiosity.

A voice in Russian from the street behind them startled him, the noise from just the other side of the closed door. He turned, seeing Udet tense next to him, the young German swallowing hard. The soldiers in the narrow hallway instinctively holding their breaths.

Hase slowly slid his back up the wall, feeling the muscles in his tired legs complain at the strain. His heart beginning to beat faster in his chest, his mouth becoming dry, the adrenalin rising within him once more.

As Hase stepped forward Hausser turned to look at him, his eyebrows raised in anticipation. He leant forward towards the young commander and whispered, 'Get the men to put their scarves over their mouths and follow me when I wave back.'

Hausser stared at him, his eyes momentarily uncertain, then he smiled and nodded slowly, placing his hand on the soldier's arm, 'Don't leave us too long young Hase…we need you.' Patting his shoulder further, he slowly broke eye contact and turned to face the other men.

Hase turned, his stomach twisting in excitement and fear. Lifting his scarf from around his neck, he tightened it across his mouth. A cool breeze drifted in through the doorway, the tentacles of cold air seeming to grasp him and entice him out into the street.

He stepped gingerly forward to the left of the door, clearing his throat. Raising his voice, he shouted, 'Russians coming out, don't shoot comrades!'

Behind him in the hallway, Hausser forced a wry grin, hearing the emphasis Hase placed on his Ukrainian accent.

There was a brief pause, the silence only broken by Tatu shuffling his boots on the wooden staircase, his calf muscles aching from the position he had adopted.

Hase took a deep breath and shouted again, 'Russians coming across the street, don't shoot comrades!'

He squinted further, straining his ears to hear any response. Then he heard distant voices to his right, some shouting of commands, then 'Proceed comrade...don't shoot men, Russian infantry ahead!'

Hase pushed himself forward, his heart beating loudly in his chest and his mouth dry, he ran half crouched into the light. His legs feeling heavy as his boots crunched glass on the cobblestones, he darted to the left, jumping over an abandoned ammunition box.

Hausser had grimaced as he turned his face, seeing the young soldier run out through the doorway, his ears listened for the sound of gunfire. Behind him the door handle moved on the thick door leading into the hallway. Meino clenched his teeth, his palms becoming moist with sweat.

Hase slipped on landing on the cobblestones and slid on the glass fragments, his body coming to rest half under the smouldering armoured car, his rifle clattering onto the street beside him. The metallic tinkering of machine gun fire on the front left side of the armoured car indicated the gunner in the tall storage buildings had seen a Russian soldier run out, but his line of sight was obstructed by the smoke and angle of the warehouse roofs.

Hase gasped as he realised he was now safe from the German guns, turning himself slowly and cautiously, moaning at the scuffed pain in his legs and knees from falling on the cobblestones. Lying on his front beneath the armoured car, he slowly and pensively crawled forward to the rear right wheel of the vehicle. Behind him he could hear the Russian soldiers further down the street return fire against the machine gunner in the storage building, forcing him to duck away from his position.

In the building behind him, Hausser slowly raised his weapon towards the doorway further down the hall, the handle twitching as the Russian soldier on the other side attempted to open the door. Turning, the soldier shouted across the street, indicating for the men opposite to come towards him, his shout cut short as Meino fired a burst of his submachine gun through the door, hitting the Russian soldier several times as he fell backwards into the road.

Hase stretched forward beyond the rear wheel of the armoured car, his hands reaching over the cold cobblestones and grasping the sides of a manhole cover. The oily dirt was caked round the thick steel cover and it slipped under his nails as he attempted to gain leverage on the heavy disc. Retrieving his bayonet from his belt, he furiously began to scrape the dirt from the gap between the cobblestoned road and the thick steel cover, spurred on by the burst of gunfire behind him.

Placing the bayonet on the road, his fingers moved into the gap he had created, grasping the sides of the steel cover once more. He exerted pressure, his arms tensing as he tried to lift the heavy lid...but it wouldn't move...seeming to be stuck fast.

He sighed, frustration rising within him, retrieving the bayonet again, his fingers bleeding from scraping against the rough steel. Jabbing the long knife back into the narrow gap he had created, he began scraping feverishly again, trying to clear enough space to form a more suitable grip, the sweat beginning to run down his face as he felt the panic begin to rise within him.

An explosion in the street the other side of the door caused Meino to fire another burst of his submachine gun. Russian voices echoed in the hallway as the soldiers began to gather in the street outside, their caution at approaching the door evident, delaying their attack.

A frustrated groan rose from within his chest as Hase struggled with the steel disc, his fingers being cut on the rough steel as he desperately tried to gain a grip on the cover. He heard the clanking as another burst of machine gun fire hit the armoured car's metal plate, the bullets ricocheting off to the left and front of the disabled vehicle.

Explosions and crumps from the warehouse opposite forced him to duck his head, dropping his bayonet, his hands rising up over his helmet. Dirt and roof fragments showered down onto his body and the cobblestones around him, with dust and smoke billowing out from the burning building and enveloping him. He slowly lifted his head, spitting dust from his mouth as he opened his eyes. Nicu slid across the cobblestones next to him, his boots narrowly missing the Russian's outstretched right hand. Looking up, the young Romanian winked down at him, and thrust his bayonet into the gap between the cobblestones and the steel manhole cover.

Invigorated, he grabbed his own discarded bayonet from next to him and jabbed it into the gap opposite Nicu's weapon. Hearing another burst of machine gun fire from the building behind them, their eyes met. With a nod, they both simultaneously pushed down hard, hearing a scrapes as the bayonets forced their way between the cover and its housing, the heavy metal disc jolting upwards.

Smiles widened across the two men's faces as they pushed the thick metal cover off to the side making a heavy scraping noise as the encrusted metal grated across the cobblestones. The smiles dropped from their faces as the fragrance of stagnant water and excrement rose from the dark opening. Nicu leant down, his hands placed either side of the opening, his head slipping into the hole, stretching down into the shaft beyond. He checked from side to side and retracted his head again, smiling briefly at Hase to indicate the tunnel below was clear.

Nicu twisted his legs round and sat on the edge of the manhole as a shell burst further down the street behind them. Ducking slightly as they were showered in dirt, he turned to look towards the doorway, shouting, 'Hausser!' Picking up his rifle from the road, he dropped into the opening below, his hands grasping the top rung of a metal ladder leading seven metres down into the dark sewer.

Hausser twisted his head, looking out of the doorway, his face grim. Turning back, he glanced at Udet excitedly, 'Go!'

Udet slapped Petru's shoulder and both men darted through the open doorway, Udet struggling with the bulky blanket as Hausser grimaced incredulously. Meino fired another burst into the entrance doorway and backed towards Hausser. As he passed the bottom of the staircase, the commander's hand dropped onto his shoulder, 'Get out there...we will hold here.' Hausser whispered over his shoulder, the Croatian nodded and turned quickly to run past the officer into the dim light.

An explosion upstairs brought dust and plaster falling from the ceiling, a dust cloud drifting down the stairs, enveloping Tatu. Bullets splattered across the right wall, the plaster showering Hausser as the Russian soldiers outside fired through the closed door at an angle.

Tatu turned and looked at the commander from his position on the staircase, his vision obscured by the dust cloud, his voice strained, 'Time to go, Hausser! I will cover you two.'

Hausser nodded, 'You follow quickly, don't wait around here.' He turned to face the young soldier knelt by the wall, his rifle pointing at the door, 'Come on Albrecht...let's go.' The young commander turned briskly and ran out into the light, glimpsing Udet drop the bulging blanket down through the manhole before scrambling after it.

A loud crunch resounded round the hallway, then another, the rifle butts smashing on the other side of the door one after the other. Albrecht fired, the rifle kicking upwards in his inexperienced hands, the bullet piercing the door and hitting one of the Russian soldiers in the shoulder, knocking him backwards.

The door splintered as the crashing continued. Tatu rose from his position on the stairs and descended a step, jumping the last two to the floor in the hallway, his large thick jacket rising behind him as he leapt. Albrecht pulled the bolt back on his rifle, his hands shaking as Tatu turned and fired a burst of his PPSH submachine gun down the hallway, the bullets splattering into the frame and thick wooden door.

Grabbing Albrecht's shoulder, he propelled the young German forward through the back entrance as he heard the door buckle behind them, the wood cracking in the frame. Firing another burst with his left hand as he pushed Albrecht forward with his right, they emerged into the dim light.

Bullets spattered across the front of the armoured car as the two men lunged towards it, the Russians further down the street returning fire at the position high in the building. As Tatu and Albrecht reached the right corner of the armoured car, Tatu looked down, seeing the dark opening below them on the cobblestones. He spun round, raising his weapon, firing a burst at the doorway, his weapon clicking as the magazine emptied. A Russian infantryman at the opening ducking back inside the hallway, the bullets hitting the frame next to him.

Tatu reached for another magazine, seeing Albrecht raise his rifle to cover the doorway, the young German shouting desperately at him, 'Get into the sewers, I will cover!'

Tatu swiftly knelt and turned his body, inhibited by his large jacket, his right boot placed on the top rung of the ladder leading down from the manhole and into the shaft to the sewer. He looked up as he descended the steel ladder, 'Come straight after me.' A look of desperation forming on his face.

Albrecht fired across into the hallway, the rifle kicking upwards again in his hands. Pulling the bolt, he grinned, his eyes sparkling, the thought of him holding back the Russian infantry heightening his adrenalin. As he pushed the bolt forward, a Russian leant out quickly from the doorway, his rifle raised, the bullet whipping past Albrecht's ear. The Russian then ducked back in.

Startled by the shot, Albrecht fired again, dropping to his knees and swinging his legs over and into the manhole. The smile dropping from his face as a grenade bounced across the road some feet from him, his eyes widening as he frantically pushed himself down the ladder rungs.

Catching his helmet on the rim of the manhole, his head knocked backwards as he hastily descended the steps, lowering himself into the manhole shaft. His breath was caught in his chest and his heart beat loud as the explosion above threw dust and debris down the hole, the metallic pings from the impacts loud on his helmet.

A panic fuelled smile began to form on his face once again as he quickly descended, the adrenalin rush running through his head and body once more. He shouted as his boots clunked on the metal ladder, 'Get going, they are through the door.'

As he got nearly to the foot of the ladder, he felt the relief begin to run through his body, the urgency and excitement still in his actions. He looked up at the circular light above as he reached the foot of the ladder, his boots splashing into the flowing water in the bottom of the sewer pipe.

His eyes suddenly widened in terror as the small black oval shape disrupted the circular light, the dark object dropping over the side of the manhole and falling towards him. His mouth opened as adrenalin intoxicatingly shot through his body, his voice hoarse, 'Run!'

Chapter Twenty Three: Through the Darkness

Tatu was about ten metres further down the dark narrow tunnel when he heard the squealed shout from behind him, 'Run!' Spinning round, he saw the grenade drop from the light, instinctively throwing himself forwards, his weapon discarded beside him, hands reaching behind his head to protect his neck.

Further along in the dark sewer, the other soldiers turned, seeing the flash as the grenade landed on the ground at Albrecht's feet. The explosion propelled the young German into the metal ladder, his nose shattering as it struck one of the rungs, the broken bone propelled upwards into his brain, killing him instantly. Metal fragments from the grenade pierced the back of his legs and lower back tearing through his internal organs as his lifeless body slowly slid down the ladder and came to rest in a heap, slumped at its base.

Petru screamed, propelling himself back towards Tatu, the stale and polluted water splashing around his boots. Russian voices echoed around the tunnel from the opening as Udet raised his rifle towards the light cascading into the tunnel.

As Petru reached the fallen Tatu, he roughly grabbed his countryman's thick jacket and pulled him upwards, half dragging him down the tunnel. Tatu groaned loudly, reaching out and grasping the barrel of his weapon as his boots dragged through the putrid water.

Two more grenades fell through the opening, one clunking against one of the steps on the ladder and falling forward of the other. The concurrent explosions sending a wall of sound echoing down the tunnel, the blast wave following, constrained and concentrated by the wet tunnel walls.

Petru twisted as he dropped Tatu into the slurry, throwing himself forward as he heard the blast, putrid water thrown up from the explosion falling over them. The soldiers further along the tunnel turning to protect their faces, the shrapnel hitting the tunnel walls either side of the explosion.

Tatu immediately raised his head from beneath the water spluttering and spitting the foul liquid from his nose and mouth. He gasped for air, winded by the blast, determination pushing his body upwards and dragging his weapon along with him.

Before him, Petru had risen to his hands and knees, his mind stunned and disorientated by the blasts. Tatu grabbed his friend's collar roughly, pulling his countryman with him as he trudged along the dark tunnel, pushing his boots through the putrid water. The relatively narrow sewer walls were circular on either side, brick smeared with dried excrement and frost, the central channel on the slime covered floor filled with putrid and darkened slurry.

Before them, Udet had turned back and was aiming his weapon at the exit from the manhole shaft opening some twenty two metres away, a shaft of dim light illuminating the ladder from above. A Russian infantryman twisted his body in the upper shaft, ducking his head into the tunnel from the covered ladder and keen to see into the sewer, encouraged by the sight of a dead soldier slumped at the foot of the ladder.

Udet raised his weapon slightly to his right eye and fired, the rifle kicking back into his shoulder. The shot echoing round the wet tunnel walls, a slight metal clunk as the bullet hit and forced its way through the Russian's helmet. The Russian infantryman's head fell limp, a lifeless arm dropping through the manhole shaft opening, his legs caught on the upper rungs of the ladder.

Hausser moved back down the tunnel, forcing his boots through the water, roughly grasping Petru's left arm and lifting him upwards. The three soldiers struggled forwards as Petru tried to gain his footing, the brick tunnel's floor covered in murky slime under the water. The commander adjusted his stance as Meino pushed past him in the enclosed width of the tunnel, his MP40 raised and pointing at the opening further down the sewer.

Nicu and Hase were further along the darkened tunnel, their bodies silhouetted in a shaft of light cascading across the slimed brick from a narrower right side drainage pipe. As the three soldiers approached, they could see the stress on the two men's faces, their eyes wide and saddened at the spectacle of the broken body at the foot of the metal ladder.

Meino fired a burst from his MP40 as he saw shadows pass across the light coming from the manhole shaft into the sewer, then the dead Russian infantryman's upper body slowly disappeared upwards as his countrymen dragged him from the opening.

The Croatian turned his head slightly, the smell in the tunnel pungent, 'We have not got long Hausser, I think the Russians are getting ready to attack again.' Then his eyes moved back to the top of his weapon as he looked down the length of the barrel of the MP40 towards the shaft opening.

Hausser leant forward slightly, peering to the right into the shaft of light, his right arm still supporting Petru. The smaller tunnel extended for approximately thirty metres at a slight incline, with a grille covering the end. The water running between his boots converged at the junction of the tunnels and then flowed down the incline to the end. The side tunnel was empty and the commander now realised they were only a short distance from the banks of the Volga.

Stepping forward, Hausser and Tatu trudged on, still holding most of Petru's weight as he struggled to regain his coordination, the blasts having caused some concussion. The water was now flowing against them, forcing them to drag their boots through the slime lining the slippery brick floor to the tunnel. Nicu and Hase advanced before them, their rifles at waist height, seeing a similar shaft of light from the right some two hundred metres ahead along the gloom of the tunnel.

Behind them, Meino and Udet backed along the tunnel, their weapons raised and ready to protect the others. Udet had attached the wrapped blanket through his belt and the contents, the metal helmets, occasionally clunked against his leg and the wall of the tunnel as he stepped backwards.

Two more explosions occurred on the floor of the tunnel near the open manhole cover, with Albrecht's broken body smashed by each blast wave and fragmentation. The noise wave echoed towards the group, bouncing off the walls of the tunnel and dislodging dirt, crusted excrement and dust from the brickwork.

The forward group slowly and gingerly approached the shaft of light in front of them, noting the tunnel beyond continued to a bend about forty metres beyond the dim daylight. The putrid water at the junctions of two tunnels was swirling as they got nearer, the flow interrupted from the right.

Hase leant forward, glancing round the brickwork into the light in the narrow side tunnel. Noticing a dead body slumped against the tunnel wall, he looked beyond the gruesome sight and saw the light at the end was uninterrupted, the grille having fallen off. Bricks and debris lay high at the end, preventing the water from escaping and forcing it back along the tunnel. As he slowly glanced around, he read the scrawled sign painted on the wall opposite in Russian lettering. Turning his head, he coughed with the stench as he opened his mouth, then spoke, 'Hausser, this tunnel leads to the tall buildings, we are nearly there.'

They slowly gathered in the smaller side tunnel, with Udet and Meino covering the main tunnel. The distant sounds of occasional rifle fire and machine gun bursts echoing around them from the broken opening at the end.

Hausser walked slowly down the tunnel towards the light and turned to face the soldiers, a faint smile forming on his lips as he looked across them, 'God in heaven, you men look terrible.' He proclaimed.

The unshaven, dirty faced and soaked uniformed soldiers fleetingly grinned back in response, their eyes dark with exhaustion. Petru smiled briefly in response to the grins, his tired body leant against the tunnel wall next to the scrawled sign, his head aching and ears ringing from the explosions.

Hausser placed his hands on his hips, his face becoming stern, 'Let's remove the Russkie uniforms, or what's left of them, we are very close to our men now.' He slowly began unbuttoning the grey padded tunic, the men observing the white outline of the cross outside his field grey uniform beneath. Noticing their stares, his hand instinctively reached up and lifted the metal decoration to his throat, dropping it back under his uniform for it to rest on top of the felt Russian underwear.

They slowly and wearily removed the dirty grey Russian uniforms with Hausser and Nicu relieving Meino and Udet for them to complete the task. Looking back down the tunnel, the commander observed that the Russians had not attempted to follow them. The fire from the tower and tunnel having deterred them and upon receiving differing orders, they had retreated.

Udet smiled triumphantly to himself as he removed the blanket from his belt, unwrapping it and handing the men their original helmets. The soldiers nodded in appreciation as they accepted their national metal headwear, placing them carefully on their heads as a final addition to their uniforms.

As they fastened the helmet buckles under their chins, Hausser turned from the wide tunnel, checking each man's appearance briefly. Trudging through the water between the men, he avoided looking at the dead body as he stepped over the outstretched legs. The Russian corpse's head bent into his chest, dried encrusted blood covering his chin.

The men watched as the young commander's silhouette receded towards the light, his MP40 held loosely in his right hand. As he approached the end of the smaller tunnel, he cautiously lowered himself to a crouch, arriving near the end and stopping just short of the debris and incoming light. The broken brick and rubble a result of a shell hit several days before.

Hausser listened intently, feeling the cold, fresh air on his face and hearing the running water in the tunnel and the rippling near the debris. An explosion flashed in the distance as he looked out from the narrow tunnel, his eyes squinting in the light.

The commander was able to see through a gap that continued for a short distance after the debris, the obstruction caused by a section of the roof of the tunnel collapsing. In the distance, through the remains of the tunnel, past the lying snow, he could see an expanse of water…his heart beating faster as he realised before him was the river Volga.

Then he froze, hearing another sound. He strained his ears again, hearing more…a smile gradually forming on his lips. He cleared his throat quietly, and shouted out, 'Nicht Schiessen, Deutsche Soldaten.' Placing emphasis on his Berlin accent.

There was a pause, the faint sound of the water lapping around the debris the only noise. Then a voice echoed through the tunnel as he received a reply, 'Kommen Freund!'

Hausser moved slowly forward and looked up to his right, seeing a smiling soldier cautiously lower the rifle now pointed at his face. Excitement rose within him as he grasped the outstretched hand that was then extended towards him, the hoarse cheer behind him in the tunnel forcing a broad grin onto his face.

Chapter Twenty Four: The Italian Connection

He could vaguely hear the rumble in the distance, his mind wandering in its slumber…then he heard it again, distant yet meaningful. The whoosh was instant, the explosion higher on the outside of the building causing the ceiling plaster to crack, the dust drifting down onto the sleeping soldiers below.

Hausser's eyes flickered, then opened, seeing the cracks in the scuffed ceiling above. His eyes followed one of the dark lines as it weaved across the stained and dirty plaster above him. In places, the plaster had fallen away completely revealing the thin strips of wood nailed to the beams above, the technique a fast and easy way of preparing the surface to hold the plaster mix.

His limbs ached from the previous few days and he felt the tiredness in his arms and legs through the dull pain. As his mind drifted, he became aware of the dull throbbing in his head, the symptoms of sleep deprivation and the continual exposure to noise.

Slowly the distant sound of gunfire filtered through his ears, the battle raging further round the Volga bend to the north…yet it was quieter here, almost dreamlike after what they had experienced. As his mind adjusted, the colours becoming more vivid, he realised it was still light, the small high broken window in the room providing the dim illumination of dusk.

Alertness filtered into his head through his drowsiness, his mind trying to resist, to block out the oncoming reality. It was a futile effort, the immediate noises of the sleeping men around him beginning to become apparent, to filter through his dwindling resistance.

He considered he had probably slept for two or three hours as it was still light. The men, exhausted from their ordeal, had succumbed to the desire to sleep after eating. The rations they had been provided with as a welcome to the building having been consumed ravenously by all.

Next to him, Petru stirred, then lapsed back into a deep sleep, his snoring light as he turned and lay on his back. On the other side of Petru, Tatu was deep asleep, his thick long jacket wrapped as a pillow under his head.

Hausser slowly rose to a seated position, his elbows on his knees. The drowsiness he felt was almost overpowering, but his senses were now alert. Looking round the small storeroom high in the building, he observed Hase lying with his back to the outside wall, his eyes clamped shut. Udet was asleep on his back, his legs bent due to his close proximity to the wall and being near Hase's head.

Next to Hase lay Meino, his eyes flickering in dream, the Croatian deep asleep, another soldier sleeping lengthways along their heads, Nicu. The young Romanian's deep breathing indicating an exhausted slumber and beyond him their weapons leant against the office wall. Across the floor lay the discarded office materials, paper, pencils and order sheets, left by the clerks as the original occupants fled the building during the German advance on the city some three to four months earlier.

As Hausser sat there scratching his head, he felt the 'swimmy' mental feeling of exhaustion, his mind confused as the final stages of his alertness returned. He stretched forward, the dull ache in his back momentarily dispersing as his muscles extended and contracted. Placing his right hand on the floor, he gingerly rose to his feet, the aches in his limbs slowing his actions. Leaning down, he retrieved his helmet and carefully stepped over Tatu's outstretched legs. Placing the helmet on his head, he collected his MP40, raising the strap over his right shoulder and carefully opened the door to the small room, quietly closing it behind him as he exited.

The large 'L' shaped fifth floor room he now stood in housed the wounded, many lying sleeping or subdued in the failing light. The several broken windows and holed wall at the far end providing enough light to see the extent of the old storage space. The room stretched past the small side office space he had been sleeping in, the floor covered in the wounded soldiers as they lay against the walls and across the thick wooden floorboards. Glowing oil lanterns were placed sporadically across the room adding to the light.

Several men were bandaged heavily, their pitiful moans and coughing the only sound. Water bottles lay next to each casualty and he briefly acknowledged the soldier at the far end of the long space tending to an injured man's bandages.

He stepped carefully across one of the sleeping wounded men, towards his objective, the door at the far corner of the room which lead to the stairs. As he reached the doorway, an infantryman appeared before him, the man slightly out of breath having just ascended the steps.

The man had no helmet, and a matted mess of black hair, his eyes glancing round the room, then focussing on the young German officer, 'Ah…Herr Leutnant, I have come to get you…the commander will see you now.' He retorted, a cheeky grin on his face.

Hausser looked him up and down, considering the man's uniform strange for the location, he observed it was dirty and of poor quality. The man's skin was slightly tanned, with a clear complexion, 'What unit are you from soldier?'

'248th Autieri Group, Herr Leutnant. We are transport drivers and were delivering supplies to the southern suburbs when the Russkies attacked. We are cut off now, I think.' The man replied, his dark brown eyes staring at the German defiantly, his face unshaven.

'You are Italian?' Hausser asked surprised, now hearing the accent to the man's German.

The soldier seemed frustrated, his eyes saddened, 'Yes, Herr Leutnant. There are only five of us here…well four now. We run messages and cook. It seems the commander does not think we are good enough to fight here, even though we are good enough to die on the cold steppe against the communists.'

The commander smiled at the soldier's frustration, thinking of the meal they had eaten earlier, 'Well if you fight like you cook, you may be better than he thinks…that was a splendid meal earlier. What do you call it?'

The man's eyes softened, a slight grin crossing his face, 'That was our A.M.R.P. Ration food, Spaghetti con Carne with Biscotti. I am glad you enjoyed it, we had a lorry load when we arrived, but you greedy Germans and Romanians eat too much! There is not too much left now, soon you will have to resort to the pigswill your own armies provide!' His grin broke into a wide smile, his eyes flashing.

Hausser chuckled, 'Still Italian humour comes through, eh? What's your name?'

The man stood to attention, his smile remaining, 'Corporal Barsetti, Herr Leutnant. But you can call me Luca if you wish, sir.'

The young commander nodded, 'Good Luca, let us go and see this commander then. I will try and persuade him to give you a rifle to fire if you wish.'

The darker Italian's eyes brightened, 'I wish so, Herr Leutnant. I was quite a shot back in Italy...I was only moved to transport for arguing with my commander, the pig!'

Hausser grinned, 'Well you have spirit, let's hope it sees you into old age. Now let's see this commander of yours, apparently he was too busy when we arrived.'

The Italian turned in the doorway, 'Follow me, Herr Leutnant. I will show you something on the way to our beloved commander.' The sarcasm clear in his voice, he started to descend the stairs outside the doorway, grasping the metal bannister as he progressed.

Leutnant Hausser slowly followed Luca down the stairs, his body aching. Reaching the floor below, he watched as the Italian ducked below a hole at chest height in the building's exterior wall and walked, half crouched into a small room to his right before the stairs continued downwards. To the left lay the door leading into the fourth floor storage area, the floor below where he had been sleeping, the room of similar dimensions to the one above. Glancing left, Hausser saw several Romanian and two German soldiers cleaning and preparing their weapons. At the end of the room he observed the machine gun position that had fired from the building earlier, the German gunner lifting sandbags to strengthen his cover.

Hausser turned back and replicated the young Italian's actions, cautiously entering the small darkened room to the side of the stairs, considering there must be similar rooms on each floor, probably the former offices for political officers or managers.

The room had sustained severe damage, the result of a shell hit. The far inside corner was covered in a dirty and smeared tarpaulin, which slowly moved in the breeze, an indication of a hole in the structure behind it. In the right corner sat an oil lamp, its dim glow partly illuminating the area. In the centre of the room, a shattered desk, broken in two down the middle with a smashed chair on its left. The walls were dark where flames had scorched the plaster as a result of the explosion with burnt and discarded papers lying around the floor. To the right and left of the tarpaulin were some empty ration boxes, stacked to provide seating next to the makeshift curtain. The young Italian made his way carefully across the obstacles and sat to the right of the curtain, indicating with his hand for Hausser to join him, on the opposite side of the tarpaulin.

As the commander slowly lowered his tired body onto the ration boxes indicated to him, Luca leant over and extinguished the oil lamp, reducing the light in the room to near darkness. Hausser stiffened, uncomfortable with the situation, straining his eyes to accustom them to the gloom.

Luca leant further forward, his voice reduced to a whisper, 'Keep your head down, Herr Leutnant. We are not too sure who is watching us up here. Please do not look out for too long in case a sniper is within range.' His hand reached behind him, retrieving a small pair of field binoculars, offering them to the German commander.

Hausser took the field glasses from him and nodded slowly, becoming accustomed to the poor light, his intrigue growing.

Luca smiled briefly, aware the commander was becoming curious. He leant towards the commander and slowly reached up, grasping the edge of the tarpaulin next to Hausser, 'Are you ready?'

The young commander smiled, enjoying the intrigue the young soldier was creating, 'I think so.'

'Good.' Luca relied, pulling the tarpaulin back towards him quickly, 'Welcome to the Volga bend!'

The dim light of dusk made him blink as it hit his pupils, the light brighter than his eyes had become briefly accustomed to. Snowflakes flurried into the room, a cold breeze reacting to the cover being removed and drifting across his face. The vacuum and slight change in temperature pulling the flakes through the large shell hole in the wall, the breeze now free to carry them through.

As Hausser opened his eyes again, he looked out of the opening high in the storage building. Outside the snow was slowly beginning to fall, the flakes gradually descending to earth as far as he could see.

As his eyes became accustomed to the change in failing light, high clarity returned to his vision as his adrenalin began to rise, the panoramic sights before him causing the hairs on the back of his neck to twitch.

The sky was grey with heavy snow clouds, the sporadic flurries of flakes in the air an omen of the forthcoming weather conditions for the night. Below the window lay the wide expanse of the Volga River, its banks some twenty metres from the back of the building. The large bend in the river lay before them, slightly to the left, the river turning sharply as it negotiated the terrain. Two wooden jetties stretched out into the water, the wooden and metal supports frozen into the ice that embraced both river banks. In the centre of the river, some fifty to seventy five metres wide in places, flowed the icy cold water of the Volga, the surface carrying scattered debris and bodies southwards.

Hausser's eyes followed the river as it stretched out northwards, the city of Stalingrad to the left as far as the eye could see, the horizon glowing red. Smoke plumes and tracer fire rose into the dusk sky all across the city, the landscape lit up by the many fires burning out of control. As he watched, explosions erupted in a variety of places across the torn city as shells dropped to their targets. The Russian field guns firing from across the river on the east side into German held positions.

The sounds of distant war filtered into the room, echoing off the walls. The cracks of single shots blurred with machine gun fire and the crumps of explosions from shells and hand grenades. Mesmerised, almost entranced by the scenes and sounds of utter destruction before him, he slowly raised the field glasses to his eyes.

Adjusting the zoom on the binoculars lenses, he narrowed his eyes to look through the glasses, focussing on the right bank initially. He could just make out some men loading a small barge on the river's edge, the figures walking gingerly across the ice. Further to the right, the distant flashes of the field guns firing distracted him momentarily, but any sight of their position was disrupted by trees and damaged buildings near the riverbank.

As he moved his vision to the left, he saw the surface of the river with floating items and bodies littering the dark water, propelled by the strong current. His curiosity was aroused as he glimpsed an item bobbing in the water, the small object seeming to be swimming against the current from the west bank to the east. Straining to recognise the object in the river, he hesitated, then realised what the item was. A dog was swimming in the freezing water, the small terrified animal attempting to escape the battle torn city.

He exhaled slowly, considering that only men now would remain in the devastated city, the animals attempting to flee a war that had become the epitome of hatred, a man made hell on earth. Lowering the glasses from his face, he rubbed his tired eyes, then raised the binoculars again, his fascination overcoming the momentary exhaustion.

Far in the distance on the left bank, he could see small figures offloading another barge, the exposed walk from the water's edge to the riverbank across the ice adding pace to the men as they carried supplies and weapons. Above them on the higher bank stood some bedraggled civilians and wounded soldiers, awaiting their turn on the barge before it returned across the river.

He scanned the burning city to his left, seeing the flashes of explosions and flames flickering in the buildings of the city. The puffs of smoke that rose from an apartment block as small calibre shells hit the outside, the small flashes of submachine guns in windows and on streets, the eerie reflections across walls casting shadows and unknown images of fear in the fading light.

Realising he had little viewing time left with the darkening sky, he adjusted his position to view the riverbank to his left. The jetties and stone walls bordering the iced river could provide some cover from the fighting in the city if they were to attempt to move from this position. Moving the glasses slowly southwards along the river's edge, he noted a distant metal ladder ascending the high stone wall from the iced river, some two hundred metres from the sharp turn in the river. Lifting the glasses slightly, he could see beyond the ladders position into the streets beyond, his view now a forty-five-degree angle. The fighting seemed to be in these streets beyond the ladder, his realisation that this was perhaps the front line or limit of Russian advance northwards.

'Herr Leutnant...' Luca stated, concern evident and rising in his voice as Hausser rose from his position to get a better view from their vantage point, the commander's eyes and concentration fixed through the field glasses.

'Just a minute.' The young commander stated as he squinted through the glasses further, trying to identify something in the street beyond the ladder, his view obscured by the corner of a building.

Plaster exploded across the room as the high velocity bullet zipped three inches past the front of Hausser's face, hitting the wall just next to him. The sniper on the other side of the river having noticed slight movement through the shell hole in the storage tower as he scanned the buildings opposite through his sights.

Hausser propelled himself to the right, landing roughly amongst the fragmented rubble and burnt paperwork strewn on the floor, the field glasses dropping from his grip. Luca pushed the tarpaulin back across the opening as another bullet ricochet off the outside cement just right of the opening. The young Italian dropped to his knees next to the German commander, checking his body for injury.

Hausser shook his head, the rough impact with the floor stunning him momentarily, a jabbing pain shooting down his right arm. He looked up, seeing the Italian's cheeky smile as he reached out to help him up, 'Perhaps enough for today, Herr Leutnant. The Russian sniper will be watching the gap more closely now I think, good job he is not a great shot today.' The Italian grinned as he saw the officer was not hit.

Hausser raised himself to a seating position, his hands shaking. The anger rising within him at his own careless actions, the tiredness reducing his alertness, 'Yes, enough for now. Let's not give him another chance...perhaps we should go and see your commander now?'

The Italian nodded, smiling as he helped him to his feet, 'He is on the third floor below, planning our further defence. Let's go and talk to him, he wanted your report.'

The two soldiers slowly trudged across the small room towards the door, Hausser rubbing his bruised right arm, with the Italian holding his left for support.

In the forest on the other side of the Volga, the Russian sniper grinned ironically in defeat. He considered he had fired in haste as the figure in the opening moved, scolding himself for the over eager reaction. His grin slowly faded as he thought of the fright he had given the enemy soldier some two hundred and fifty metres away. As the light diminished further, he pulled the blankets and branches further around him as a shield against the dropping temperatures. His tally for the day was two, but the dark would bring the opportunity of silhouettes against the fires, making his aim easier...this night's hunt was just beginning.

Chapter Twenty Five: Hauptmann Becker

Hausser's boots clicked together as he saluted the captain, his dusty and dirt covered uniform an open display of the adventures they had experienced, 'Leutnant Hausser reporting as requested, Herr Hauptmann.'

The captain smiled wearily, returning his salute, his uniform creased but relatively clean by comparison. The red wine covered cuffs and insignia to his jacket indicating he was a captain of the military police or a Feldgendarmerie Hauptmann. Slowly he lifted a metal ration cup to his lips and drank greedily from the contents.

The captain stood at a desk at the back of the third floor of the storage tower, a radio and operator positioned to his left in the corner of the small office. The small room was dimly lit, with a flickering oil lamp on the desk and one next to the radio. The captain's eyes were dark and bloodshot with tired lines underneath, the outward signs of exhaustion. His matted greying black hair unkempt from a nervous habit of running or rubbing his hand across the top of his head. On the desk lay his steel helmet, with a metal gorget (Ringkragen) lying alongside.

A pile of radio message signals lay on the desk, with the captain's luger pistol sitting on top as a makeshift paperweight. Placing the metal cup back on the desk, the captain reached for a cigarette from a packet next to the cup and raised it to his mouth. As he lit the cigarette, his hands shaking, his eyes surveyed Hausser, looking him up and down. Slowly he raised his left leg and sat on the corner of the desk facing him.

'I am Captain Becker, please be relaxed.' He indicated to the young German commander, 'It seems you have had quite a journey here, Leutnant Hausser. Have you got any information about the Russian strength facing us here?' The captain narrowed his tired eyes as he spoke, rubbing them with the fingers of his right hand.

Hausser shifted uneasily, the dull pain in his right shoulder throbbing as he tensed his arm, 'They have several hundred soldiers in the town below, probably getting ready to attack. What is your strength here?'

The captain smiled briefly, 'Not many, forty men give or take, there are about twenty eight in this building and maybe ten or twelve in the smaller storage building next door, which has fewer windows. In addition, there are fourteen wounded so far, we have held out for a couple of days now. I am hoping the counter attack from the north will commence soon otherwise I think we may have some difficulty holding our position.'

Hausser raised his eyes, 'This counter attack...has that been confirmed?' He indicated to the radio operator in the corner who had now turned to look at him.

'Not as yet, it's more a natural presumption on my part at present. It is only natural for the High Command to order a counter attack to rectify the enemy's incursion.' The captain looked around, surveying the sandbagged windows in the large room surrounding the office, 'Until then we will just have to hold out.'

Hausser's expression changed, the frustration beginning to show on his face, 'Incursion! This was a full scale offensive; the Russians are apparently several hundred kilometres to our rear. One of their officers advised me they had now cut us off in Stalingrad, what have you heard on the radio?'

The captain's eyes widened in horror, his tired face confused, 'We could be surrounded? They have told me to hold out and await reinforcements or further orders.' The captain hesitated, seeming to consider the situation briefly, 'Mind you, that was yesterday, since then we hardy get a reply, we are just told to await further instructions. What do you think that means?'

Hausser shook his head slowly, 'I am not sure, there may be so many things for them to deal with that you have become a low priority. If the city is surrounded, then I doubt there will be any reinforcements coming, you may even be alone here.'

A shell hit the roof of the storage tower, dust falling gradually from the ceiling of the room in places, some landing on the paperwork on the desk.

The captain's expression became grave, his darkened eyes seeming moist as he looked at Hausser, 'I have wounded here...we need reinforcements or a counter attack to relieve us. We cannot break out...the enemy is too strong and we would never make it with the wounded men. My duty is to keep my men as safe as possible until we are rescued.'

Hausser's expression became grim, then his eyes lightened, 'It is very quiet at the moment. There is no shooting, so perhaps you have some time.'

The captain shook his head slowly, glancing at his watch, 'No, the Russians negotiated a two hour ceasefire and offered me surrender terms. I cannot get a reply from command advising me whether I can accept or not...they keep saying they will radio us back soon. The Russians said they would care for our wounded if we surrendered.'

Hausser looked curious, 'When do the two hours' end?'

The captain slowly stood up, his expression sad, 'We have ten minutes left.' Turning to the radio operator, he gestured with his right hand, 'Try them again please corporal, ask if we have permission to surrender...or even if there will be a relief effort.'

The radio operator turned in his seat, adjusting the buttons on the radio as he leant forward placing the earphones over his head. As the man spoke softly into the microphone, the captain indicated for Hausser to accompany him into the larger room. As the men walked slowly out of the corner office, several German and Romanian soldiers stood to attention, their positions next to the sandbagged windows, their weapons ready in their hands. The captain dropped his cigarette, stepping on it as they walked.

The two men walked slowly towards one of the sandbagged windows, a small gap between the obstructions at eye height for a soldier to fire out of. Next to each window were placed candles to assist reloading and visibility in the darkened room. As they approached the window, the captain indicated to the German soldier standing next to it, 'Please give us a minute...go and sit with the radio operator and report any messages as soon as they come in.'

The middle aged soldier nodded, his stubbled face grim. The captain slowly leant against the frame of the window, his eyes glinting in the candle light. He turned to Hausser, his voice lowered, 'You are an experienced soldier, where as I am a military policeman with limited combat experience. What is your consideration as to what the Russians will do now?'

Hausser breathed deeply, thinking for a second, the candle light flickering across his features. He drew breath and looked the captain in the eyes, 'I think they will probably attack you tonight. If you do not surrender, they will want this building secured on their flanks so they can move more men up north into the city.' He glanced briefly through the gap in the sandbags, seeing only a few lights in the darkness below, the shadows of the buildings reaching out into the distance. Turning back, he sighed, his voice hushed, 'They will probably come in the darkness...that should reduce their casualties. Once they are inside I think you will be overwhelmed, you have too few men to resist the hundreds we saw.'

The captain nodded grimly, his features becoming stressed as he ran the shaking fingers of his right hand through his hair, 'What do you suggest?'

The young commander thought for a moment, turning to look out through the gap once more. Slowly he began to speak, 'I think I saw a possible escape route earlier, but it will be difficult if not impossible to escape with everyone. Once the Russians get an idea that you are trying to leave, they will throw everything at you...we may lose everyone. One thing for certain, the wounded will not be able to escape, some of those I saw are too badly hurt.'

The captain sighed, 'I understand. What can we do to delay or stop them?' His eyebrows rising.

Hausser glanced back through the gap. Speaking softly, he stared out into the dark streets below, 'Barricade all the entrances, booby trap the stairs and inflict as many casualties as you can. But that will only buy you more time I think, and there is little or no time to prepare. It will also infuriate them so when they do come in, they may not take any prisoners at all…are you willing to commit to that course of action?'

The captain nodded again, digesting what Hausser had said, then his face lightened slightly, 'I understand…the escape route you suggested, could we get the men out in groups?'

Hausser considered the captain's question, 'Perhaps…it may take a couple of hours though and we would have to move quickly. What about the wounded?'

The captain swallowed, his eyes widening, a decision formulating in his mind, 'I will stay with the wounded…they are now my men and I am responsible for them. Once you have got as many men away as you can, I will surrender to the Russians to save them. I will ask for a couple of volunteers to stay with me to help.'

The young commander turned his head to look at the captain, seeing the strain in the man's eyes, 'That is a brave decision and one that could save the men. If that is what you want, I will try and get as many men away as possible.'

The captain nodded, his resolve returning as he reassured himself of his decision, 'Then it is decided. Gather your men Leutnant, I will give you some of my men to take along.' He paused, a brief smile forming on his lips, 'They will be your men once they leave this building, Hausser. Let us hope the Russians do not get wind of our plan.'

Hausser looked at the captain, admiration in his eyes for the man's decision, 'Yes sir, if I may suggest we place your men in four groups, the first group to follow us once we have secured the escape route?'

Captain Becker nodded, forcing a faint smile, 'Yes Hausser, I will see to that. Take the mad Italian Luca with you and a couple of others. Once you secure the route, will you be sending someone back to collect the next group?'

Hausser grinned briefly, 'Yes of course, sir. I think the best place to leave from is next to the sewer exit we came in from, it is covered by both buildings. Did you secure the sewers? I asked one of your men to pass the message on when we arrived?'

The captain nodded, 'I put three men down there, that's all I could spare.'

The young commander pursed his lips, 'As we begin to leave we will need to keep fire up from the top windows even if the Russians are not attacking, that will help to perhaps convince the enemy we are not up to something.'

'I will arrange that...a good distraction will be provided. We will drop hand grenades out to confuse them.' The captain smiled weakly, 'I wish you good luck, Hausser, and thank you for your advice.' He stretched out his hand to the younger man.

Leutnant Hausser was slightly surprised by the gesture, but shook his hand firmly, 'I will try my best for you sir.'

'Sir!' The raised voice drifted across the room, startling both men as the soldier appeared at the doorway to the office.

Captain Becker turned abruptly, 'Yes, what is it? Have they finally replied?'

The soldier stood at the doorway, his eyes wide with adrenalin, 'Message from Sixth Army Headquarters sir.'

Captain Becker straightened, his demeanour becoming stern, 'What is it?'

The soldier paused, clearing his throat, 'Message reads sir, Sixth Army regrets there are no reserves available to assist you. No relief effort possible at this time. Russian offensive forces are operating to the army's rear restricting operations. Hold position for as long as possible and consider breakout attempt. In the event of situation deteriorating or not warranting breakout, you are granted freedom of action as local commander. Surrender should only be a consideration if situation becomes hopeless.'

The captain turned to the younger commander, his voice resolute, 'It is decided then...gather your men and start the escape, Leutnant Hausser.'

The young Berliner nodded, turning to glance out of the gap once more, his voice firm, 'Yes Sir, we will leave as soon as possible.'

As he looked out over the darkened town below, he stiffened, glimpsing some distant flashes on the horizon high beyond the buildings and streets that stretched away from the water's edge. Seeing distant smoke trails above the closely grouped flashes the adrenalin swept through his body, an electric charge sweeping up his spine. Turning to the captain, a look of desperation forming on his face, his voice rising in alarm, 'Katyusha's firing, get away from the windows.'

Both men pushed themselves from the window, lunging to the floor, their hands rising over their heads. As they did so, Hausser could just hear a muffled panicked shout from the floor below, 'Panzer Alarm! Enemy tank in the street!'

The building shook as the rockets hit the upper floors, throwing plaster and debris from ceilings onto the men in the rooms below. Next to the radio operator, the oil lantern fell from the top of the radio set, igniting on the floor as it smashed, the operator jumping backwards to escape the flame. On the top floor, still smouldering from the fire earlier in the day, half the ceiling collapsed completely, already weakened from the damage it had sustained.

Hausser held his hands over his head as the plaster dust and fragments fell onto his back and helmet. He glanced sideways down the rectangular room, through the falling dust to see the sandbags in the far window fall inwards, the building movement dislodging them. Falling onto the machine gun and gunner as he lay curled on the floor below the window, the man's body shuddered, his arms pushing the bags from his back as he swore. Bullets sprayed across the ceiling causing further plaster and cement to fall as Russian machine gun fire from the street entered the open window.

In the small office, the radio operator and soldier were throwing sand and dirt from a nearby bucket onto the burning oil, the light from the flames highlighting their silhouettes and shadows as it flickered through the open doorway.

An explosion on the outside wall broke Hausser's stare, the Russian SU-5 Self Propelled gun firing at the building from the opposite side of the wide thoroughfare some seventy metres away. A metal clank echoed across the darkness as a gunner on the ground floor opened fire on the tank with a small anti-tank rifle.

Captain Becker struggled to his feet, an outstretched hand assisting Hausser to stand, 'Time for you to leave my friend.' The captain shouted, dust and dirt now covering his tunic. He leant forward as another shell hit the building, dust billowing around him, 'Take six men and secure your escape route, Herr Leutnant. I think our time here is now short.'

Hausser nodded, spitting dust from his mouth, 'I will get my men...we leave immediately.' He turned and walked briskly to the doorway to the stairs.

Behind him, Captain Becker turned to his men, pointing to the open window, 'Re-barricade that window, and keep your heads down. Return fire when you can men, I want no heroics tonight...we just hold the Russians off. There is a way out!'

The soldiers nodded grimly, rising to positions next to their selected windows and peering out through gaps in the sandbags. The captain moved towards the small office, seeing the fire was almost out, 'Get on the radio...see if the guns in Stalingrad can provide some artillery fire to support us.' He pointed to the soldier next to the operator, 'You, check the floors for casualties, tell the men they will be leaving soon. I want four volunteers to stay with me and the wounded to surrender to the Russkies once the rest are away. Understood?'

The soldier nodded, his face grim, 'Jawohl, Herr Hauptmann!' Saluting, he moved quickly past the captain and headed for the door to the stairs.

Hausser stood on the third floor landing as another shell hit the outside of the building, throwing dust down from higher in the structure. Sporadic gunfire from the ground floors echoed in the stairwell as the soldiers fired at movement in the streets. The metal clank of a small anti-tank rifle firing at the thick front armoured plate of the Russian SPG filtered in through the broken windows.

As the German soldier pushed past him to ascend the building stairs, Tatu appeared inquisitively at the turn in the stairwell above, his PPSH 41 submachine gun in his left hand. 'What is going on, Hausser? This does not look good, Russian soldiers are in the streets heading this way.'

The German commander looked up at him, seeing the eagerness and excitement in the Romanian's eyes. Hausser cleared his throat, 'Get the others, and choose three Romanians to come with us. Meet me at the sewer exit entrance, we are leaving!'

Tatu nodded, turned and disappeared back up the staircase. Hausser began to descend the steps to the ground floor, gunfire now echoing around the stairwell from below. As he reached the second floor, Luca emerged from the right side room, concern on his face. Seeing Hausser, a brief smile crossed his face, 'What are we going to do, Herr Leutnant?'

The young commander looked at him, 'Get yourself a weapon, Luca, you are coming with us to secure an escape route.'

The Italian nodded, his eyes widening at the command, 'Yes sir!' Turning quickly, he disappeared back into the gloom of the side room.

As Hausser turned to descend the next few concrete steps, Luca reappeared from the darkness of the room, a Russian Mosin-Nagant rifle brandished in his right hand. Reaching out he stopped the commander by grasping his arm with his left hand, handing Hausser some MP40 ammunition clips. Then he turned back into the room and began rummaging for rifle ammunition amongst the stores in the darkened office.

As the German commander descended the next set of concrete steps, tucking the clips into his belt, he shouted over his shoulder, 'Meet me at the sewer exit to the building Luca, bring three men.'

Luca shouted from within the darkened room, 'I will be there shortly, Herr Leutnant!' The Italian had just located the appropriate ammunition box and was pushing handfuls of bullets into his pockets, tunic and a knapsack he found next to the ammunition crates. Eventually emptying the ammunition box, he grasped a Romanian metal helmet and ran from the room.

Several more rockets hit the upper stories of the building as Hausser reached the ground floor. Dust and plaster poured down the stairwell as he grasped the metal hand rail with both hands, the building seeming to shake even at ground level. Hearing boots on the staircase of the floors above, he pushed himself forwards to the right, towards the side office on the ground floor.

Behind him, there was another clank as the anti-tank rifle fired again at the Russian SPG in the street. Rifle shots and submachine gunfire echoed around the building as the soldiers within fired out at any movement in the streets outside.

As Hausser stood in the doorway to the small side office, the soldier in front of him spun round, his hands grasping his rifle tightly at chest height. He was breathing heavily, the adrenalin rushing through his body, 'F..Firing in the sewer, sir! The Russians are attacking!' As he spoke, a shell from the Russian SPG across the wide street exploded behind him just outside the room opposite, the shrieks of pain from a wounded soldier resounding off the walls around them.

Hausser walked towards the outside doorway of the small room, used to check delivery paperwork and the drivers or boatmen in as they delivered their cargo. The doorway had been two thirds barricaded with sandbags and furniture and he passed the sentry beginning to pull some of the furniture aside. The soldier leant forwards and promptly began helping him, pulling the table on its side away from the sandbags. As they moved the table, Hausser addressed the private, their eyes meeting, 'When my men come…tell them I will be just outside.'

The soldier nodded, 'Yes sir. Are you going to get help?'

Hausser frowned, his voice lowered, 'I doubt it…we hope to get round the river bend. Once we secure that point, we will send men back for you and the others.'

The soldier nodded grimly, 'I think we have not much time now sir, the Russians are massing for an attack.' He hesitated, his eyes saddening, 'Good luck sir.'

The German commander nodded grimly, then turned and grasped a chair, removing it from its position, gaining closer access to the sandbags. As the furniture was finally removed, Hausser slowly clambered on top of the barricade, a blast of cold icy air enveloping him as he rose above the obstruction. Glancing from side to side to check if the area was clear in the darkness, he half crawled across the top of the sandbags. Once through the opening, he dropped out of sight, landing with a crunch in the frozen snow outside.

Chapter Twenty Six: The Rubber Dinghy

Hausser landed roughly in the frozen snow, the crisp top of the blanket of flakes crunching under his boots. He hesitated, crouching on the bank, his breathing heavy. To his right, a freezing breeze swept over him, the slight wind coming in from the eastern side of the river Volga. He looked round, seeing the snow decline away from him, down the bank towards the frozen river. Glancing left, the darkness of the street was some distance away, the firing echoing in the passageway between the buildings.

A burst of submachine gun fire resounded from the opening in the roof of the smashed sewage pipe, below him to the left. The other sounds of war were further to his left, the sounds bouncing off the walls of the two buildings.

He shivered slightly as his body adapted to the more exposed lower temperature, his ears listening to the sporadic fire from within the building behind him. Grasping his MP40 in both hands he slowly lowered his body onto the snow, nudging himself down the slope towards the rubble strewn opening to the sewer tunnel.

His body slipped on the icy slope, sliding the last couple of metres down the incline, his boots breaking his descent as they made contact with the rubble and sides of the fractured tunnel. Gingerly, he lowered himself over the edge of the shattered sewer entrance and dropped onto the rubble a metre below.

Another burst of submachine gun fire to his left startled him briefly, the noise far louder as the sound echoed off the walls of the tunnel. Pushing himself to a crouched position, the muscles in his legs complaining at the strain, he slowly advanced into the darkened tunnel, the stench sweeping into his nostrils. As he stepped into the water, it seeped into his boots through the stitching, the severe temperature making him draw breath. The putrid water swirled around his boots as he pushed them along the floor of the sewer, a thin ice beginning to form on the surface.

Flashes from another submachine gun burst at the junction of the sewer lit up the tunnel briefly. Near the junction he saw two German soldiers, both crouched in the freezing foul water. As he slowly and carefully pushed his feet through the slimy water, feeling for footholds, one of the soldiers leant out and fired again down the main tunnel to the left. The muzzle flashes lit up the side tunnel again, revealing the dead Russian soldier he had seen earlier in the day, his body contorted in the same position.

Hausser paused, wary the men were at a high state of alertness. Swallowing to moisten his lips he called out in a low voice, 'Deutsche Soldat!'

One of the soldiers spun round, hearing the commander call out, his weapon ready and raised. Slowly lowering his rife as he saw the silhouette in the tunnel, he gestured for Hausser to approach with his right hand, a strained whisper coming from his lips, 'Komm!'

The German commander shuffled through the water towards the soldier as the other leant out into the tunnel and fired another short burst, the muzzle flashes illuminating the darkness in the tunnel for a couple of seconds. Glancing down, he carefully stepped over the outstretched body, looking up as he neared the two soldiers at the junction in the tunnel. The darkness in the sewer prevented him for making out their features, but he could just distinguish their shapes as he approached.

Crouching next to the soldier that had beckoned him forward, Hausser whispered, 'How far away are the Russians?'

Russian bullets whipped through the tunnel before them, impacting on the wall of the turning in the tunnel to their right. The soldier adjusted his position uncomfortably, 'Further down the tunnel...they keep trying to advance but we have this approach covered. They have been dropping smoke to try and get forward, but I think we can hold them here. We have killed several.'

Hausser nodded, his feet feeling numb in the cold water, 'Have you got enough ammunition to keep them back?'

The soldier paused as the other man leant out, firing a short burst from his MP40 again, the flashes briefly illuminating their faces, 'We have enough I think...we also have some grenades if they get much closer. The Russkies have got as far as the next side tunnel but they won't get any further tonight.' He grinned, 'The tunnel to the right has collapsed round the bend, so the Russkies can't get in that way. I can only guess what will happen up top if they attack in force though, we have nothing to stop tanks.'

The young commander pursed his lips, 'I thought there was three of you down here?'

The soldier paused, his voice straining with emotion, 'There was...Manfred is over there.' He indicated by outstretching his hand into the darkness to Hausser's right, 'He got hit in the throat coming back from checking the collapsed section round the bend, falling face down in the water. We couldn't get to him in time with the crossfire. All we could hear was him slowly drowning in this poisoned water.'

The German commander sighed realising the soldier's pain. There was silence for some seconds before he spoke again, 'How are you able to stay down here in this freezing water?'

The soldier slowly smiled again, his voice now a whisper, 'There was a rubber dinghy in the warehouse, we cut sections and wrapped the rubber round our boots before we came in here, didn't you?'

Hausser shook his head, smiling ironically, 'I didn't think of that.'

The soldier's voice became concerned, 'Best not stay too long then I think...frostbite is not pleasant. We will hold here...how is it up top?'

The young commander moved his weight across his body from one leg to the other, his thigh muscles beginning to ache, 'I don't know how long they can hold out. I am going to lead some men round the bend in the river and see if we can create an escape route for most of you.'

'Fantastic! Shall we just wait here for you then?' The soldier replied, a hopeful grin forming on his face.

The soldier behind him turned, his MP40 lowered, 'That's the best news I have heard in the last week, how long before you come back for us?' He raised his weapon again, leaned out and fired another burst into the dense smoke at the far end of the tunnel.

Hausser smiled briefly, waiting for the firing to stop, 'Hopefully one hour, it will depend how much resistance there is along the river.' Bullets splattered across the wall opposite throwing dust and grime across the dark tunnel, causing the men to duck back instinctively, the Russian infantry returning fire in the darkness.

The soldier in front of him retrieved an MP40 ammunition clip from his belt and held it aloft for his countryman to collect, his voice becoming solemn, 'I think it is time for you to leave...you will get frostbite otherwise. We will hold here...you have a long walk ahead of you on those feet. Remember to collect us please.'

Hausser nodded, turning, 'I will remember, try and keep them out of the side tunnel if you can.' Rising from his crouched position, the German commander cautiously stepped over the outstretched legs of the body and began forcing his numb feet through the slimy water, the cold now biting at his ankles in the sodden boots.

As another burst of submachine gun fire echoed across the walls, Hausser made his way carefully towards the debris at the end of the tunnel, seeing tracer fire cross the river in the distance. Looking back briefly, he raised his hand as a gesture towards the men in the darkness, hearing a whispered, 'Good Luck' in return.

As he reached the rubble, he slowly lifted his right foot out of the slurried water, placing it onto the fallen bricks, hearing a clank from the aging anti-tank rifle echo across the walls of the buildings either side, followed by the metallic pings of bullets hitting the Russian SPG across the road to his rear.

Grasping the side of the broken tunnel, he looked up and saw Tatu extend a hand to him. The Romanian smiling as he grasped his arm, helping him out of the darkness.

Chapter Twenty Seven: Prelude to escape.

As Hausser straightened up from the climb out of the sewer, he glanced around in the gloom, the gunfire from the street behind him causing concern. Tatu pulled the strap of his PPSH 41 over his shoulder, 'The men are waiting inside, Hausser. I thought it best to keep them under cover until it is time to leave.'

The German commander nodded, his exhaled breath now forming into clouds of condensed air in the dropping temperature, 'Let's check the route before we start out. It will be even colder on the riverbank, have they all got their balaclavas and gloves?'

Tatu turned to look towards the river, running his hand over his moustache and grinning, 'I told them to get ready for the cold...they should all have the kit we issued them with. It is unfortunate we left the greatcoats in the carriers...if we had not been dressed in two layers of clothing, we may have remembered them.'

Hausser glanced around further, then faced the Romanian, 'The extra kit would have just slowed us down, perhaps none of us would be here if we had been wearing the greatcoats, they are too cumbersome.' He indicated towards the river as the Romanian quartermaster turned to look at him in the gloom, 'Let's go and check the route we will take.'

Both men looked cautiously north along the alleyway between the two storage towers, their breath forming clouds between them in the freezing temperature. Behind them, sporadic fire both in the sewer and from the defenders in the buildings echoed between the walls of the towers. Before them, the land rose slightly before falling away, the decline leading to the banks of the frozen river. Broken brick and debris from shellfire lay across the end of the opening, half covered in frozen snow, on top of the remaining part of the broken sewer tunnel, providing possible cover and a vantage point.

Freezing air enveloped them as a breeze drifted between the towers, the air seeming to cling to their bodies in a cold embrace. As they slowly approached the end of the buildings, both the German commander and the Romanian quartermaster lowered themselves to the ground, unwilling to provide a target to anyone observing from the city or eastern banks of the river. Lying just behind the crest of the rubble, they slowly edged forward until they could just see over the debris and broken cement, wary of exposing themselves to possible fire.

Tatu's eyes widened in shock as he took in the sight before him. On the left, the city waterfront stretched out before them following the river bend, the burning buildings lighting up the snow and ice that stretched from the walls that bordered the city to the water's edge. Gunfire and explosions echoed distantly from around the bend in the river to their left as the ferocious fighting in the lower suburbs continued into the evening.

The flames' reflections flickered off the waves of the freezing river as it flowed southwards, carrying debris and bodies with the strong tide. Set into the waterfront walls were a variety of piers and jetties, the wooden and metal support pillars embedded in the frozen ice and snow. Their distance from the flowing water now up to a hundred metres due to the freezing temperatures. The ice slowly encroaching towards and into the water from either side as temperatures dropped further, increasing the strength of the water's flow and undercurrent.

On the east side of the river, opposite the city and hidden from view in trees and dispersed between the few buildings, the flashes from Russian artillery and Katyusha rocket batteries fired sporadically towards Stalingrad. The subsequent explosions sending dust, debris and broken bodies into the air as they landed throughout the streets and atop buildings in the ravaged city. Flashes as high explosive rounds landed across the city lit up the night sky occasionally causing buildings to topple, burying and crushing soldiers and civilians alike in the ruined remains. There would be no one to rescue such casualties and many would be attacked and consumed by the rodents or vermin that now roamed the city unchecked.

Occasionally, further north, shells would land to the east or on the iced bank of the river. The German batteries desperately attempting to deter or hit Russian reinforcements or boats preparing to cross the Volga with equipment or supplies. Firing at known or suspected boarding points on the water's edge, the power of the Wehrmacht artillery now severely reduced as ammunition rationing had been introduced earlier in the day.

In the far distance, they could just make out the shadows and silhouettes against the snow of bedraggled grouped civilians sheltering below the waterfront walls. Their fear of the battle raging in the city forcing them out into the severe temperature that many would succumb to during the forthcoming night. Numbers of the remaining under-nourished city inhabitants were hiding in cellars or in sewers and the people on the ice were usually fleeing fighting that had broken out in their darkened hiding places. There was now nowhere to hide or seek sanctuary in the burning city.

Tracer bullets flew across the river in both directions further north as machine gunners on either side reacted to movement or shadows they glimpsed in their binoculars. The crack of sniper fire and other small arms fire seemed to be continuous background noise to the sights before them, the remaining spirits of the two men seeming to slowly ebb away as they watched...to be gradually replaced by grim determination.

Hausser turned to Tatu, his voice lowered, 'We will keep close to the wall along the river...that should reduce the chances of being seen in the darkness.' He shifted his position uncomfortably, trying to see further around the bend, 'There is a ladder some distance around the river, we will go back up into the streets there and fight our way back to the German lines.'

Tatu nodded grimly, his thoughts distracted. Then he sighed, his voice strained, 'These are inexperienced troops, Hausser. We cannot expect them to hold for long without support. Maybe only one or two groups will escape before the communists overwhelm them.'

The German commander turned to face him, the Romanian quartermaster's solemn face hidden in the darkness, 'We have to try, Tatu. We owe the men that.'

The Romanian shook his head in frustration, hearing sporadic fire and an explosion behind them on the front of the building as he swallowed hard, 'Time is too short now. I wish you well my friend, but I think it best for me to stay here for now. I will send out small groups as you signal us. We will buy you the time you need to get as many as possible away.'

Hausser exhaled heavily in annoyance, the condensed air drifting before him. Considering for a few seconds, he slowly nodded, 'Very well, Tatu, if that is what you think is best. But you follow on as soon as you can...we will need you around the river bend. Buy me a little time, put a spotter in the damaged room above and I will signal you when the next group should leave...we will clear the way and secure the exit from the bank. If all looks hopeless, get everyone that can move out and we will try and cover your own escape.'

The Romanian smiled briefly, 'I had better not keep you then. I will send the first group out in a moment.' He extended his hand, Hausser slowly reaching out and grasping it, 'Good Luck, Herr Leutnant.' Tatu shifted uneasily and pushed himself backwards, slowly rising to a crouched position, he turned and ran towards the doorway, his footsteps crunching on the iced snow.

Hausser sighed, his emotions drained, hearing the gunfire firing out from inside the building to his right, he moved his body sideways across the snow. Cautiously, he crawled back from the mound of debris and rose to his feet. Considering the situation briefly, he grasped his MP40 tightly and slowly approached the corner of the storage tower, dropping onto his right knee, he awaited the men assigned to the first group.

Tatu ran through the small office, the guard moving to the side to let him pass, his weapon held tightly, his face solemn and pale with fear.

As Tatu entered the main building, he stopped at the foot of the stairs, a group of about ten soldiers before him either stood in the foot well or sat on the stairs. Breathless, he looked around the group, seeing all the men had covered their faces and were wearing overcoats or an additional layer of clothing.

The building shuddered as an artillery shell hit the right corner, dust and plaster falling down the staircase and landing on the collected group. Tatu drew breath, his lungs hurting from the exertion in the frozen temperature, 'Right, the first group needs to leave. I will stay and help hold back the Russkies.' He looked around the group observing their initial hesitation, pointing to the nearest soldier in German uniform, seeing the fear in the young man's eyes, 'You! Move outside, the rest follow him. When you get out there, turn to your right and report to the German officer next to the riverbank.'

The young soldier swallowed, nodding, his eyes wide. Moving slowly, he passed the Romanian quartermaster and moved into the side office, lifting his rifle from his shoulder. The other soldiers, both Romanian and German followed him, filing past Tatu. All carried grim expressions beneath the scarves wrapped round their mouths.

As the soldiers shuffled through the side office, Nicu stopped before Tatu, 'What do you want me to do?'

Gunfire echoed around the stairwell from above as the defending soldiers reacted to movement in the street. Tatu glanced into the next large room, seeing the Romanian and German soldiers on the ground floor cautiously peering out into the darkness through gaps in their barricades.

Tatu turned back and smiled at Nicu, 'Time for you to leave too, my friend. Hausser will need some help with the others.' The Romanian quartermaster placed a hand on the young man's shoulder, 'Be careful...stay close to the officer...keep him safe.'

Nicu nodded silently, 'Yes sir. We will clear the way for you.' He blinked as if to clear his eyes, then turned and proceeded into the small office.

The Italian then side stepped past Tatu, his knapsack bulging with supplies and ammunition. Winking at the Romanian as he caught his eye, 'Now I have a weapon, it is time for the Italian Army to enter the fight.'

Tatu grinned with surprise, 'Plenty of spirit then, keep that head safe from snipers and don't damage that helmet...it is Romanian property!' His voice lowered as the Italian passed him, 'Take care out there! I want some more Italian cooking when we get out of here.'

Luca nodded as he proceeded into the office, a grin forming beneath his scarf, 'It may not be restaurant quality, but what do you Slovaks know about that?'

Tatu shook his head, the smile falling from his face as he turned to face Hase, 'Dumb insolent Italians!'

Hase looked into the Romanian's eyes, seeing a determination, but also sadness. He stretched out his hand towards him.

Tatu grinned again, seeing the soldier's reaction. Leaning forward, he flung his arms around the younger man, holding him tightly for a second, his voice shaking, 'Take care young Hase.' Pushing the young soldier to arm's length, he looked him in the eyes, 'Now go and help your friend, quickly.' He pushed him sideways towards the office.

Hase stopped in the doorway, looked back at the two other men in the stairwell, then to Tatu. Breaking eye contact, he turned and walked briskly through the office and out into the night.

A concerned look crossed Tatu's face, 'Where is Meino...our Croatian?'

Petru cleared his throat, 'He is up on the third floor, trying to teach these policemen and cooks how to defend properly!'

Udet rose from his seated position on the stairs and descended the two steps to the ground floor, wincing as the movement from the dull pain in his ribs. Looking at Tatu, he reached up, grasping the rifle strap on his shoulder and removing the weapon. Turning to Petru, he spoke softly, 'Let's give the Russians a battle to remember then.'

Katyusha rockets hit the roof and front of the upper stories, the explosions deafening as the sound wave passed down into the foot well. Dislodged dust and plaster fragments fell from the walls and ceiling above, showering the men as they instinctively ducked their heads. Slowly the soldiers straightened up, the two older Romanians turning and looking in disbelief at the young German, Tatu leaning forward and gently pushing him in jest, 'Pig headed Berliners...so you want to stay with your uncles?'

Beneath his scarf, a smile cautiously formed on Petru's face, his eyes drifting to Tatu as he indicated to Udet, 'What floor do you want us on?'

Chapter Twenty Eight: The Russian Storm

Tatu shook his head, 'No, I don't think so. Udet, you must……'

'Smoke! In the street! Smoke!' A shout from the large ground floor room forced the three soldiers to turn abruptly. Tatu advanced into the spacious storage room, the dim illumination from the oil lamps flickering across the wide room. Small bursts of submachine gun fire echoed through the building from the upper floors as the gunners fired out at any shadows or movement.

Petru and Udet followed Tatu into the warehouse, their weapons held in both hands, noticing the large sturdy double wooden doors at the far end barricaded with sandbags and furniture. Stopping at the first window on his right, Tatu stole a glance through a gap in the sandbags.

Outside in the darkness, he could see the smoke rising from the three canisters lying in the road and against the building exterior wall. As his vision in the empty street was gradually obscured by the rising clouds, he turned to the soldier that had uttered the alarm, a puzzled expression on his face, 'Where is the tank?'

The Romanian soldier at the next window interrupted, brandishing the antitank rifle in his hands, a grin forming on his young face, 'He reversed back round the corner, sir. I think we killed one of the gunners and damaged his tracks…not sure he is happy!'

Tatu nodded, running his hand across his moustache, 'Good! Now get ready…the Russians will be coming any moment.'

The smile fell from the infantryman's face as he heard the bolts on weapons nervously being pulled by the soldiers behind him. The soldiers checking their weapons were fully loaded.

Tatu slowly walked round in a circle in the centre of the room, his voice raised as he heard further smoke canisters falling and rolling on the cobblestones outside, 'The Russkies will be attacking any second, they are waiting for the smoke to reach the upper floors before rushing us. We need to hold them off to have any chance of escaping.' He stopped briefly, looking across each of the faces of six apprehensive soldiers in the ground floor warehouse. Indicating with a nod to Udet and Petru, he continued, 'We will back you up if you have to reload or are struggling…just shout out!'

Tatu paused, allowing the information to sink in, then he continued, 'If we lose the ground floor we can probably hold them for some time in the stairwell, but our chances of escape will be then slim.' He smiled comfortingly at Udet, the young German's eyes showing the lines of stress. Indicating to the double doors at the end of the room, he continued, 'The Russkies will try and come in through the end doors, through the office beyond the stairs, or in through the windows. If they get near to the windows, they will probably try and drop grenades through…we must prevent this or throw them back out.' Noticing the smoke begin to drift in through the gaps in the sandbags, Tatu realised there was little time left to talk, sighing he looked across the determined faces of the listening soldiers, 'That's it comrades, we stop them or we die, understand?'

The clicking of boots pulled together echoed round the room, the chorus of 'Yes sir!' uttered from each soldier.

Tatu smiled briefly, then his demeanour became solemn, 'Good Luck men.' Turning abruptly to Udet, his eyes narrowed, 'Udet, go upstairs and get them to drop grenades out of the windows as the Russians attack. Tell them to keep down though and not to throw them too close to the side of the building. Russian snipers will be watching the windows as soon as they attack.' Tatu hesitated, as if to consider something, then spoke again, 'Ask Hauptmann Becker for a couple more men, get them to cover the sewer and the office entrance…we are too weak there I think.'

Udet nodded, turned and strode swiftly from the room, ascending the stairs two at a time, the metal hobnail studs on his boots clicking on the cement steps.

Hearing a distant whistle outside, Tatu reached into the pocket of his large overcoat. Pulling out a new magazine for his submachine gun, he shook it to check the weight and changed it with the existing drum on his PPSH 41. Pointing to the windows, he raised his voice, the strain evident, 'Here they come men, give them everything you have.'

He watched as the soldiers nervously re-assumed their positions next to the windows, most briefly glancing out into the smoke. The rattle of the MG34 above them started, the gunner firing blind into the smoke. Then another MG34 commenced firing bursts from a different part of the building.

Footsteps could be heard descending the stairs, and Petru noticed two men reach the ground floor, turning to their right. Tatu moved towards the second, middle window, his submachine gun held low, then he heard the distance rumble from the south. Shaking his head in exasperation, he exclaimed, 'Incoming artillery, stay down! The Russkies will come straight after the artillery hits. Get Ready!'

He watched as the men along the windows drew breath, a couple swallowing hard as they lowered themselves to the sides of the windows. Tatu ran his hand across his moustache, his apprehension rising. He thought hard to clear his fear, the adrenalin coursing through his system. Considering the Russians must be about to throw a large number of soldiers against them could be the only explanation for the delay in the attack, taking some time to brief the squad leaders and organise the assault. Looking up he caught Petru's eye, realising his countryman was thinking the same from his expression.

Heavy calibre artillery shells smashed into the tower, hitting the upper floors and roof. The building shuddered, whole sections of plaster and cement falling from ceilings onto the floors and infantrymen below. Oil lamps were knocked over with the impact, their contents spilling out and spreading rapidly across the floors. The oil igniting and causing small fires that the soldiers stamped on in attempts to extinguish the flames.

The wounded on the fifth floor lay frightened and apprehensively against the walls for cover, the Italian soldier assigned to orderly duties attempting some encouragement. As the shells hit, beams and cement from the ceiling shattered and collapsed on the helpless men, huddled together. One of the last shells exploding on the floor above, having penetrated the weakened roof. The immense explosion blew a hole in the ceiling, the ensuing blast wave killing most of the wounded men, their ear drums and lungs perforating, being unable to resist the physical shock imposed on their weakened bodies by the blast constrained within the room's walls. The barricades on the windows, sandbags and supply boxes were blown out of the openings, dropping into the street below. The Italian orderly, hit by the falling masonry was also killed in the blast, his broken body thrown brutally against the northern wall facing the river in the shock wave.

The two upper floors now caught alight after the high explosive shelling. The flames initially rising dramatically into the night sky as destroyed oil supplies, stores and wooden beams instantly combusted and burned out of control. A hoarse cheer rising from the on-looking Russian infantry in the streets below, the sight providing welcome encouragement after consuming their pre-attack vodka ration.

Below ground, in the sewer, the young German military policeman was picking his way cautiously along the tunnel having entered from the collapsed section. The twenty-year-old had only arrived at Stalingrad the month before and had been posted to the southern suburbs two days before the Russian offensive began. Previously he had been assigned to guarding rail wagons and supervising prisoner groups, far from the front lines, which ill prepared him for this experience. He gripped his rifle tightly as he advanced towards the junction in the tunnel, his knuckles white against the weapon beneath his gloves. His breath now short and shallow, his adrenalin seeming overwhelming as it heightened his senses and made him light headed and slightly nauseous.

The freezing water seeped into his boots as he pushed his feet carefully through the poisoned slurry and thinly formed ice towards the two soldiers at the junction. He froze as the sounds of the explosions entered the narrow tunnel behind him, echoing off the walls to either side, his heart beating loudly in his chest and mouth dry. The stench had been overwhelming at first, but this had been rapidly overcome by his increasing fear as he realised the Russian attack was imminent. He heard the distant 'Hurrahs' as the Russian infantry emerged from cover, throwing more smoke grenades towards the storage building in an attempt to blind the defenders.

Before him, one of the soldiers in the tunnel had leant out slightly, squinting into the darkness that extended off down the sewer tunnel. The smoke seemed thicker than previously and this drifted towards and around them in the darkness. Unable to make out any shapes or movement, he slowly raised his MP40 once again to fire a burst along the tunnel. As the smoke swirled around him, he strained his ears for sounds of movement, the noise of rifle and submachine gun fire from above ground distorted in the tunnel, preventing him from making out any distinct sound.

He leant out further, adjusting his body to allow him to lean more into the main tunnel, his eyes and ears struggling to identify a noise or movement in front of him. The feeling of disorientation beginning to seep into his mind as the smoke and darkness eliminated any vision. Then his eyes widened, his mouth opening to shout an alarm as he heard the metallic 'whoosh' before him. The oncoming flames filling and lighting up the tunnel in front of him as they surged towards him. His pupils tried to adjust to the extreme light and his mind screamed at him to move back into the side tunnel, to safety as the flames engulfed his body. The chemically induced fire swept across his body and around him and past him down the tunnel. The intense flame and heat seared his skin, burning it from his bones instantly, his uniform igniting and combusting with the chemical fuel. The burning liquid poured into his body through his nose and mouth, instantly searing his throat and lungs and enveloping him as his body twisted in an attempt to deflect itself from the oncoming wave of light and fire. The intense agony from both inside and outside his body briefly overcame him as he passed out and fell sideways into the main tunnel, his body still burning ferociously. His body writhing and twitching in final unconscious agony in the sewer water, the struggling ceasing as the fire burnt though his organs, cooking them…he died within seconds.

The soldier behind him in the side tunnel instinctively threw himself backwards, the side of his face scorched by the surging flame. He landed in the putrid ice and water, the rifle falling from his grasp, the terror overcoming him, the intense cold of the water an extreme shock to his body after the searing heat. As he struggled to raise himself from the water, spluttering, his frightened shout echoed through the tunnels, 'Flammenwerfer!'

As the soldier in the water some ten metres before him flayed around in an attempt to rise from the slurry and ice, the young German military policeman's eyes widened in horror and terror. The burning body lying at the intersection of the tunnel illuminated the sewer before him. Flames burned on the walls and surface of the water as the chemicals were consumed by the fire. Dried excrement, dust and dirt also ignited in the intense heat, the flames burning for a short time on spots on the walls and the rounded roof of the tunnel.

In panic, his heart beating wildly in his chest, he dropped his rifle. Reaching frantically to his waist, he grasped the stick grenade in his belt, pulling the cold metal from between his tunic and thick leather belt. His hands were shaking in terror as he unscrewed the base of the grenade, hearing the splashing of water to the left of the intersection as the Russian infantry advanced. Pulling the cord that fell from the unscrewed base, he tossed the grenade forward, the metal stick hitting the right wall of the tunnel and bouncing into the middle of the intersection, coming to rest next to the burning body.

A spurt of flame shot along the right wall as the soldier pressed the trigger on his weapon of flames, the Russian combat engineer's stance to the left of the corner to limit his exposure to fire. The young German fell backwards into the polluted water as his body twisted to avoid the oncoming ignited chemicals propelled along the wall. The intense cold seeming to grasp at his body as the poisoned water enveloped him.

The grenade's explosion at the intersection of the tunnel killed the approaching Russian flamethrower instantly, igniting the metal canisters of chemicals on his back. The subsequent fireball engulfing the cautious infantry advancing behind him, their screams echoing across the walls. The fire surged forward along the tunnels, igniting the dried dirt and soldiers alike as the chemically induced flame sought out further victims.

The flames in the side tunnel shot along the right side of the sewer roof, the angle of the corner of the intersection saving the two German infantrymen a similar fate to the Russian soldiers. The German nearest the intersection had turned and was scrambling on his hands and knees away from the corner, the slurried water splashing onto the walls on either side. As the fireball receded, he rose desperately from the water, attempting to run, forcing his legs through the freezing liquid. His sight was obscured by the returning darkness, his right eye blinded, the side of his face burnt from the chemicals. He was disorientated, his panic to escape back down the side tunnel overpowering. Advancing blindly, he fell headlong over the outstretched legs of the Russian body, falling face down into the freezing water, his outstretched arms breaking his fall, a shriek of panic coming from his swollen lips.

Hands roughly grabbed the back of his tunic, pulling him forward. The younger German military policeman gripping his countryman's wet uniform and dragging him along the side tunnel. Behind them, the screams of dying and critically wounded Russian soldiers echoed across the slimy walls of the sewer, the still burning chemical patches and bodies casting flickering shadows and light around them. As the two men struggled up the rubble that lead from the sewer, the cold air enveloped them, sending chills across their bodies. To their upper right, the infantryman at the delivery doorway was leaning out firing his rifle towards the street behind them as they scrambled up the iced slope. The soldier at the doorway turned his head as they approached, the fear evident on his face, 'Get inside, quickly!' As they struggled through the doorway, one supporting the other, the submachine gun fire and rifle shots were loud around them. Screams of wounded from the street drifted along the alleyway as they struggled into the office to the side of the storage tower.

Tatu glanced to his right to see the two men struggle into the stairwell, then fired a burst from his submachine gun out through a gap in the sandbags, the muzzle flashes illuminating his face. As he looked back to the stairwell, the young German military policeman shouted to him, desperation on his face, 'The Russians have the sewer!'

As the two men struggled to ascend the stairs, Udet pushed past them on his way back down. Reaching the doorway, he looked across the large storage room, seeing the soldiers fire from their individual windows, then duck back behind cover. Shouts in Russian could be heard from just the other side of the wall as the first wave of surviving infantry reached the building, still disorientated in the smoke.

Udet hesitated, seeing Tatu fire out of the window again, then shouted at the Romanian, 'A German Battery in Stalingrad is ready to fire, Tatu. Where do you want the artillery?'

Tatu glanced round at him, moving his body from the window, desperation on his face, 'Bring it down just the other side of the street...drop grenades out of the windows!'

Udet nodded, turned and started to hurriedly ascend the stairs, pulling himself upwards with his gloved hands on the cold metal hand rail.

Petru glanced out through a small gap in the barricade on his window, the swirling smoke before the building obscuring his vision. Shadows moved through the smoke as he raised his rifle, firing at a silhouette in the cloud, the shadow falling backwards onto the cobblestones.

The sounds of engines revving from the street alerted Tatu to a new danger, he stooped and glanced out of a gap in the sandbags, his adrenalin rising further. The smoke billowed in through the gap as he blinked to clear his eyes. Seeing the burning debris on the cobblestones, the smoke slightly dispersed, he glanced at the shapes across the thoroughfare. His spine tingling as he noticed the distinctive silhouette of a Russian field gun being manhandled by its crew emerging from a side street of the buildings opposite.

The clatter of tank tracks rattled over the cobblestones as the silhouette of a T34 Russian tank swept out from behind the buildings and field gun, the armoured vehicle abruptly turning to face the storage tower. A flash in the smoke as the 76mm tank's turret gun fired, the high explosive shell hitting the front of the building near one of the windows. Plaster and debris shot across the room as Tatu instinctively ducked, the taste of plaster dust in his mouth as some of the sandbags toppled from the window.

Rising again, he fired through the widened gap, hearing screams from the street as the burst from his submachine gun hit several advancing Russian infantrymen. As he ducked away from the opening, bullets poured through as the Russians fired back, the bullets slamming onto the ceiling and walls at the back of the room.

Explosions echoed through the building as grenades bounced onto the tarmac, tossed from the upper windows. Tatu raised his weapon, firing blindly through the opening, the screaming of men and gunfire echoing in his ears. Looking quickly around, he saw two of the defenders lying on the warehouse floor, blood seeping from wounds they had sustained. Hearing the 'Hurrahs' from Russian infantrymen outside, he realised the second wave was now moving towards them, the gunfire from above in the building heightened as the machine gunners fired desperately into the smoke filled street below. The 'pings' as bullets bounced off the T34 opposite distinctive through the other sounds of war.

Hauptmann Becker appeared at the foot of the stairs, an MP40 in his hands. Seeing the Romanian quartermaster look across at him, he shouted desperately, 'Artillery incoming, they only have one salvo to offer us though!'

Tatu nodded, his teeth gritted. Rising slightly and glancing out into the street, his eyes widened as he saw the shadows of the gun crew opposite step back from their field gun. One of the gunners shuddering and falling as he was hit by machine gun fire from above. Tatu's desperation rising, he turned, screaming 'Get back!'

The flash from the field gun was followed immediately by an explosion, the shell hitting the exterior wall in front of the foot of the stairs. Tatu stared through the doorway as the wall implode inwards, Hauptmann Becker and the soldier behind him disappearing as the brickwork and masonry blew into the figures, engulfing them. Dust and cement fragments flew sideways into the wide room, forcing the remaining defenders to duck their heads.

The T34 fired again, the tank jolting backwards with the force. The shell smashed through one of the first floor windows, exploding inside, killing three of the German defenders in the storage room as they attempted to repel the Russian attack.

Bullets poured through the broken barricades as the T34's machine guns opened fire, the lead projectiles flying above the defenders heads as they ducked for cover, splattering against the back wall.

Tatu gulped, realising the situation was hopeless, firing another blind burst of his submachine gun through the opening he turned, shouting to the remaining soldiers in the room, his voice hoarse, 'Get up the stairs, we can't hold them here!'

The screams from outside in the street were drowned out as more artillery shells struck the upper floors of the building, shaking the structure. Plaster dust and fragments billowed from the ceiling around them, the dust now thick on the floor. The soldier next to Tatu rose and began to run towards the doorway to the stairs, spinning round as he passed the window, then falling backwards as he was hit in the chest and shoulder by machine gun fire from the T34.

Tatu scrambled across the floor towards the opening, hearing Petru shout at the remaining men in the room to follow them. As he reached the doorway, he turned, leaning into the corner of the room, raising his PPSH 41 to cover the other men's retreat. Seeing the three remaining soldiers scramble across the floor towards him, their faces contorted in terror with bullets flying above them through the windows. Petru was making his way along the side of the wall, some five metres away as the first grenade fell at the back of the room, thrown in through the broken barricades from a Russian leaning against the outside wall.

'Grenade!' Tatu shouted as the first man reached him, turning his face from the expected blast and raising his hands in protection. The other two German soldiers were desperately scrambling to get closer to the doorway as the grenade exploded, the fragmentation hitting one on the side and rear as he tried to get to the opening. The soldier slumped onto the floor, his hands clenched and back arching in pain as he reached out towards Tatu, his eyes desperate.

The other soldier was covered by his countryman's body and reached the doorway just behind Petru. Two more grenades flew into the room through the openings in the barricades, clattering across the floor and coming to rest against the far wall. Tatu pushed himself to his feet, turning and running through the opening as the explosions ripped through the room behind him.

Petru was firing through the opening in the destroyed wall as the quartermaster came through the doorway. The shell hole was roughly at waist height and was of about a metre in circumference. The surviving infantrymen from the ground floor storage room and office were now climbing the stairs quickly, their desperation to escape causing them to push against each other. Tatu turned, looking back into the darkened room. Seeing the bodies lying across the floor, he raised his weapon to chest height to cover any eager Russian infantry men that may attempt to climb through the windows.

As Tatu stared into the room, his eyes darting across the floor and walls as the bullets from the T34 flew through the windows, the wooden doors at the far end of the storage area blew inwards as the Russian engineers outside detonated their charges. The barricades that had been stacked across the double doors flew inwards, clattering across the cement floor. The debris lay scattered across the floor near the now open double doorway, one of the doors hanging weakly from its hinges as the other fell from the broken metal supports. Further smoke canisters and grenades clattered across the floor as the Russian infantry either side of the large door prepared to storm the area.

Tatu slapped Petru's shoulder, firing his PPSH submachine gun at the wide opening on the other side of the area. 'Get up the stairs! This floor is lost!'

Further explosions in the room they had exited occurred as the grenades timers ran out. The fragmentation killing any remaining wounded in the room that had been desperately clinging to life, their prone bodies shuddering with each blast. Sporadic firing from the open doorway splattered across the walls on either side as the Russians prepared to enter the ground floor.

Tatu turned away, hearing Petru's footsteps on the stairway. Opposite he glanced a Russian infantryman advancing into the office, his rifle raised. Reacting quickly, he raised his submachine gun and fired a short burst. The man screamed as the bullets entered his chest, falling backwards onto the scattered sandbags.

Tatu grasped the handrail on the stairs, pulling himself upwards as he heard the shouts echo in the room behind him, the Russians making each other aware of their positions before entering. Glancing down as he mounted the first step, he saw the body of Hauptmann Becker to the side of the stairs, his uniform covered in rubble and dust. Blood was on the floor around his body and the infantryman lying prone next to him, the explosive blast and shell fragments having probably ended their lives.

As he quickly ascended the steps, he saw Udet and Petru above him, half concealed behind the next set of stairs, their weapons pointing down towards the stairwell to cover him. As he passed them, he could hear a

'Whoosh' of shells fly past the building and land in the streets to the south of the tower. A faint smile crossing his lips, the German artillery had finally arrived...unfortunately too late, he mused to himself.

Machine gun fire echoed down from the floors above as the gunners fired out into the street, attempting to prevent further infantry from reaching the building. Tatu could hear the explosions outside as the salvo of German artillery landed amongst the streets opposite, hitting several Russian squads grouping to advance. The engines of the T34 revving as the shaken tank commander decided to distance himself from the artillery's target area.

As he passed Udet and Petru crouched on the stairs, the young German spoke, 'You are in command now Tatu!'

As Tatu wearily ascended the next few steps, passing two more soldiers, he replied, his voice tired, 'Of what?' He hesitated wearily, composing himself and turning on the steps, 'Move most of the men to the third floor...leave only a couple on the first and second floors, that should reduce their tank and gun targets, their guns cannot traverse that high. Get more men to cover the stairs, it's their only way up now.'

He looked back at the young German, seeing the man's wide eyes with fright, 'We have a short respite I think, they will regroup before storming the stairs. Drop grenades out of the windows when you see smoke. Use grenades on the stairs when they try and come up. I am going to see how Hausser is doing along the river...there is still hope.'

Chapter Twenty Nine: The Lower Bank of the River Volga

Hausser had waited in the biting cold at the corner of the storage tower, turning only from the sights of the devastated city beyond the Volga bend as he heard the crunch of boots in the iced snow behind him. As the group of soldiers gathered around him, he noticed their eyes widen as they looked out across the river. The burning buildings and battle raging on the west side of the Volga a visible surprise to most of the infantrymen.

Exhaling heavily, he addressed the assembled group, the condensed air from their breath swirling around the men, 'We will make our way along the riverbank as quickly as we can.' He stated, the men watching him apprehensively, 'Stay close to the walls of the river, this will conceal our shadows. If you venture too far from the wall, the snipers may see you against the snow, do you understand?'

The soldiers slowly nodded solemnly, their expressions grim as they looked beyond him in awe at the fires and fighting further north along the river.

Luca stepped forward, 'Shall I get some men from the storage building next door?'

Hausser considered the proposal for a second, 'Yes, get half of them, there is little time left now...I think we had better get as many men away as possible.'

Luca nodded, his teeth clenched, 'Yes sir, I will catch you up.' He turned and slipped through the other men, heading for the building next door.

Hausser turned back to the assembled men, 'Keep your voices down as we make our way along the river, we don't know where the Russians are...let's go!'

The commander turned and slipped out from the side of the building, feeling the colder air grasp his body as he slid down the slope towards the frozen riverbank. Slowly the soldiers followed, their footsteps deliberate on the iced surface, all wary of slipping and potentially injuring themselves.

Reaching the riverbank wall on the opposite end of the alleyway, Hausser hesitated and waited for all the soldiers to join him. The burning buildings casting light across the ice leading to the river...below the wall, they were in almost complete darkness.

Slowly their eyes adjusted to the darkness and they were able to see a brief distance in front of them, the intense cold beginning to penetrate their extra layers of clothing and seemingly bite at their flesh.

Moving carefully along the base of the wall, Hausser occasionally stopped to check the men behind him. His breathing was shallow and he felt his stomach twist with apprehension. Passing the corner of the second storage building he looked up, seeing the dark shadow of the solid structure above them. Swallowing hard and attempting to remove the lump from his throat as he passed across a narrow gap between the storage building and the next structure, this building in darkness.

Reaching another sewage pipe set into the cold dark wall, he cautiously glanced into the narrow tunnel, its end obstructed by a wire mesh grill. Seeing only pitch black in the tunnel, he held his breath and advanced across it, the sounds of gunfire further round the river becoming slightly louder.

As they progressed, he approached a jetty stretching out from the wall, the shadows of the wooden and metal structure becoming larger as they neared. Turning, he realised Nicu was behind him, indicating for the young Romanian to stop, he edged forward to the first pillar of the structure. Listening intently, he could hear muffled Russian voices from the alleyway above, the sentries staying back from the cold water's edge to claim limited comfort against the exposed temperature.

Turning to check the group behind him, he indicated with his right hand for them to approach cautiously, pressing his finger to his lips and pointing upwards. As the group reached him, they passed individually, crawling under the structure on the ice and cautiously pulling themselves forward across the cold snow.

As the second last man reached him, Hausser realised Hase was following the group, moving his head cautiously from side to side to check the surroundings for any threat. Hausser hesitated, then grasped the soldier's shoulder as he drew near, whispering next to his ear, 'Wait here for a short time Hase, make sure that impetuous Italian does not alert the Russians above us.'

Hase turned to look at him, nodding, his voice lowered and hushed, 'Yes sir, I will wait for them.'

Hausser lowered himself to a crawl and pushed himself across the snow under the jetty, feeling the cold seep through his uniform and Russian underwear as his body moved across the ice. Emerging from the pitch black beneath the structure, he joined the waiting group of men, their apprehension clearly rising as they turned to progress.

Hausser slipped through the waiting soldiers, assuming his position at the front again. The wall was beginning to gradually turn to the right as they reached the bend in the river and he could now make out a number of other jetties in the distance.

Glancing upwards, he saw the building above them was in darkness, the towering structure containing stores and foodstuffs for shipping north on the river, the stock now rotting in its boxes. As he cautiously passed the building, the lower section of the Volga bend began to turn towards the northwest, exposing the snow's surface to additional cold from the icy breezes drifting across the river.

Checking his footing more carefully for fear of slipping down the heavily iced slope to the riverbank, he turned to place his back against the wall, feeling the freezing stone against his body as he drew breath. The soldiers behind him adopted similar positions, grasping each other's shoulders to steady themselves.

As the wall turned further towards the north, Hausser glanced back towards the storage tower, his heart sinking, stomach twisting as he glimpsed explosions against the dark building, the flames from the roof shooting upwards and spreading into the air. Stopping for a second, he realised Udet was not with the group, his lips pursing under his scarf, 'Pig headed stubborn Berliners!' He mouthed to himself as he considered the battle that was raging in the storage tower.

The sights from the storage tower spurred Hausser on as he started pushing the pace along the side of the wall, side stepping in the ice and pressing his weight onto his left foot before progressing, ensuring he did not slip. The soldiers behind him were scrutinising the ice for shadows of the steps the previous man had taken and adopting these in the darkness.

Approaching another jetty, Hausser pushed himself from the cold stone and leant against the first support pillar, creating a gap for the soldiers to proceed between him and the wall. Slowly each man dropped to a crawl to fit under the pier and progressed through the darkness under the wooden structure, their bodies sliding slightly on the ice.

As the last man passed him, Hausser looked back down the riverbank, squinting to see if he could make out Hase and the group from the second tower. Unable to see anything in the darkness, he shook his head in frustration, turned his body and crept below the pier, crawling across the iced snow to the other side.

As he emerged from beneath the other side of the pier, he re-joined the group of soldiers collected on the iced snow. The bank was now more gradual as it declined towards the ice at the foot of the slope and the men were grouped around the pier supports awaiting his arrival.

Hausser hesitated, straining his ears as he thought he heard a sound, muffled laughter emerging from the building above as the Russian platoon housed in the darkened structure gained some rest from the extreme temperature and fighting during the day. The Russians were drinking heavily, and their conversation and laughter drifted from the building to the listening soldiers below.

A rifle crack echoed from the roof as a sniper fired out across the river bend, his position cold and isolated on top of the building. The sounds of gunfire and shell explosions drifted across the ice as the lower Volga river wall started to bend round towards the north.

Hausser pushed himself from his crouched position and started to walk carefully along the base of the wall, feeling for footsteps of the soldiers ahead of him on the ice. As they advanced some twenty metres further, he froze as he heard a 'puff' from above them. Looking up, he caught his breath as a flare rose into the sky. He dropped to a crouched position, his heart beating loudly in his chest as he watched the glowing projectile rise into the frozen air. His fear rose as he tried to anticipate where it would land, possibly illuminating the soldiers and exposing them to fire if it landed too close.

On the eastern side of the river, the Russian sniper raised the binoculars to his eyes, the flare from his countryman on the rooftop opposite an agreed prior arrangement to enable him to check the riverbank for enemy soldiers. As he adjusted the zoom, he gradually moved the glasses along the bank from a point in the city opposite back down the river as it bent round towards his position. Checking the darkened piers individually, he then lifted the binoculars to check the trajectory of the flare, then lowered the glasses again. Shivering below his blankets and the bushes he had placed around him, he scanned the opposite bank again for movement. Seeing nothing, he placed the binoculars onto the bushes concealing his position before him. Slowly he reached behind for his ration pack.

Hausser exhaled gradually as the flare dropped slowly onto the ice further up the riverbank, the breeze guiding the projectile towards the burning buildings in front of them. The flare glowed brightly and intensely as it landed on the ice further up the river, beyond the next jetty as he slowly rose from his position and backed against the wall again, feeling the cold stone against his body.

Edging forward, Hausser could now just make out the gap in the wall he had seen from the storage tower, the flames from the buildings in the street above lighting the edges of the stone around the entrance to the street, now some one hundred and fifty metres further from their position. Below the wall would be the ladder he had seen through the binoculars, now obscured in the darkness.

As the group moved further, they approached the last jetty before their potential exit and escape from the riverbank. Hausser slowed as he approached the darkened structure, the cold now becoming intense to the exposed men. As he crouched to go below the pier, he glimpsed darkened frozen bodies beneath the structure on the ice. Grasping his MP40, he cautiously edged nearer, pointing the weapon towards the prone figures, cautiously watching them for movement.

As he ducked under the platform, the realisation was the bodies were of civilians, frozen in death's embrace. He swallowed as he observed the bodies were mostly small, of young children that had hidden from the fighting, their parents leading them to potential safety from gunfire. The exposure to the elements providing no mercy as their body temperatures dropped dramatically. He grimly counted five children and one adult, considering they had been eagerly awaiting someone to come and rescue them or to tell them the battle had passed…that they were now safe…that perhaps their rescuer had been killed before getting to them.

Crawling forward, he carefully but forcefully pushed the frozen bodies aside, moving them further down the decline. Considering their innocence as they waited, their hopes of rescue high as they slowly dropped into a warm sleep in the cold. Two of the bodies were frozen on the surface of the ice and he reluctantly applied pressure with his boot to dislodge them. The bodies slipping gradually across the frozen snow once this was achieved, a slight noise as the iced grip on the corpses gave way.

As the other soldiers passed, several closed their eyes, the bitterness of the scene causing them to become aware of their fragile existence in this environment.

Hausser waited for the men on the other side of the pier, wary the experience could disturb some of them. Slowly they all emerged onto the iced snow, the condensed breath from their exhalations now hanging in the air. The commander indicated for them all to gather round as he spoke in a whisper, 'We are nearly there...so don't make any mistakes now. The Russians are in the streets around us and probably between us and our lines even when we get off this bank.' He looked across the soldiers darkened faces as he spoke, noticing most were quite withdrawn from their vacant expressions, the early signs of exposure. Continuing he drew breath, 'When we get up the ladder, move away from the edge quickly and to the sides of the street, this will reduce the chances or sniper fire. Keep low, even lie down on the road until I can make a decision what to do next.'

He watched as individually the soldiers slowly nodded, his apprehension high as he considered their potentially limited combat experience. Turning thoughtfully, he moved at a crouch towards the wall, now feeling the cold in his thigh muscles. He realised they now needed to get off the exposed bank quickly if they were going to be able to fight in the streets beyond the ladder....exposure was now also a deep concern.

Moving along next to the wall, Hausser hoped Hase had not waited too long for the follow up group, the temperature now bitterly low. He considered that even his young Russian friend would struggle if left out too long in the bitter dropping temperature.

Glancing out onto the ice, he observed the flare had now died, the last 'whisps' of smoke rising from the projectile as it lay on the white iced surface.

The commander increased his pace along the wall, a freezing breeze from the east now drifting directly onto them as they progressed north. His boots slipped occasionally on the ice, but the decline was now very slight, so this limited his chances of falling. As they trudged forward, he occasionally glanced back at the group, checking their progress. He observed a couple of soldiers had fallen slightly behind, but decided the distance remaining was too slight to justify stopping to regroup.

Approaching the ladder, his uneasiness faded. Grasping the cold metal with his gloved hands, he stepped onto the first frozen rung and started to ascend towards the street.

Back in the small fourth floor office of the storage tower, Tatu scanned the bank of the river bend with binoculars through the shell hole in the wall. Below him, sporadic gunfire echoed in the stairwell as the Russians tried to gain an understanding of the strength they faced before attacking. The occasional explosion within and outside the building indicated the grenades the defenders were using to deter the attackers, a stock of grenades that were now beginning to run out.

He tensed, lowering the glasses for a second as he heard a grinding noise above him in the building. The noise becoming slightly louder, then silence. Raising the glasses again, he scanned the ice as it bent around the river, looking for a shadow or silhouette. Seeing nothing, he began looking along the river wall silhouetted from the fires beyond.

A smile crossed his lips as he thought he glimpsed something against a gap in the wall, then he ducked his head as shells exploded above him on the roof, a shower of dust falling from the ceiling above him. Raising the glasses, he looked again…seeing nothing, he reluctantly dismissed his earlier thought.

As he lowered the binoculars from his eyes, he heard Udet's shouting in the stairwell, a desperation in his voice, 'Tatu, come quickly, we need your help.' Dropping the binoculars, he ran his shaking hand over his moustache and grasped his PPSH 41 submachine gun. Turning abruptly, he ran from the office.

Chapter Thirty: Der Kessel

Hausser slowly and carefully clambered to the top of the metal ladder, the cold from the rungs beginning to seep through his gloves. He moved his boots slowly and purposefully, aware that the hob nails in the soles could make extra noise on the metal rungs.

Approaching the top of the ladder, he carefully raised his head over the top rung so he could peer into the street beyond. As his eyes adjusted to the light from the burning buildings on either side of the narrow street, he took in the sights before him.

The street was approximately seventy metres long, ending in an intersection with a main road. To either side were low two storey buildings, probably apartments and houses for the many workers and political officers that had resided in the city. Flames licked from most of the windows and doorways, the signs of heavy fighting during this and the preceding days. Several doorways were open, smoke billowing from within some as he looked on.

In the middle of the street, some thirty metres from him, sat a disabled German armoured car, an SdKfz 221 facing away from him. He had glimpsed this vehicle through the binoculars he had used from the storage tower, and was curious as to the vehicle's condition. Looking from his hiding spot, he examined the armoured car, seeing the dead gunner slumped in the upper hatch, his body bent backwards after being hit in the face by Russian bullets. Several bodies lay further down the street, the victims of vicious hand to hand fighting.

The vehicle was sat at an angle, its axle damaged, with both right tyres punctured. Beyond his sight, the front radiator had been punctured from Russian machine gun fire, but he was encouraged to see the main cupola machine gun was still in the open hatch, pointing skywards as the gunner's body had fallen backwards, wedging the weapon in its current position.

At the end of the street, next to the intersection, were some twenty Russians, some crouched next to the right corner, others stood behind them or in the middle of the street, all positioned some distance before the main road. From their stances, he realised they were in a state of high alertness, either preparing to attack to the right or readying to receive a counter attack.

A shell burst occurred to his left, causing him to duck below the top of the wall instinctively. As the dust and debris dropped onto the street in front of the wall, he slowly lifted his head again to further look down the street.

Tracer bullets zipped across the junction beyond, the Russians ducking back from the corner of the right wall. A brief smile crossed his lips as he realised the tracer fire was coming from the right, that these were German machine guns firing. The sounds from the streets and buildings in the immediate vicinity were of small arms fire, rifle shots and bursts of hand held submachine guns, broken only by the explosions from grenades.

Excitement rose within him as he realised the German lines may only be a short distance to the north. The Russian infantry's obvious tenseness seen in their stances and body movement indicating the German force opposing them was potentially strong or even superior to the Russian numbers.

He carefully descended the ladder again, his hands now cold in their gloves. As he reached the foot of the metal ladder, he turned to face the assembled group of soldiers, seeing the cold in their eyes, with a couple visibly shivering. Addressing the men, he kept his voice to a whisper, 'There are Russians in the street above, but it is the only way I know into the city.' Facing Nicu, he placed his gloved hand on the young Romanian's shoulder, 'Nicu, there is a German armoured car above, try and get into the hatch and see if the machine gun works. Keep your head down and only fire on my command.'

Nicu nodded obediently, 'Yes sir...are we close to our lines?'

Hausser paused, looking across the faces of the other men, 'Yes, I think so. The Russkies seem jumpy, so we had better be careful...they still outnumber us. It will be a short fight without the turret machine gun.' He swallowed, concerned with the fighting ability of the men before him, 'The rest of you take cover when we get into the street, use doorways and the buildings that are not ablaze, but stay close, splitting up will only weaken us.'

He watched as the men nodded slowly, their adrenalin rising, fear entering their eyes. Hausser continued, 'Once we are all in position, we will open fire. Then attempt to move through the buildings to our right, do you understand?'

The soldiers nodded, a couple whispering, 'Yes Sir.'

Hausser looked across the men again, then slowly turned, moving the MP40 on its strap to assist him climb the ladder again, 'Good, let's go.'

The commander slowly climbed the ladder again, feeling the metal tense as Nicu stepped onto the bottom rung behind him. Reaching the top of the ladder, he glanced out into the street again, his teeth clenched.

The vision before him was the same as before, the Russian infantry, some in white winter camouflage cautiously stood or crouched at the end of the road, their weapons held tightly and at the ready. The sounds of sporadic fire in the streets to either side rose as he lifted himself above the top rung, grasping his MP40 in both hands and ran at a crouch to the back of the armoured car, his heart pounding in his chest.

Crouching at the rear of the vehicle, he glanced over the right wing of the armoured car, seeing the Russians were still concentrating on the junction. Looking round further, he saw his small group of soldiers rise from the top of the ladder one by one and adopt positions either side of him. To his right, a German infantryman cautiously dropped to lie on the street, his position next to the deflated rear wheel. A Romanian crouched next to him glancing over the left side of the vehicle and Nicu pushed between them, carefully grasping the black shoulder straps of the dead gunner above him on the vehicle.

Over to the left, two Germans lay on the street, their rifles pointing towards the assembled Russians, and to his right a Romanian cautiously crawled forward towards the first doorway, his rifle held in his right hand.

The heat from the burning buildings on either side of the street provided some comfort to the group of soldiers, their faces feeling some brief warmth from the fires, wisps of steam rising from some of their uniforms. Behind them, a cold unforgiving breeze drifted in from the Volga, sweeping down the street and across the Romanian, German and Russian soldiers.

Nicu tugged the dead gunner's body, achieving little as the corpse's boots were wedged in the copula of the armoured car. Gritting his teeth, the Romanian pulled again, applying more force as the body finally broke free from the vehicle, sliding down the cold metal from the open turret. The machine gun moved as the dead gunner slipped from the vehicle, the barrel of the weapon dropping slowly as the body that was propping it up was released. The soldiers averted their eyes as the dead gunner's shattered face passed them, frozen skull and brain fragments falling onto the street around their feet. Frozen blood covering his black uniform, a sign of the elevated and exposed position he had died in.

Further tracer bullets whipped down the main street, across the intersection, then a whoosh as a shell followed the machine gun fire. Hausser's adrenalin jumped as he considered the German or allied force had heavy weaponry or even tanks, his realisation this would probably be the front line some metres to their right.

Nicu carefully laid the dead gunner onto the cobblestones, swallowing against the rising nausea from his stomach. He began cautiously clambering onto the back of the armoured vehicle, the cold from the metal plate seeping through his padded clothing.

As the young Romanian stretched his hand out to grasp the machine gun, his body lying across the back of the vehicle, a Russian soldier innocently walked out from a doorway on the left, two ammunition boxes in his hands. The Russian sensed something and turned to face them, his eyes widening in horror as he recognised the German and Romanian uniforms. Turning back and starting to run, he dropped the boxes with a clatter and shouted a warning, raising his hands to retrieve his rifle from his shoulder.

One of the Germans on the left fired his rifle, the Russian falling forward onto the cobblestones, the bullet entering his back. The cracks of rifles to either side of Hausser followed, felling three of the Russian soldiers at the end of the street.

Hausser leant out from the armoured car, raising his MP40 and firing down the narrow street, two more Russian soldiers falling. The inexperienced rifleman next to him on the ground fired, the rifle kicking upwards, his bullet missing the Russian infantry as they dropped to the ground, turning to return fire.

Submachine gun bullets flew across the street from the open doorway on the left, hitting and killing the German soldier in the doorway on the right, his body slowly sliding down the frame he was propelled back into it, blood pouring from his mouth.

The rifles cracked again after the soldiers reloaded, hitting two more Russian soldiers as they lay on the road, their cries of agony echoing between the buildings.

Nicu grasped the machine gun, twisting it towards the Russian infantry and pulling the trigger. The gun clicked as the firing pin shot forward, the gun empty of ammunition. Nicu groaned in frustration, hitting the ammunition chamber on top of the weapon. He pulled the trigger again, the weapon clicking again, empty. Ducking his head as bullets clanked across the armoured car's front metal plate, he slipped back off the back of the vehicle, reaching for the rifle across his back.

Bullets clattered against the armoured car and cobblestones as the Russian infantry opened fire. A shell burst off to the left, showering the Germans and Romanians with debris and dust. Hausser fired blindly out from behind the armoured car, hearing a scream off to his left as one of the German infantry was hit in the shoulder, his body jerking backwards.

From the doorway on the left side, a Russian leaned out, aiming his PPSH 41 towards the armoured car. His body jolting and falling forward, the Romanian next to Hausser seeing the enemy soldier and twisting his rifle round, the weapon recoiling back into his shoulder as he fired, the bullet hitting the Russian in the heart.

Tracer bullets flew across the end of the street at the junction as Hausser fired out from the back of the armoured car. The rifleman at his feet fired as bullets whipped around them, flying past them and over the walls behind.

The shouts of 'Hurrah' came from the doorway to the left as six Russian infantrymen surged out of the building, turning to face the Germans and Romanians at the end of the street. The German to the left fired his rifle hitting the front Russian who spun backwards, then his face jolted backwards as a bullet from a well-aimed shot at the end of the street entered his skull through his helmet.

Nicu was knelt behind the armoured car and fired at the Russians running from the right, hitting one, then he rose to defend himself as the enemy ran towards them, screams of hatred coming from their open mouths as they charged.

Hausser stepped back from the carrier to turn to face the oncoming charge, his weapon at waist height as he fired a burst. The pings of enemy bullets hitting the armoured car almost deafening as they increased in ferocity. Glancing down the street, he glimpsed the other Russians rise, some twelve men, and start to run towards them. One fell backwards as he rose, the German lying at Hausser's feet firing his rifle as the Russians began their charge.

Hausser rounded the left side of the carrier, between Nicu and the other Romanian, his teeth gritted and mouth open, the Russians only five metres away. He fired a burst from his MP40 and three of the Russians fell in front of him, their weapons clattering onto the cobblestones. His eyes widened as more Russians exited the doorway, then started charging towards them, bayonets flashing on the end of their rifles. A Russian officer marched out behind them, a look of determination on his face, his pistol raised. Hausser swallowed hard, the intense feeling of desperation rising within him.

The Romanian in front of Hausser stepped out in front of him, swinging the butt of his rifle across above the metal plate of the armoured car and hitting the Russian bearing down on Hausser in the face, the man falling away to the left unconscious, the blood from his shattered face splattering across their tunics.

The German soldier next to the right wheel rose from his hiding place in panic, turning to run back to the ladder as his desperation to escape overcame him. As he emerged from the side of the vehicle, a rifle shot from the end of the street hit him in the shoulder, his body falling sideways onto the cobblestones.

Nicu was backing slowly towards the ladder, his hands shaking as he attempted to reload his rifle, desperation on his face. Hausser fired a burst of his submachine gun at the Russians charging towards them, felling two, then the gun clicked empty.

The Romanian in front of him screamed as a bullet fired from one of the charging Russians hit him in the chest, the man falling backwards against Hausser who instinctively tried to stop him from falling to the ground.

The Romanian twisted his body before Hausser, grasping the commander's tunic as he turned, the spittle from his screaming mouth spraying across Hausser's face. As the Leutnant looked beyond the man leaning against him, the charging Russians were closing in, some six metres from him, their bayonets seeming to stretch out towards him. He felt the emotions drain from him, the feeling of ultimate failure and impending defeat approaching.

The lead Russian was looking straight into his eyes as he closed towards him...then he was gone, falling to the left along with the charging men behind him, their bodies shattered with multiple wounds from machine gun fire. Each man was hit several times from the high velocity machine gun, their bodies jerking as they fell to the left, the forceful impacts throwing their bodies sideways. The Russian officer fell forward, his mouth opening as the bullets exploded through his chest, his pistol clattering onto the cobblestones.

Hausser fell backwards as the injured Romanians weight caused him to overbalance and his legs to buckle. Bullets smashed into the front of the armoured car as Hausser landed roughly onto the cobblestones, his head jerking backwards with the impact and hitting the street. Behind him, Nicu had dropped to his knees, desperately grasping for the bullet clip he had dropped when trying to frantically reload his weapon.

Hausser pushed himself up, stunned and dizzy at the impact his helmet had made on the cobblestones. Glancing under the armoured car as his head lifted and seeing the front wheels at the end of the street, the tracks behind it. Recognition flashing through his panicked swirling mind as he saw the distinct wheels of the half tracked vehicle, the wheels of a German Sdkfz 251 Hanomag armoured transport, the front gunner spraying machine gun bullets across the Russians in the street.

Behind the Hanomag a German Panzer III tank drove past slowly, its machine guns firing southwards, German infantry sheltering behind the tank as they advanced. Then the young German commander's vision became misted as his body buckled. He passed out, his helmeted head falling back onto the cobblestones.

His mind drifted as he heard a sound, the sound seeming to come nearer. Then his senses began to clarify, as he felt the gentle slaps to his cheek, 'Herr Leutnant?'

His eyes flickered open, not recognising the German medic kneeling over him. The medic's face turned away, the white circle on his helmet with a red cross within seeming to swirl cloudily as he looked, 'He is awake now!' The medic shouted.

The sounds of shelling and machine gun fire in the distance to his left filtered through the mist in his mind, then got louder as if he advanced mentally towards the noise. Rifle cracks and shell bursts entered his mind further to the south as his alertness returned, the medic turning back to look down on him. Above the medic's face Nicu looked over his shoulder, a faint smile crossing his lips, 'Welcome back Leutnant Hausser.' The young Romanian stated.

Hausser's mind sharpened, 'M...My men?' He started to push himself upwards, the 'swimmy' disorientated mental wave hitting him as his body rose to a seating position, the medic grabbing his arm to prevent him from falling backwards. The commander glanced around, seeing several German infantrymen in the street cautiously inspecting bodies and helping the wounded.

'They are all dead or wounded, sir.' The medic retorted, 'Let's get you to the Hanomag.'

Hausser shook his head, feeling the mists clear slightly, 'N...No, on the river. We must get them.' He replied, biting his lip and drawing blood in an attempt to get the pain to clear his mind.

The medic slowly and carefully helped him to his feet, placing his arm under Hausser's shoulder to steady him, 'On the river?' He retorted, his voice adopting a questioning tone.

Hausser turned and looked back towards the wall facing the river, pushing his feet across the cobblestones with the support of the medic, he struggled towards the building to his left, stammering, 'Where is Nicu?'

The Romanian patted his shoulder reassuringly, 'Here...Herr Leutnant. I have some binoculars.' He pushed the glasses into Hausser's shaking hands.

Hausser reached the wall of the apartment block on his left, leaning as he faced the river, some six metres from the wall. The medic stood next to him, supporting his weight, 'Come now, sir...let's get you to the Hanomag.'

Hausser sucked air through his nostrils, the feeling of nausea rising within him, 'Not without my men!' He slowly raised the binoculars to his eyes, blinking in attempt to focus his sight through the lenses.

As his eyes slowly focussed, he gradually moved the glasses to see along the riverbank wall. Frustration rising within him as he was unable to make any shapes or silhouettes out in the pitch black. Then he moved the glasses along through the darkness to the storage towers, seeing the first in complete darkness.

He lowered the glasses from his eyes and shook his head as he felt the 'swimminess' return to his senses, the signs of concussion evident to the medic.

Raising the binoculars again he scanned the second building, seeing the fire rage on the upper two floors and lowering his gaze through the binoculars to the base of the building, desperately attempting to make out any shadows or silhouettes of soldiers potentially escaping from the structure.

As he watched, flames shot out from the sewage tunnels either side of the large storage tower, the billowing smoke and fire shooting out across the riverbank and ice. Then the sound waves hit them, a distant rumble moving across the corner of the river.

Raising his view to the burning building, he saw it shudder briefly, then dust and smoke pour out of the shell holes in the river side of the building. The flaming roof seemed to drop, then shudder again, the large storage tower collapsing inwards. Smoke and flames shot into the air and the structure imploded as its shattered floors and walls fell inwards and downwards. The Russian engineers in the sewers having blown up the foundations, the building collapsing completely.

The soldier staggered as the man next to him fell, the full weight dropping onto the medic's arms, the binoculars clattering as they fell to the cobblestones. Leutnant Hausser had collapsed unconscious.

Thank you for reading this book, I hope you enjoyed the experience as much as I did writing it.

Please investigate the following adventures currently available or in production from the author:

World War Two:

Bloody Iced BulletBloody RattenkriegBloody Kessel

Bloody Stalingrad (Trilogy)Bloody Kharkov I

Bloody Kharkov IIBloody Citadel

Bloody Red Storm RisingBloody Retreat to the Dneiper

Science Fiction:

The Last Marine in the GalaxyThe Red Leopards of Zaxon B Galaxies

Collide: First ContactPlanet Genocide I

Zaxon B: The Final StrugglePlanet Genocide II

Fantasy:

Blades of the UndeadBlades of the Iced Warrior

Crime Drama (Dark Humour):

Blood and HungerBlood and Insurgency

Bloodied London IBlood and Intoxication

The Hong Kong ScotsmanThe Werewolves of New Hong Kong

Historical Drama:

The Last Highlanders

Sequel Outline: Bloody Rattenkrieg

Leutnant Hausser will return in Bloody Rattenkrieg. The brutal final battle for the streets and buildings of Stalingrad as the Russian armies close in around 'Der Kessel'.

As the German Luftwaffe desperately attempt to supply the starving, freezing and devastated city from the air, defenders from a number of nations, cold and hungry, will continue fighting overwhelming odds.

Historically, some of the most vicious fighting the human spirit ever experienced.

During the struggle for survival itself, against nature and a viciously motivated enemy, the German soldiers and their allies finally gain an insight into the true evil of the regime their uniforms represent.

Only the promise of a relief effort and their bleak prospects of survival forming an individual human's primary motivation...hope.

In six months, one of the largest military operations in history with the ultimate goal of securing unlimited oil supplies and defeating Soviet Russia...had failed. Along with the myth of German military invincibility.

Thank you for spending the time reading what I have produced. My hope you find the work as enjoyable as I find writing it.

Authors Note:

This is written in beloved memory of my late father.

Someone who always encourages you to follow your dreams, promotes happiness and strength as well as helping in everything you wish to achieve is rarely recognised in full until their gift is gone.

Unfortunately, I also lost one of my best friends in 2014, one of my dogs, a Black Lab, Doberman, and Chow cross called Taxi. He was often a troubled individual, having had a very difficult start in life before we met him, but a very loyal, loving and understanding companion in his own way.

It was an honour for me to share twelve years with him.

Sometimes, it is extremely difficult to fully appreciate the gifts and love others convey to us until they are gone. But with the strong memories and loving experiences they shared and conveyed to us, it becomes easier to appreciate just how uniquely special they were and just how important their affection was. I will miss them both very much.

Contributors:

I would like to thank two of my colleagues for their voluntary assistance with this project.

Juri Heikinen, for his help with some of the most intricate details of the book geographically. His contributions through searching Russian websites and other Russian language sources for the smallest details I was determined to get exactly correct, have been of immense assistance.

David Axell has also volunteered some considerable time assisting me with this and future projects, talking over additional ideas and potential sub plots. He has also provided valuable input on some of the wording used to assist me in the endeavour to create as close as possible account to reality.

Printed in Great Britain
by Amazon